HELEN FRIPP

the

PAINTER'S
GIRL

bookouture

Published by Bookouture in 2022

An imprint of Storyfire Ltd.
Carmelite House
50 Victoria Embankment
London EC4Y 0DZ

www.bookouture.com

ISBN: 978-1-80314-123-7
eBook ISBN: 978-1-80314-122-0

"If you ask me what I came into this life to do, I will tell you: I am an artist and I came to live out loud." Emile Zola

To Rosalie, who inspired a life-long love of art and poetry in me.

CHAPTER 1

A zebra careering down the boulevard Montmartre! Mimi Bisset had grown up on the streets of Paris and life overflowed onto the winding alleys and boulevards for everyone to see at some point or other, but this was definitely a first.

A gaggle of girls screamed as they stepped out of the laundry with armfuls of dripping linen. The terrified beast bolted, knocking over Paulette's flower cart and taking out an entire row of stalls, leaving a trail of rolling fruit, roaring men in leather aprons and chaos in its wake.

Mimi fixed the hoopla in her mind to draw later. Colour, excitement, theatre and a wild lost thing – all her favourite images in one wonderfully unlikely event.

She tightened her sinews for the task ahead. The braying animal rushed straight at her, eyes flashing, kicking up its hooves. She stood her ground and calculated its speed, then fell into perfect step with its canter. *One, two, three...* a pull on its glittering circus bridle, a meticulously timed leap and she was on its back, focusing every fibre of her body to stay in tune with its furious bucking.

'Hush, my exotic friend, clck, clck, hush, hush,' she soothed. Thanks to her job at the stables, she knew exactly what to do.

The zebra quietened at the familiar tug on his bridle, Mimi's reassuring knees pressed tight on his ribs, steering him through the crowds.

'That's right.' She smoothed his flanks; he was hot and damp with fear and exertion. 'Ignore them. It's just you and me. Walk on, slowly now. Just let me take charge and all will be well. Hush.'

He slowed, wheezing, to a trot and the astounded passers-by began to clap. She pressed a finger to her lips to silence them, afraid they'd spook him again. But she couldn't resist a regal, triumphant wave at the admiring crowd before she turned down a quiet alley. The way they looked at her, like she was a goddess from another world, set her on fire. Never mind her drab, torn dress, she was the queen of Paris at this moment. The early-morning sun catching her black hair was her crown, her eyes were emeralds and her strong body never let her down.

The Cirque d'Hiver – the Winter Circus – was the talk of Paris and she knew exactly where to find it, in the spot it returned to every year, at the flat ground at the bottom of the Butte, the hill of Montmartre. It was the place where the *beau monde,* the beautiful people of Haussmann's smart new boulevards, rubbed shoulders with the likes of Mimi from the filthy backstreets. She was delighted that her ridiculous zebra had crashed into her life, presenting her with an excuse to enter that hallowed land.

Before she got there, though, there was one person she just *had* to show off her curious tamed beast to. She picked her way through the maze of backstreets, saluting the people she'd known all her life as she passed by on her exotic steed, pretending nothing was at all amiss, carefully steering her fugitive away from the deep open sewers. As she passed the old convent with the high gates she'd scaled so many times in her childhood, the girls screamed in delight.

'*Salut!*' she yelled. 'School will dull your brains. Any girl with an *ounce* of taste should catch a zebra!'

The exasperated nuns waved her on, but her old teacher, Soeur Benedicta, pulled her habit over her mouth to conceal a smile.

At the Moulin de la Galette, the night was only just over. A skinny girl in a shimmering dress with a pinched face slammed the stage door, her make-up lurid in the morning light. She'd be running to her job at the laundry. A man in an expensive top hat jerked awake in the doorway. He rubbed his eyes, still clearly drunk. Mimi pulled a face at him to exaggerate the surreal sight he was witnessing. She imagined the picture she'd paint of the scene, framed in gold, like the ones she'd seen in the Louvre with Rafi. She'd only be able to outline this one in borrowed coal on the pavement, though, until her two jobs at the stables and the laundry earned her enough money to buy colours.

Rafi was where he always was, outside his windowless studio room, perched on a crate, at a makeshift desk made of bricks and planks, writing on scavenged scraps of paper.

She stopped close enough for him to see, but he didn't rouse him from his work. He never heard her coming unless she shouted his name, he was always too absorbed in his writing. Her dear friend since childhood. He wore a tweed cap, like the ones all the would-be writers and intellectuals wore to mark themselves as part of the tribe. He'd found it with Mimi on the ground outside the Moulin de la Galette, and now he was never without it. He was as skinny as everyone in these parts, and his high cheekbones and trimmed beard added to his carefully curated scholarly air, even though he was from the gutters, like her. Neither of them intended to stay there, though. They talked into the night about how they would escape these mean backstreets. He would be a writer, she a great artist.

'Meet Tif,' she called to him, letting go of the reins and presenting herself with open arms.

'What the hell?' Rafi grinned as he took in the sight. He didn't look as shocked as he should have. He was used to Mimi and her outlandish surprises.

'Short for *fugitif,* escapee,' she said, bowing grandly.

'I didn't mean the *name,* I meant the actual zebra, with you riding it,' he laughed.

She jumped down, clutching the colourful bridle as Tif brayed. 'Come and say hello.'

'No thanks, he looks suspicious enough of me, and that's quite a set of gnashers he just bared. You're the one with a way with horses.'

'He just senses your fear,' she teased.

'And he's not mistaken. I'll leave you two to your new-found friendship.'

'You know we've always wanted to go to the circus? I present our ticket for two, Monsieur.' Mimi swept a curtsey.

Rafi carefully secured his papers with a stone, jumped up and kissed her hand.

'Then I shall gratefully accept, Mademoiselle. We'll leave the carriage and go on foot, I think. The day promises to be lovely.'

They both looked up at the gathering rainclouds.

'Perfect,' replied Mimi. 'I believe the zebra knows the way.'

Mimi's senses were firing, committing every single detail to memory. The shabby camels with their flabby humps, the fortune teller's tent covered in stars like a church basilica, the glint of spangles where the breeze caught the trapeze girls' dressing gowns as they strolled across the grass.

'He doesn't take kindly to strangers. How did on earth did you catch him?' the stable boy asked.

'I help at the stables in Montmartre. They always ask me to break in the tricky ones.'

'She does the same with men, too,' laughed Rafi.

'Hey!' She thumped her friend.

'You must be fast,' said the stable boy admiringly. 'Zebras are mad buggers when they're scared, and I heard he was causing chaos.'

'That's what everyone does on the street when they're scared. You just need to stay calm, show them some love,' Mimi replied breezily.

That's how she and Rafi had found each other, both of them running scared on the streets. Rafi was an orphan, and her mother was a drunk. She had no idea where her father was, but rumour had it that he was an Italian acrobat at the circus. That's where she'd got her olive skin and supple body, so he'd left her something at least.

Mimi had always furiously guarded Rafi, saving him the meagre scraps from her dinner, sneaking him into her room on the nights the frost traced patterns on the inside of the tenement windows. They'd creep, clutching hands, past her unconscious, snoring mother, who reeked of alcohol and men's sweat most nights.

She didn't blame her mother. Who wouldn't want to blot out such misery? She'd done her best for Mimi and that accounted for the men, which in turn accounted for the absinthe. The one thing she'd never asked of her daughter was to contribute to the family coffers in the same way. It was the fate of many of her friends, even if they had a job as a laundress, or a seamstress, or a flower girl. None of it was enough to raise a family, especially if your child's father had dropped you back into the dirt like one of the sequins Mimi foraged from the streets outside the Moulin de la Galette.

She kept a collection of rescued things, each one representing a friend who had been lashed into poverty and prostitution like a leaf on the storm, through no fault of their own. Bits of crockery, shards of coloured glass, the sequins that scattered carelessly like confetti from the starving dancing girls' dresses in the back alleys, all made up her secret collection. Most prized amongst it all was a child's doll, dressed in yellow silk. That was waiting for her future life.

Thinking about it all at once – the injustice, the way that society sneered and turned its back on the slums and only gave opportunity to their own – was too much for one person to bear. So, she made it her mission to just live for the moment, trust in nothing and no one, apart from her own mind and body, and Rafi of course. Her revenge for losing at the life lottery of wealth and position was to enjoy every moment of just being alive, and that's exactly what she was doing right now.

The caravans here at the circus were gilded and painted and to her eyes they were like the old masters at the Louvre Museum. Mimi mentally saved these to draw later, too. What a portfolio of happenings in just one day! Life could be hard, but beautiful and strange in equal measures. You just needed to reach for the light at every opportunity. So when a man dressed in red coat-tails, carrying a whip and top hat rushed by, Mimi flashed her eyes at him, and he stopped to tilt his hat like a cavalry soldier addressing a lady.

'Can we see inside?' she asked the stable boy.

'It would be a bit churlish of me to refuse the zebra tamer of Montmartre, wouldn't it?' he replied with a wink. 'Come on, they're rehearsing on the trapeze for this evening's performance. There's a new performer, Jules Léotard, who's practising a triple somersault for the first time. There's no safety net. I bet you'll scream.'

Inside, the stable boy showed them to the seats high at the

back of the tent and told them to not so much as *breathe* for fear of them disturbing the trapeze artists' concentration.

'I'll come back and find you in a bit,' he told them.

'I wish I had a pen and paper,' whispered Rafi as the boy scurried off. 'I don't want to forget a moment.'

'Look!' Mimi hissed back, pointing at a girl in a glittering costume. Someone switched on the gas lights, which edged the ring and hung high up in the top of the tent, lighting the space in dramatic shafts. The girl scaled the net, arms and legs splayed like a frog, and with each movement, the gaslight flashed a different shade of the iridescent peacock blue she was wearing.

Without colours to paint with, Mimi always worked hard to capture the luminosity of any tableau she'd collected in her mind's eye, using monochrome light or shade. The zebra would be easy for once. But how she wished she could capture this spectacle when she returned to the dim gloom of her little room in Montmartre.

A man climbed up behind the trapeze girl, light and supple as a spider. This must be the famous Monsieur Léotard. Mimi had made it her business to observe everything about the world, and even from here, she could tell that every muscle was honed, and that was how he gave the impression of effortlessness.

The pair climbed to the top of the net, then the girl stepped onto a narrow bar, high as one of Haussmann's new ten-storey buildings.

'I already can't watch. You know I get vertigo,' whispered Rafi. Mimi grabbed his arm in agreement, transfixed.

The girl nodded across the tent, and it was only then that Mimi saw the man in the red coat-tails who'd tipped his hat to her, standing on a bar on the opposite side of the high space, holding a trapeze. The girl swung out on her trapeze: and let go. Rafi and Mimi stifled a gasp. But she caught the bar the coat-tailed man had timed perfectly for her and joined him on the other side.

Monsieur Léotard grabbed the empty trapeze the girl had flung back his way. The pair swung, twisted in the middle and swapped trapezes.

'Bravo,' shouted red-coat as the pair flew through the air, caught each other's wrists and defied gravity with meticulous, stomach-turning style and precision.

Mimi drew in her mind's eye the exact curve of the trapeze, the number of centimetres they could risk in their turns before they missed. She felt the visceral thrill of their supple muscles controlling their every move, every synapse engaged in the moment, the reassuring satisfaction of skin on skin as they caught each other exactly before they fell. Beauty and skill and daring wrapped up in perfect, powerful beings.

It was September and the Paris sky outside the tent was a mean grey, but in here the creamy canvas and bright lights made a different world, where unlikely dreams came true. Rafi was always telling her not to take risks, to stay safe. But in the circus, risk was beautiful, awe-inspiring. A place where an eye for a spectacle, a strong, quick body and mind and an appetite for danger could make you a living.

'Mimi, did you hear a word I said?' Rafi whispered.

She was so absorbed, she'd forgotten he was there for a moment.

'What did you say?'

'I can read your mind. You want to be up there, with them, pitting your wits against death, don't you?'

'Why not? I can do a backflip from a standing start and I can jump across ten bollards in a row on any boulevard and never miss my footing.'

He rolled his eyes at her presumption and they giggled.

The performers scaled down to the sandy ring, clapped their hands, sending up clouds of chalk to catch the light. When the stable boy came back to join them, he pointed Mimi and

Rafi out to the man in the red coat-tails and he beckoned them over.

'I hear I have you to thank for the return of our runaway,' he smiled.

Mimi curtseyed. 'No beast too exotic or wild. Animal tamer extraordinaire at your service.'

'You're certainly a slip of a girl to be handling a frightened animal in a busy street. We are very grateful to you, and your friend here.'

Rafi shook the man's hand. 'I'm just the accomplice. She's the mastermind of the operation. Pleased to meet you.'

'Louis Dejean,' said the man. He regarded them. 'You both look like you could do with a good square meal. To thank you for your service, I'd like to offer you a season ticket to our winter circus, which includes dinner at the bar once a week.'

Mimi shot Rafi a warning glance not to look *too* grateful, even though it was beyond anything they could have dreamt of before she caught her zebra. This was too fortuitous not to try to turn to even more advantage.

'I'm Mimi and this is Rafi. That's so kind of you, and I'd like to accept on behalf of Rafi, who is currently working his way through a sack of dried beans for his supper most evenings. But as *my* payment, I would gratefully accept a position in your stables. I can assure you of good references from the mews in Montmartre and I have the added advantage of being able to perform a handstand on the back of any horse stabled there, which is frowned upon mostly, but here I'm sure would be acceptable, and perhaps even encouraged?'

Monsieur Dejean laughed and glanced at the stable boy, who shrugged.

'We could always use someone to help with the mucking out, I suppose.' He turned to Mimi. 'You'd have to roll up your sleeves like the rest of us.'

'Like I say, I know stable work.'

'You wouldn't be the first wild thing we've taken in off the streets of Paris, and there *is* a certain spark in you that we might be able to train.' Monsieur Dejean smiled.

As they emerged from the tent, Rafi whistled. 'How did you do that?'

'If you don't ask, you don't get,' said Mimi.

She looked up at the sky. A weak sun loomed, unable to break the clouds, but it must be about midday. A pang of hunger stabbed. She hadn't eaten yet today, but she'd feast on her good fortune and the sights of Montmartre instead.

As they climbed the Butte, they stopped to watch a funeral procession pass. A gilt carriage, four glossy black horses, reins decorated with crimson pom-poms. Inside was a child-sized coffin piled high with flowers and trailing behind, walking in step to the funeral drum with a small crowd of friends and relatives, was the mother, dressed in shabby black, not much older than Mimi. Her cheeks were still rosy, but her eyes were ancient. Despite the pomp, this was a pauper's funeral, the child no doubt the victim of disease and poverty, like half the children born here. The mother perhaps had a rich benefactor, maybe the child's father, to pay for such relative splendour.

Rafi crossed himself. Mimi knew he'd be railing against social injustice, another tiny life lost to inequality.

The procession was melancholy and bizarre and sumptuously cruel, like life, and Mimi swallowed a lump. This could so easily have been her fate, if she had not made certain choices.

She shook off the thought. *Just think about today, about now, about what God has given you for free, and use it well*, she told herself. It was the only way to survive.

CHAPTER 2

The bells pealed across the rooftops and invaded Mimi's dream. She counted five and blinked sleepily at her latest pictures on the wall. A circus tent: bunting adorning the guy ropes, the fortune teller's stall covered in stars, a girl high up on a trapeze. A job at the circus!

She slumped back into her pillow. That was only a week ago, but everything had changed so much since then. No rush to get to the laundry today.

Every inch of available wall space was covered in her drawings, which were organised into friezes – all scenes of Paris she collected. She'd leave here one day, and her wall drawings were the only things she'd miss in this dingy room where her mother had died in her arms, pockmarked with syphilis.

She could choose not to do the same. That was her *maman's* legacy to her. Determination was an inheritance better than any money. She was healthy. That already made her an out-and-out winner in Montmartre. More, she was smart and daring and drawn to the light, figuratively and emotionally. All she had to do was make sure the light wasn't dangerous, like a flame. Or even better, she'd *be* the flame.

The shouts and arguments had already started in the rickety tenement. Bare floorboards and thin walls were all that separated her attic room from her fellow residents. On the ground floor, the butcher slammed the door, shaking the whole building, and clattered out in his clogs and leather apron, leaving behind a weary wife and five hungry children. The old widow's songbirds in the room below Mimi's chirruped a welcome dawn chorus. The poor old soul had lost her grip on reality and screamed for her dead husband all night. Mimi had learned to sleep through that particular nightmare. Sandwiched between the widow and the butcher were the two girls who danced at the Moulin de la Galette by night and took gentleman callers by day. Like the widow's songbirds, they were bright, gaudy and delightful, kept for cheap entertainment, with fleeting, captive lives ahead of them. Her mother couldn't have been too much older than the girls – sixteen – when she had Mimi. But she made herself believe that it was passion, not commerce, that created her. That her papa whispered love and dreams and hope to his beautiful lover in the Parisian night.

Her little room was basic; at least, that's what she liked to call her clean-scrubbed hutch. A dripping sink with a rusting pipe, a worn little table where she sketched, prepared food, sewed and filled the chipped china bowl for washing. On the far wall, a cupboard containing her two dresses, crockery and box of treasures.

A cat-like stretch shook off the damp night, and she got up. The cold floor stung her feet, but every morning, she took care to be glad. The blood was coursing through her veins and every new day was a possibility, a question mark just waiting to be answered. She briskly smoothed the eiderdown across the narrow bed, pulled on her best dress, then took the box to the table to open it.

She lifted out the little doll in the yellow silk dress and

propped her up to watch the proceedings. 'I'll come for you one day,' she whispered, repeating her daily ritual.

Amongst the bits of pretty china, glass jewels, buttons and scraps of Chinese silk was a broken mirror, edged with faded gilding. Balancing it on the table, she pulled her fingers through her tousled black hair by way of a brush and pinched her olive cheeks. Rafi told her that her wide-set green eyes looked wicked even when she didn't mean them to, which would get her into trouble one day. Too late for that.

'A better life,' she said to her reflection, another part of the ritual she did every day. Her mother smiled back in agreement with the same green eyes.

A low sun promised a bright September day through her little window, the rooftops rosy with the first rays. First, the laundry to give her notice, then a rare day of leisure. A whole day, with no work to do before she began at the circus tomorrow. She and Rafi had an array of delights planned, all free of charge, and courtesy of her great benefactor, Paris.

Down on the street, the world of Montmartre was already busy. Ragpicker children worked the gutters outside the tailor shops, pulling scraps out of the filth, menaced by the gangsters who supervised them.

'*Salut!*' she called to them, willing them to grow stronger than the men who stood over them.

Further up the hill, the narrow streets grew wider and sunnier. Serving girls hurried past in white bonnets, men in blue smocks pulled goods carts, or headed to the blacksmith's, or the gypsum mines on the open slopes. The unseen work that fuelled the lives of the *beau monde*.

At the laundry, screeches of laughter and shouts rose up through the humidity, the steam engine flywheel adding to the din. The whole place smelt of damp and soap and bleach as women bent over the rows of hot tubs scrubbing and beating on washboards, working hard to get the lipstick out of toffs' collars,

cooing and envious over the expensive silks and light cottons
dumped carelessly into laundry baskets in ladies' boudoirs
without a second thought about who might scrub it all away.

The concierge shuffled out of her glass booth with a blue
bag of bicarbonate and cake soap, but Mimi shook her head.

'Not today. Not ever! I'm starting at the Cirque d'Hiver
tomorrow. I rescued their zebra.'

The concierge shrugged, unimpressed. 'Circus, is it? Heard
that one before. You'll be back the moment he drops you for the
next *grisette*. Mind you save enough money for the soap or
you'll be out on the streets. I'm not a charity.'

Miserable old sow, thought Mimi as she squinted through
the steamy fog.

The butcher's wife was already there leaning over a tub,
skirt tucked between her thighs to reveal red stockings and
battered lace-up boots. Her arms were red raw with her days at
the laundry, as were most of the women's here, droplets clinging
to their hair and clothes.

At their usual place by the big windows, Mimi found her
friends shouting over the din, opaquely illuminated by the sun
filtering through the milky fog.

Paulette was easy to spot with her bright copper hair. She
was petite with a voice like a foghorn and told the dirtiest jokes
in the laundry, and that was going some.

Henriette stopped her beating and beckoned Mimi over.
The vaporous air curled her soft blonde hair and her cornflower
eyes were round as child's, but her gaze was hard and cynical.

'Go on, tell her,' urged Henriette.

Paulette let her washing float in the tub and put her hands
on her hips. 'They're building a hollow elephant with a stage in
it outside the Moulin de la Galette, and I'm playing the guitar
for the belly dancers. Imagine all those toffs getting off at girls
dancing in an elephant. They'll know what a crescendo is when
I've finished with them.'

'They'll be paying double for a top F,' screamed Henriette, doubled over laughing.

Paulette had taught herself guitar and her playing was beautiful. Despite the jokes and chat, Mimi knew this meant a lot to her friend.

She smiled. 'Never mind a top F, what about the trills? You can keep those going all night!'

'You're disgusting,' shouted Henriette. 'Where's your soap? You can share my tub,' she said, shifting across.

'No need. I can go one better than the belly dancers in the elephant. I've got a job at the circus.'

Paulette was well known for 'borrowing' her customers' dresses before she returned them, laundered, and her brazen stare could fell a lord.

'Who is he?' said Paulette. In their world, it was usually a man who made anything happen in return for favours – nights out, jobs, new dresses. Basically, anything that wasn't just about staying alive.

'A zebra, if you don't mind,' replied Mimi grandly. She embellished the story about her brush with a crazed striped fugitive, promised faithfully she'd get them tickets and went off to meet Rafi at the Gare Saint-Lazare, leaving the laundry behind forever. How many girls had she seen triumphant with their ticket out of there, only to return battered and broken, or selling matches drunkenly on the corner of boulevard de Clichy? She'd be different.

Rafi was never late – and there he was standing under the station clock, wearing his best waistcoat, a darned but nevertheless white shirt, and his intellectual's cap. She always *was* late, so she ran, waving in apology.

He beamed when he saw her and extended his arm. 'Madame?'

'How sweetly polite.' Mimi smiled. 'Lead the way.'

The station was a grand building, like a chateau, but anyone could go in. They stepped through the arch onto the busy concourse and stopped at the departure board Someone had a talent for a written flourish with their flawless chalk calligraphy. Whoever created this on a daily basis was probably paid a pittance by the railways and went hungry most nights, like her. But you didn't need to be rich to have the soul of an artist.

'Trouville, Deauville, Rouen, Le Havre. Hmm, let me see. I believe Trouville is delightful at this time of year, but Deauville is the only place for the races and I'm dreadfully bored of lovely hotels and sandy beaches and lobster, with nothing else to do,' said Mimi.

'You're right. I've got more money than sense and that gold spoon up my arse is bothering me, so I'd rather chuck it all up on a bet than use it to actually help anyone who might need it, like a dying child or one of those grubby scuts at the poor house. The less they litter up the streets, the better.'

Mimi sighed. 'Rafi, can't you just pretend, for once?'

'And can't you stop dreaming?'

Couldn't he understand she never would?

She turned to face him. 'No one could have dreamt up my zebra, and look where that's got me. You don't always have to be glaring into the gutter.'

Rafi bowed and kissed her hand. 'Come on then, Deauville it is, for the races, Mademoiselle. I believe the train is about to depart.'

They went promenading, right to the far end of the platform. The iron and glass roof was as magnificent as a cathedral. Ladies wore crinolines and big floppy hats tied with ribbons even though it wasn't Sunday and their skin was so clear and clean, like a doll's. The dolls chatted and looked out for the train and didn't even care if their skirts skimmed the dirty platform. Why would they when they had the likes of her to wash it off? Porters hefted leather trunks with gold padlocks and men in top hats shook out newspapers as they waited on the benches, with nothing better to do than catch up on their stocks and shares, la-di-da.

'Now,' shouted Mimi as the gleaming beast of a train rounded the bend with a husky toot. Mimi and Rafi stood right at the tip of the platform and screwed their eyes shut as smoke billowed to fill the station. The engine roared, showering them with smuts, coming to a breathless halt just short of the buffers. Standing in their cloud, looking back on the shadowy figures getting off the train, meeting lovers, greeting friends, was like watching a secret story unfold.

But seeing the children reuniting with their parents, burying their little faces into their mother's skirts, delightedly kissing papa on both cheeks, was the loneliest feeling in the world for Mimi.

She chased away the thought and imagined her escape from the life that she was in. To be going somewhere, away from Paris, whisked to a different place in a matter of hours was unimaginable. What was it like by the sea? What colour was the air? Did the clouds scud faster across the sky with the breeze off the ocean?

The steam subsided and the last passengers hurried onto the train. Doors slammed, women waved their handkerchiefs out of the windows and the guard blew his whistle. Another train left the station without her, and with it a world that seemed so impossibly out of reach. It's not that she wanted to go anywhere in particular, but to be one of those people, speeding out of Paris purely for leisure, to see the world outside of the slums, was so beguiling.

'I think we'll stay in Paris today after all, don't you? I do believe today is the bird market on the Île de la Cité. The birds are international, from all over the world, and I might even find a feather for my bonnet.'

They left the station and headed for Notre-Dame. *One day it will be me stepping onto that train in a crinoline so wide I'll hire a porter to shove me through the door,* thought Mimi.

On the boulevard Haussmann, the beautiful people paraded. This was one of the new boulevards, named after the architect himself. Everything was uniform, and there were rules for every building, Rafi told her. Never mind the medieval winding streets and crumbling buildings of the old Paris; a certain layout must now be followed. Rafi had read all about it – every ground floor was for commerce, every second floor was the 'noble' part with wide running balconies and beautifully crafted window frames, then another floor with a less grand balcony, then at the top an attic for the servants, all made from creamy-coloured limestone with shiny slate rooves. The effect was boulevards wide as rivers, filled with sunshine and it felt so clean. Through the big windows, the chandeliers and gilt chairs were like looking in on heaven. They were only a couple of kilometres from Montmartre, but it could have been a thousand.

'Watch!' said Mimi.

She jumped up onto a smartly painted bollard, caught her balance, focused and leapt. She made ten in a row easily, sure-footed on each tiny, slippery landing.

'See?' she said to Rafi, jumping down from number ten. 'I said I could.'

'I never doubted you, Mimi. And I can actually watch you safe on those bollards, rather than have to witness your rooftop leaps.'

'Safe is for wimps and losers,' she scoffed, exhilarated.

'Then I'm happy for you to count me among them. I know you too well. You've got your sights set on that trapeze, haven't you?' Rafi replied. He always could see right through her.

'First stop: zebra shit. Destination: flying through the air in a blaze of glory. Why not?'

'You're brave and beautiful, a rare, singular being, but you refuse to see the world as it really is. Jesus, Mimi, you're deluded. You've chucked in a steady job at the laundry – who knows how long things will last at the circus, and you've fought so hard to be independent.'

Mimi spun a pirouette to ward off his words, her arms outstretched to embrace the world. He was just worried about her, but being sensible didn't break you out of your fate.

'I have to try. I refuse to be a drudge or a prostitute and at this moment in time a stable job at the circus is a dream come true. Who cares about security or being sensible? Come on!'

The next stop was another dream of hers, to be an artist, accepted by the powers-that-be.

Rafi rolled his eyes, but fell in step with her breakneck pace.

They turned the corner to the rue Bonaparte and there it was, the École des Beaux-Arts. Girls from the slums dressed as shepherdesses and men posing as soldiers were already outside the tall gates and snaking around the corner, gossiping and jostling for position. More hopefuls looking for a ticket to a different world, desperate to be picked as artists' models for depictions of battles or classical rural idylls.

There was a time when Mimi wouldn't have thought twice about scaling the closed gates and taking a look around. Now she was nineteen, the only way she'd ever get through those gates would be as a model. But imagine what it would be like to be the one actually *choosing* the model. Spending your whole day with colours and paints and canvas and not even worrying about the cost or time it took.

Through the gates, the cobbled courtyard, surrounded by galleried walkways, looked impossibly grand. The fountain in the middle scintillated the light and she'd heard the galleries inside were vast marble halls. Funny how she could reach her hands through the wrought-iron gates, just a few centimetres separating her from the other side, but it was a world beyond her reach.

'When I'm a great artist, I'll invite you to my *vernissage* here, at the Académie's Salon exhibition,' Mimi said to Rafi.

'And I'll take you for a ride on my magic carpet,' said Rafi. 'It's actually against the law for a girl to join the Académie, so even with your imagination, it would be impossible to exhibit at the Salon.'

'Don't say that word impossible to me, you know how it makes me stubborn.'

Why did Rafi always have to state the obvious? It was true about the Académie and the Salon, but rules were made to be broken in her experience. He could be so dour and she'd hate him for it if she didn't know it was just his way of trying to protect her.

'Nevertheless, it's the truth. I can't help that, even if it does upset you, which is the last thing in the world I ever want to make you. You can forget at the bird market. I believe that is our final destination in our tour of Paris?'

'Us circus girls need our beauty sleep and I have to be up early tomorrow.'

They strolled in silence along the banks of the Seine. Cormorants sped past barges loaded with wine or fruit and vegetables, exotic wares sailed in and out of the capital from far and wide and tug boats chugged past *bateaux-lavoirs* – the laundry boats where the girls used the river water to wash laundry by day and where men arrived with flaming torches to light their way onto the boats at night.

They crossed themselves at Notre-Dame. Haussmann's big new square outside the cathedral allowed them to stand back and take in the beautiful old sight, admire the recently added embellishments of the newly carved gargoyles, chimeras and fantastical statues. Theatre and beauty again. It was everywhere if you knew where to look and it would never run out, like money or food or kindness. Life was a feast for the taking if you closed your heart to hurt. And Mimi tried to do that every day.

They strolled in contemplative silence to Île de La Cité, which was part disease-ridden slum, part Haussmann dream and part big, gaping holes of dirt and rubble where the slums were in the process of being razed to the ground.

Rafi scowled. 'All the old character's being sanitised and the people that lived here are being pushed out. Remember the dentist who sang opera so loud he could drown out his patients' screams? Who's going to pull teeth for free now? The man who looked like a floppy-haired Angel Gabriel who played the accordion like a god? His Jack Russell could dance a jig better than the girls at the Moulin. The street doesn't even exist where that Irish shoeshine could add up any numbers you threw at him in seconds. He should have been at the Institut Français, but God knows where he's ended up. Those old soldiers who played chess under the trees and cried for lost comrades but were always fed by people who had the least? All bulldozed out to make way for what?'

'You speak like I draw. It's all in vivid colours in your head,' said Mimi. 'But I love the grand new buildings and wide boulevards. You can breathe in a place like this.'

'The only reason they've widened the streets is so that they can march a full battalion on the poor. In the revolution, you could barricade a street and keep the oppressors out,' he said gloomily.

Mimi took off his hat and ruffled his hair. 'What misery goes on in there!?'

'Give that back!'

He tickled her to make her let go and caught her in his arms when she collapsed. They both felt it, she could tell, but she pulled away. She needed a friend, not a lover, and she couldn't risk Rafi ever tiring of her.

CHAPTER 3

Tif flattened his ears at her, a far cry from the frenzied beast she'd calmed on the boulevard Montmartre.

'Here,' she breathed as he nuzzled the grass she always brought him from the top of the Butte, where it grew sweetest. The markings on his face were like a bold fingerprint, unique to him. He nudged her in gratitude.

The sun was barely risen and the thick autumn dew seeped through her old boots. But she didn't care. It was worth getting here early every morning so she could finish in time to see the show every night, which meant there was no time to see Rafi. Anyway, he'd just tell her she was foolish for working so hard and imagining she could change her fate just by being near to the action. Once a worker, always a worker, he always said. But the way she saw it, it was no one's business but her own, and she wasn't going to change anything by scrubbing away at the laundry and being scared of moving on. So every day for the past month, she'd whispered *a better life* to herself in the cracked mirror over the sink and blown a kiss to the doll in the yellow dress before she left to offer help on absolutely anything that needed doing at the circus.

She'd now had a month of mucking out, grooming, polishing tack, tightening guy ropes, sewing sequins, raking the sand in the ring, serving at the circus bar, entertaining the performers' children while they worked – no end of tasks for anyone willing, like her. She never tired of the circus. The performances might be the same, but the audience were different every night and their faces were a study in infinite variety. How was it that every single person was distinct from the next, each with their own particular reaction to the show, a host of human expression, relatable yet unique, every one of them alone in this world? The best crowd scenes in the Louvre were ones that reflected this infinitesimal human individuality. Some artists repeated faces in their backgrounds, but she'd never do that. She stored the circus crowds, their expressions, clothes, gestures and interactions, for the solo exhibition at the École des Beaux-Arts she'd promised Rafi. He'd taken it as a joke, but he had no idea how serious she was.

There were artists in the audience, too. Men who sat together, squandering paper and pastels and charcoal on the scenes with abandon. The bookish-looking one with the receding hairline and tortoiseshell glasses sometimes filled up a whole sketchbook in one sitting. She wondered if they were capturing the incredible scenes which unfolded every night for the École des Beaux-Arts. Did they return there each day, and turn their sketches into oil paintings? She understood their fascination. She felt it too.

Every evening from her vantage point in the wings, she'd wink at Boum Boum the clown and pull back the curtain for him to fly past on his unicycle, scowling until the spotlight caught him. The very moment he was illuminated, his smile radiated mischief and bonhomie. He'd get them all going – the children, the aristos in their top hats and silks and the shopkeepers in the back row. It didn't matter where they came from, Boum Boum had them rolling.

She swept the curtain wider for the Cossacks on their palominos, five abreast in braided velvet coats and caps, sabres flashing. The audience screamed as the fierce men mixed swordplay with gymnastics, all the while unfeasibly staying on the backs of the steeds who circled the ring.

Up on the trapeze, the rumour (which Monsieur Dejean enthusiastically encouraged) was that Jules blacked out momentarily on the third turn of his triple somersault. Ladies in the audience regularly fainted watching it. Some genuinely, others into the arms of surprised but gallant gentlemen.

After the show, exuberant boxing and fencing matches broke out amongst the wagons, while the circus dogs barked, the animals stamped in their stalls and the girls yelled their allegiances, still beautiful in their circus costumes and rouge, shivering in the night air, chattering and laughing.

But, best of all, at the end of the night, Jules and Juliet stayed on in the big top to teach her the trapeze, lowering the ropes close enough to the ground so that if she fell (which she frequently did), no harm would come to her. Rafi hadn't believed her, but now here she was, exactly as she'd intended, changing her fate, being taught the ropes and practising whenever the big top was empty. *And* she always landed on her feet, like a cat. It didn't matter how hard she'd worked in the day. She seized the moment whenever she could, late at night, early in the morning, or on anything in Montmartre that resembled a trapeze – even in the gypsum mines where ropes and pulleys were set up for the workers. Nobody, apart from Rafi, had ever helped Mimi before. Everyone she knew until now was too busy trying not to starve or die.

Today, after her work was done, Monsieur Dejean asked her to help on the turnstiles. Friday nights were always the busiest and the usual girl had run off with a regular from the audience. A lord, from London, with an estate as big as Paris, was the whisper. Mimi sent a silent prayer after the girl, who was only sixteen. Unlikely she would even get as far as Calais before he dumped her.

Jules and Juliet brought audiences in their droves from all over Paris with their daring flying trapeze act. Tonight, the crush was so bad three ladies caught their skirts in the turnstile. *No different from the rest of us*, thought Mimi as she helped extricate the expensive fabric from the mechanism. It doesn't matter how much you have; the cream will always instinctively fight for more.

Halfway down the queue, two men surreptitiously scanned the roped-off area. The taller of the two had a mop of floppy dark hair, a red paisley scarf tied in a bow at his neck and a tailcoat that had seen better days; his friend was stocky, with a broad, open face, thick, expressive eyebrows and an easy smile, wearing a silk cravat that looked more expensive than the rest of his outfit. Students, she guessed, with a swagger about them, and an air of harmless roguery. Mimi smiled to herself as they crept into the shadows and unhooked a tent peg. The one with the cravat slipped through and as the fop turned for a final scan for followers, he caught her eye, pressed his finger to his lips with an appreciative wink, then dived under, dragging his battered leather satchel behind him.

They had some sass and fun about them at least, and who was she to grass? Two less tickets weren't going to make much of a dent in the profits with this overstuffed queue of toffs pressing coins in her palm.

Inside, from her place in the wings, she saw Cravat and Floppy pull sketchbooks out of their satchels and join the usual group of artists. Tickets were beyond their pockets, but they could afford paper and pencils, maybe even paints. It was a matter of priority that she keenly understood.

She forgot about them soon enough. Jules had pronounced that tonight was the night that she was ready for the high ropes.

Her first time with the trapeze at performance height, with only her wit and body to save her.

When the final bow was taken and the crowd filed out into the night, she slipped a precious coin into the stagehand's palm to keep the ring lamps lit.

'Are you sure you're ready for this, Mademoiselle lightning-in-a-bottle?' Jules teased, crossing his arms and nodding up to the trapeze, soaring high in the big top.

Jules Léotard wasn't much taller than her, neat and dark and powerful as a panther with his southern tan and trademark tight-fitting costume which flaunted his physique. His aquiline features and chiselled good looks reminded her of a diminutive Greek god, but it was no use admiring his generous fortune in charm and grace. His preference was for the stable boys and Cossacks and cage fighters from Egypt who travelled with the circus. They were all a little in love with him. Even if they weren't his way inclined, they all wanted to *be* him.

'I'm ready.' Mimi smiled, swallowing a lump of nerves.

'Remember everything I told you, I'll watch from here, and don't let him drop you, darling!' said Juliet.

Jules was already scaling the net. The delirium and excitement Mimi had felt the first night she saw Jules and Juliet's act surged through her veins as she scaled behind him.

When they reached the platform, Jules swung to the other side and cast the trapeze back to Mimi. *Don't think.* She caught it, plunged and flew, used the momentum at the bottom of the arc to push herself up the other side to join him. She landed sure and steady, the lights making columns of chalk dust like the fairies Maman once showed her in the sunbeams in her bedroom.

You will not look down, she instructed her pounding heart.

'Stay in the moment, focus. You must have faith that I will catch you,' whispered Jules before he flew away again to the opposite perch.

She did believe, with all her heart. This was what she was made for, something different, daring and beautiful.

He gave the nod, now! She sprang, flew the trapeze in a fizz of nerves, sinews firing, twisted free, heart exploding, and Jules snatched her out of the air, his grip slick and gritty with chalk and sweat. She flexed and arched, and they pushed together to the platform, caught the bar and landed together. Below their thin pedestal, there was nothing but cold air.

He hugged her trembling body. 'See? It's safer without a net. You trust only in yourself. A net fogs the mind. You are a shooting star now, my sweet little urchin!' He squeezed her bicep. 'Made of solid rock. How do you get like this when you don't eat?'

'I devour the air like a flame and that's what makes me strong. Haven't you noticed you can't breathe when you're near me?' she laughed, exhilarated and dizzy and faint.

'Be still, my beating heart, such spirit! You will make an angel's descent to the earth for your daring,' pronounced Jules, who adored a dramatic turn of phrase. 'Bring my goddess down from the sky,' he called to Juliet, who was waiting on the ropes in the ring.

Sitting on the trapeze, legs crossed, toes pointed, arms stretched out in a star, Mimi flashed her eyes to catch the spotlight – a professional circus girl's trick – and travelled slowly down, perceiving the heights in different colours. The top was golden and viscous, like heaven, the middle was white and thin and dangerous, and closer to the ground were black clouds of soft velvet. Safe, but stifling and commonplace.

Juliet whirled her in a wild waltz around the ring. 'You did it, you did it, you did it!'

Jules sang and clapped the circus band's oompah-pah, 'Bravissimo, bravo, magnifico, exalto!'

'I don't think that's a word, darling,' said Juliet.

'Who cares!' intoned Jules in a deep bass.

Mimi wondered if this was what it was like to have brothers and sisters, or even parents who were proud of you, for no reason, apart from just being you.

'You were a vision! I have some absinthe, darlings, back at the wagon. Let's celebrate,' exclaimed Juliet.

'It's an early night for me, my little hummingbirds. My body's a temple and there are acolytes who wish to worship at my altar. Night night, my little cat,' said Jules, kissing her on the forehead. He headed off for the Egyptian camp.

'I don't drink, but thank you,' said Mimi. 'Unlikely, I know, for a slut from Montmartre, but I like to keep a clear head.' She smiled, trying not to show her distaste for the stuff she'd seen ruin so many girls at the laundry.

'Just for coffee, then, I hate to go back alone,' pleaded Juliet. She was a ghost, thin and pale and delicate, a will-o'-the-wisp of a thing, almost light enough to float like the chalk dust in the spotlight. Everyone knew her father was an aristocrat and her mother a drunk. And, strange for a flying trapeze girl, she had the most terrible jitters. At first, Mimi thought it was an act to scare the crowd, but even on solid ground, Juliet was in a constant state of agitation, jumping from one leg to the other, stifling involuntary kicks and hand flutters. St Vitus's Dance, Monsieur Dejean called it. With Jules' powerful physique, and Juliet's delicate jitters, they were the most popular circus act in town. Up there, she was magnificent. Down here, she was just a scared girl trying to make it, like her.

'I'd love to,' said Mimi.

They strolled arm-in-arm past the animal stalls, where the beasts were quiet for the night, to the other end of the field where the most successful acts were stationed. Juliet's was one of the most elaborate wagons, gilded like a carousel, decorated with a cartoon painting of her winking cheekily at the viewer from a crescent moon swing against a night sky.

I could do a better painting of her for her wagon, thought Mimi idly as they mounted the steps.

Inside, someone had lit the wood burner. It was cosy and warm and the most luxurious dwelling she'd ever been invited into, as a guest rather than a servant.

There were low lamps with pink silk shades, a polished walnut table, a dresser crammed with porcelain and thick velvet bed drapes embroidered with a 'J' in gold thread.

Juliet gestured to a red banquette at the table. It was padded and soft and Mimi sank into it gratefully, suddenly exhausted after the night's excitement. Juliet stood two glasses on the table and, with shaking hands, poured green liquid into both, then rested two flat slotted spoons over the glasses, balancing a sugar cube on each.

'Not for me.' Mimi smiled sleepily.

'It just seems so unfriendly only pouring one. It's a charming little ceremony, you'll see.'

Juliet lit the sugar cubes, then stood back to let them sizzle and melt into the green spirit, pale face aglow. Everything about her was delicate and refined. A true aristo's daughter.

When the sugar was melted, Juliet added water and the drinks turned a milky green. She held one out to Mimi.

'Your body has flown, now your mind. Wild things like you should try everything at least once. Go on, just a teensy one, for me. It won't hurt, I promise.'

Mimi felt heady after her trapeze success and it was so luxurious and comfy in this cocoon of a wagon with Juliet. Why not just this once?

The drink was bitter and sweet and oozed warmth into her.

'There, that's better, those green eyes are a little less watchful now. You know it's all right to let your guard down every now and then? You're quite the ingénue with those ebony locks and cat's eyes. All that time talking to zebras and mucking out when you could be reclining on a chaise longue in luxury, delighting any man you choose to. What's your story? Everyone has one, particularly a beautiful gamine from Montmartre.' Juliet smiled.

'I've seen what happens to those chaise longue girls. At the first sign of crow's feet or a thickening waist, they're on a street corner, selling matches and begging their gentlemen to buy their pretty flowers. Not for me. I'd rather depend on these for survival.' Mimi tapped her forehead and strong arms.

'Well, you're quite the singular little thing, aren't you? Good for you.'

Three of the milky green glasses later and Mimi's head was spinning delightfully. It really did feel like flying. Juliet downed another and slammed the glass on the table, her jitters temporarily banished by the drink.

'That's better. Now, truth or dare. I'll begin,' slurred Juliet. 'Truth: every night on the trapeze, I fight myself not to let go. Imagine the glorious release! Your turn.'

Mimi giggled, 'I felt it, too. What is that?'

'The trapeze artist's curse. Everyone feels it up there, even Jules. But you didn't tell me anything at all about you. Truth!'

'I'd rather have a dare,' said Mimi.

Juliet burnt another sugar cube and slid the glass to her. 'All right, I dare you to drink another.'

'All right, Madame Juliet. If you insist.' Mimi felt the liquid warm her bones. 'There. Now your turn again. Truth or dare?'

'Always truth, darling.'

'Who's the most wonderful man you've ever kissed?' said Mimi from somewhere inside her addled head.

At this, Juliet's mood darkened. 'My father, on the cheek, to say goodbye,' she whispered, a lone tear sliding down her cheek.

Mimi caught her mood, hugged her. 'No need to explain if you don't want to.'

As Mimi held her, Juliet got the jitters again, a bag of shivering, fragile bones in Mimi's arms.

'I was ten years old and I adored him. He cried too, but he had a wife and a legitimate child. So he left my mother and me. That's when I ran away to the circus and Jules found me. He said I was light enough to fly.'

'Just a piece of fluff. If I wasn't holding you down, you'd float away now,' said Mimi and they managed a giggle before Mimi found herself sobbing, too.

She knew how it felt to be abandoned by a parent. Her own mother had chosen drink over her, or that's how it felt until she was old enough to understand a little more. And Juliet's grief touched something even deeper inside that, however hard she tried, she just couldn't bury. How *could* a parent walk away from a child, however much society demanded it? Even if the child was tiny, and too young to remember, was there always something missing, something sad they couldn't name? Who could ever love a child as much as their own parents? She remembered the doll in the yellow dress, a lifeless connection to something so precious, so lost, that there was never a second in the day she didn't desperately yearn to find it again.

'There *is* something. I just knew it,' said Juliet tenderly, sitting back and regarding her. 'Go on. There isn't a soul in this circus who isn't running away from something. Let it out. I promise I will keep your secret.'

'I have a daughter, a little angel, but her father took her.'

Juliet gripped her hands. 'You should not have let him.'

'She's better with him. He's rich.' Even as she said it, she struggled to believe a child was better off without their mother.

'Rich is ten-a-penny. You're special, I've seen enough urchins come and go through this circus to know it. Jules is right, lightning in a bottle. There's a self-possession about you, like a coiled spring, and when you turn your quick mind to something, sparks fly. You'll find a way. You *have* to. Tell me all about her.'

Apart from Rafi, Juliet was the only soul she'd talked to

about Colette since she gave her away. It was commonplace enough where she came from, so people forgot very quickly that she'd ever had a child, but for Mimi the pain never diminished. It was still raw, and she let the tears fall in a cloud of absinthe, grief and relief. She told Juliet everything.

She thought he loved her. Pathetic, like all the other girls in Montmartre. She was not even sixteen. Jean-Baptiste had given her money, even visited her after Colette was born. He was handsome and rich, with a rakish smile and a devil-may-care attitude that she shared, and they danced away their nights in the cabarets and under the stars. His dark hair contrasted strikingly with his pale skin, making him almost pretty, and his bow tie was always slightly skew-whiff, like he'd just run to meet her from a grand drawing room. Their daughter was a perfect, determined, olive-skinned plum with a shock of dark hair like her mother's. There were days of bliss and exhaustion when he'd come and cuddle them both in her narrow bed. He bought Colette lace dresses and bonnets and tiny shoes, even a carved crib that rocked.

Mimi had cared for her like a tigress until her new-minted eyes turned from sea-blue to verdigris. Her little princess's life would be so different from hers. But Colette's father made her see how it was an impossible dream and how he loved Colette equally. Mimi could never be accepted in his world, and he couldn't countenance living in hers. It was not the natural order. The kindest thing she could do for her daughter was to let him pass her off as his widowed sister's child, recently returned from America.

It was the ultimate sacrifice in a world where Montmartre babies were more likely to die than live. Mimi choked with grief the moment she said goodbye, folded and packed the pristinely laundered little dresses and tiny shoes, buried her head in those milky soft dark curls and hummed a lullaby to the warm little plum who, at six months, was turning into a smiling peach with a laugh that melted ice.

She couldn't stop once she'd started. She told Juliet about the nights she'd lain awake, tortured by Colette's imagined screams for her *maman*. The visceral need for her, the worry she might be unhappy, the umbilical cord that could never be cut, that ran deep and painful as the fissures that snaked through the gypsum mines, and she would never be whole again.

The next morning, Mimi woke up on the banquette under a warm throw, with the full sun on her face. Juliet was watching her with her chin on her hands.

'I've been waiting for you to wake up. You are ready,' said Juliet.

Mimi blinked; her head hurt, and her eyes were swollen with tears. 'Ready for what?'

'To perform the high trapeze. I always knew that you were strong. We saw what you're capable of last night: and now you have a reason not to fall. Your little Colette. You will get her back, I know you will. So you cannot fail.'

Mimi looked around Juliet's wagon. She was the highest paid performer in Paris, earned enough to buy a mansion if she wanted. Enough to buy a house and security and a respectable life for a little family for anyone who had nerves of steel and a head for heights. Mimi had given her baby away to give her a better life, but what if she could provide that life now? And surely a daughter was always better with their own mother? She had to try.

CHAPTER 4

Two months later, Mimi still visited Tif every morning, but there was no more mucking out for her. That was the job of one of the ragpicker children, the one with the big soulful eyes and a filthy turn of phrase that she'd passed every day on her way to the circus. *One rescued, thousands to go,* thought Mimi as the boy saluted her and unhooked the latch to the stable. Thanks to her recommendation to Monsieur Dejean, he had a chance in life. She hoped her kindness to this cheeky kid would be paid forward in luck and kindness for her Colette somehow. She pinched his cheek, which was plumper after a month here, and held out the grass for her tamed black-and-white friend.

Through a miracle of luck, wit, rope burns, purple bruises, sprains and the patience of her trainers, 'Jules and Juliet on Jupiter' was now 'Alnitak, Alnilam and Mintaka', named after the three stars of Orion's Belt. Mimi was Mintaka.

She had a different costume for every day, in seven different colours. A sparkling basque sewn with sequins, a matching headdress that shone against her dark hair, tiny shorts which just covered her toned derrière, silk tights to match her olive skin, and supple leather ballerina slippers, all made just for her.

She could never have dreamt in a million years what it was like to fly through the air, hear the gasps of the crowds on the release, the cries of relief on the catch. With her hair streaming, she was a comet's tail blazing in the lights, a lithe, mythical being. On the trapeze, the laws of gravity were nothing to their little constellation of three. The moment between the 'hep' and the 'catch' was a journey across the abyss, a frisson of terror, focus and synapse, the only moment she was truly alive.

Mimi and Juliet were 'a negative of each other: unattainable heaven and delicious, wicked hell', as one review mused on Juliet's pale fragility and Mimi's contrasting sultry power. 'An act that strikes terror into the hearts of the weak and evokes the bloodlust of Roman emperors in the strong. An impossible, glittering spectacle you'll pray is over, then cry out for more,' proclaimed *Le Figaro*'s theatre reviewer, who never missed a show.

Mimi's world was now a cavalcade of dreams, where 'ghost twins' spooked the queues at the turnstiles, dogs in tutus danced, elephants paraded in Rajasthani finery and superhuman feats of horsemanship, strength, contortion, freakery, flaming chariots and glamour were the order of the day.

Monsieur Dejean could rouse the dead with his purple prose: 'Cirque d'Hiver's brightest lights... the awe-inspiring, the death-defying, the unparalleled gods and goddesses of the firmament! Alnitak the brave, Alnilam the ethereal and Mintaka the dark star.'

And with her rising star, Mimi dared to hope. In Montmartre at the laundry, she'd tried to get on with her life, and accept that she had done the best she could by Colette. But now, the thought almost hurt, she wanted it so badly. She could make her own money, make a life for herself, and bring her daughter back to live with her, where she belonged.

The girls from the laundry came to see the show, smothered her in congratulatory kisses and begged to borrow her sequinned basques. She gave free tickets and behind-the-scenes contacts to Rafi, and his interview with the Egyptian acrobats made *l'Opinion Nationale*. The Egyptian troupe had met whilst they were labouring on the Suez Canal and Rafi was lauded for his political understanding of the strategic importance of the waterway, along with his vivid descriptions of the men's lives first in Egypt, and now in Cirque d'Hiver. On the back of that, other commissions had begun to trickle through. Mimi was fiercely proud of him, but they rarely crossed paths nowadays and she missed him. He hadn't believed her when she said she'd fly the trapeze and now look at her. She enjoyed exasperating him and seeing that wry smile he did when she proved him wrong, and she looked forward to the day he saw her flying.

The circus adapted to every season and Christmas meant warm glühwein in the bar and hot chestnuts served to the families queuing for the festive spectacular. Snuggled up to their parents, the little girls were wrapped in muffs and hooded capes, the boys in knitted hats and mittens with fur collars turned up against the cold. In Montmartre, Christmas meant freezing, suffering and death, so it was easier to be happy that her daughter was just safe. Here, Christmas meant storybook happy families.

But at least she had a family now, of sorts; the circus took care of their own. It was an eclectic coming together of humans from all over the world, constantly evolving, sweeping up the odd waif and stray along the way for an unusual talent, a freakish appearance, or exceptional beauty – they were all fed, watered, loved and drawn into the bosom of the place.

That was how she came to be sitting in the darkness of Madame Vadoma's fortune-telling tent. Juliet had persuaded her that a girl with no past to speak of, no parents to ask about relations or tell her about who she was, should consult the fortune teller. Madame Vadoma offered one free reading to every new recruit to the circus, and today it was Mimi's turn.

Mimi had thought it would be a gas, perhaps even evoke a sketch that would only need charcoal to capture the dark images inside the starry tent. But now she was here, sitting in front of Madame Vadoma, she wasn't so sure. She had expected her to drop the act, like all the other circus performers did with each other when they were out of public view. Not Madame Vadoma. After Mimi blinked to accustom herself to the sudden darkness in the tent, a figure in a yashmak had gestured for her to sit with a sweep of her arm, then unveiled herself to reveal an unsmiling, ghostly face framed with long black witchy hair. Mimi shifted in her seat and hoped the worst of her secrets were safe from the woman's penetrating stare. She opened her mouth to speak, but the fortune teller held up a hand with fingernails so long they curled over.

'No talking, it blurs the vision,' she commanded.

Madame Vadoma moved a figure around a pentagon board, muttering words 'from the dead'. In the dim light, Mimi saw that the figure was an exact facsimile of her and she longed to be back outside in the sunshine.

'I see it!' Madame Vadoma's eyes flickered and her voice deepened unnaturally.

This act was a bit too convincing for Mimi's taste.

'Your papa is watching. He is your catcher through Monsieur Léotard and bids you *stai attento, mio piccolo gattino.*'

Mimi didn't dare ask what the words meant, but they sounded Italian and that made her want to cry as she remembered the rumours about her parentage, her drunken mother's fling with an Italian acrobat. She committed the words to memory to ask the Italian tumbler later.

'There are two papas. This one has a little girl with him who looks like you, but isn't you. She is screaming.'

Colette! That was enough of this old woman's cruelty. Juliet must have briefed her too well. Mimi stood up to leave.

'Sit! You'll break the spell, they'll kill you!'

She did as she was told, frozen to the spot.

Madame Vadoma moved the figure again. 'There is a brother, but not a brother. His writing will reach into the future.' The woman heaved in unearthly, shuddering sobs. 'You will die twice. Once in terror.'

'Please, stop,' begged Mimi.

Thank God, the woman snapped out of her trance and transformed into something more human. She put her hand over Mimi's.

'I must complete the reading, my dear, but don't be afraid. Death does not always mean the end. It can mean a new beginning. Hear me through, just a little longer.'

Moving the figure once more, Madame Vadoma smiled and nodded.

'Sunlight, a river, an artist's palette. A man who cultivates the weeds will bring success, but without him there will be no happiness. There, my dear, it's not all bad, but I have a warning. You must endure.'

* * *

'Hocus-pocus and nonsense,' Mimi whispered to Tif, burying her head in his warm flank for comfort. What a disturbing little interlude!

Tif stamped in agreement and the sun shone on them both, chased away the whispering shadows and filled her with optimism and warmth once more. But there *was* something that she couldn't entirely dismiss. Giacomo, the Italian tumbler, had translated 'her father's' words for her. *Be safe, my little kitten.* It had been her mother's nickname for her. How did Madame Vadoma know, and what did her father mean by it? And if that was true… did that mean her Colette really was screaming for her mother? For Mimi?

She tried to put it out of her mind. Up there, on the ropes, the exact split second she was in was the only thing that mattered.

Dressed in a new basque – red and green, for Christmas – she peeped out at the audience before going on, her nightly ritual. There were Cravat and Floppy, sketching amongst the coterie of artists. And Rafi was here too. He'd promised to come tonight for the Christmas Spectacular and take her for a glass of champagne afterwards. He actually had money from *l'Opinion Nationale,* and they'd have a drink just because they could, like a couple of *flâneurs* from the *beau monde.* There he was, scribbling something in a notepad, wearing his intellectual's cap and a new tweed jacket.

Her heart stopped when she saw the little girl in the front row. Wispy curls escaped from a green silk hairband and she was wrapped in a fur-lined winter cape, like a child in a fairy tale. It was her, she was sure. Colette! How was that possible?

Even from where she was in the wings, Mimi was stricken with longing and love for this little vision. As she stared, a striking man with dark hair and a boyishly skew-whiff bow tie leant down and whispered something in Colette's ear. Another shock: her ex-lover Jean-Baptiste. Did he *know* it was her up on the trapeze? Of course not. He had probably told her daughter she was dead.

As he whispered, Colette giggled. What wouldn't Mimi give to be on the receiving end of those giggles.

'Dear God, please give her back to me,' she whispered.

But she didn't need God, or anyone else. Colette was precisely why she was here, and she'd go out there and perform and save her money and keep going until she could provide a home and buy velvet capes and give her the doll with the yellow dress and take her to the circus. It was worth risking her life for every night. Mimi was all Mimi had, and it was more than enough, she told herself.

She didn't tell a soul, not even Juliet. Circus people were a superstitious lot, and the idea that she might be distracted by such a momentous audience member would spook them all. She could fly better now than she ever had in her short life as a trapeze artist. She'd make damn sure that Colette would never forget Mintaka.

Tonight, like every night, Jules performed his triple somersault, silencing the crowd as he lost height with each turn, and saving himself just at the nadir. She and Juliet – Mintaka and Alnilam – were once more the brightest stars in the firmament and the crowd held their breath until they were both safely on their platforms, clutching the bars. The last flight was Mimi's mid-air pirouette.

Jules threw her the trapeze, which she seized with a flourish, swooped, released and spun. Colette's bright upturned face caught her eye and Mimi beamed a split second too long at her, arched for Jules' grip: and missed.

Colette's screams ripped through her as Mimi plummeted, clawing the air, terrified at the inevitability of ground rushing to meet her. Then everything blacked out.

CHAPTER 5

The clinical smell of alcohol filled the room. Mimi opened her eyes and Rafi swam into focus, looking terrible. He smiled.

'Hello,' he said gently.

She tried to sit up, but nothing happened. Both legs and her left arm were splinted and cast. Her drawing hand was cotton wool and her limbs were numb. Sweet Mary, she wanted her mother, the one she knew when she was little, who made everything safe. A leaden lump of fear choked her. Her beautiful, reliable body!

'Jesus, Rafi, what's happened to me?'

So this explained the nightmares she'd had somewhere dark and unexplained, with only Colette's screams to accompany her.

'Why do you always have to go so far to get attention?' He gave her a watery grin.

It must be bad; he was being too kind, and he didn't want to tell her. She was back in her little narrow bed in the attic. The old widow's songbirds were counterpointing her mutterings from the floor below, and the circus pictures she'd drawn the day she rescued Tif were still there on the wall to mock her.

How had she thought that a *grisette* from Montmartre could ever escape?

Everything hurt and the brave look on Rafi's face made her tremble.

He poured something onto a teaspoon and held it to her lips. 'Here, the doctor left this for the pain. Just take it easy. Everything in good time.'

Swallowing the tincture sent her head spinning, but it chased away the pain.

'How long have I been here?'

'Two weeks, but you mustn't worry. Everything is taken care of. The circus has paid for a good doctor...' Rafi faltered.

Mimi steeled herself. She'd always faced the truth, hadn't she?

'Don't mollycoddle me. I need you to tell me the truth. Am I going to walk out of here?'

'We don't know, Mimi. Take it minute by minute and be glad you're alive.'

All those years she'd defied death, illness, prostitution, alcoholism just to end up confined to her bed? She couldn't accept it.

'Please don't cry. We'll work something out.'

'I'd rather be dead! What if I can't walk and I'm stuck forever in this hovel? I won't make a good invalid. I can't sit forever in a wheelchair bravely overcoming. I draw with my left hand. Fuck me, couldn't God or whoever makes the rules leave me with something?'

'You have me, always.'

'I didn't sneak you in here on cold nights, and half starve myself so you could eat when we were kids just for you to sit in this miserable box with an invalid.'

'You can't tell me what to do any more, you're not my big sister.'

'I can and I will!'

They laughed through tears.

'*Putain.* What the hell am I going to do?'

'You'll think of something, you always do. The circus left yesterday, but they'll be back in the summer, and they said to say that you'll always have a job with them, if you want it.'

'What, to sit on the side-lines while everyone feels sorry for me? I couldn't!'

Rafi told her everything. The moment he'd seen her miss, Boum Boum scrambling for the rubber mat which had saved her life. How the audience had gasped, Jules had cried like a baby, and Juliet was so jittery she hadn't done a performance since. They'd been at her bedside every day, but she had no recollection.

Mimi had landed on her left side. Thank God, she had no open wounds to fester in this damp room, but the bones in her left foot were broken, along with the femur, the radius and three fingers. Her right ankle was badly damaged. They didn't know whether she had internal bleeding, or a severed spinal cord, but they couldn't rule it out. He sounded like a bloody medical dictionary. That was Rafi's way of dealing with things, hiding behind the facts, away from emotions. Her heart went out to him. She had slept through the horror; he had watched the whole thing.

'Nobody could believe you pulled through... those bastards were more interested in the show than your safety.' He trailed off. 'You're alive, that's all that matters.'

She didn't tell Rafi about the recurring nightmare where she plummeted through Colette's screams alone in the dark, or that she didn't exactly remember the moment of impact, but somehow her body did, and the thought of it nauseated her every excruciating second of the day, even though she'd been barely conscious. For the first time in her life, she felt fragile, instead of invincible. That was the worst of all.

Sinking back in her pillow, Mimi stared at the wall, drifting while Rafi told her about arrangements, when the doctor would visit, how Henriette and Paulette from the laundry had arranged shifts with Rafi so she would rarely be alone. On her bedside table were two large bottles. One labelled laudanum, the other ether. She knew too many people who'd kill to get hold of these to get them through the day, injured or not. Next to them were the sketchpad and charcoals she'd bought with her first circus pay.

'Mimi?'

The light had changed; she must have been asleep for hours.

Rafi was holding an envelope. 'Monsieur Dejean asked me to give you this when you woke.' He held it out to her.

'I only have one hand – you open it.' Her voice sounded far away.

It was from that old witch, Madame Vadoma.

'If you are reading this, you have defied death and you are meant to live. Use it well.'

It was hard to stay conscious, even when she desperately wanted to. Rafi left at some point, and possibly the doctor arrived. She wasn't sure if Henriette was there crying at her bedside, begging her to eat. But the witch's words were vivid, etched in lights somewhere unfathomable, if only she could get there. *You are meant to live.* Hadn't that always been the case? But she was meant to live more than a half-life, surely?

The days and nights melded. Mimi felt her strong body turn soft and tried not to think about it. Sometimes she woke with tears streaming without knowing why. Other times, Henriette was there, bawdy as ever, relating her Tales of Toff-men, as she called them. One had a bent dick, and another had a thing for feet and all she had to do was wiggle her toes in return for a silk stole. An English aristocrat had given her ten francs and a tea caddy in return for a blow job – 'Only took five seconds, pent up like a bloody piston. I had to dodge sideways, or it would've blinded me.'

Paulette played the guitar and stayed much longer than she needed to. Mimi understood. Practice time was valuable, it was quiet in the sickroom and life wasn't that easy out there. So, whatever it took. She serviced toffs, liked Henriette, but she hated it. Loathed the smell of their lordly emissions, the arrogance, the very fact that she had to. There was money enough to share food, so Paulette took shelter with Mimi whenever she could.

It was all she could do to keep the girls' hands off the laudanum. There were a couple of times when they all took some and lay around giggling and cosying up, revelling in the dizzy feeling and delicious release. After that, she was firm with them: no laudanum. But not quite so with herself. Conscious and unconscious, she relived the moment over and over when she reached for that trapeze and missed. Laudanum soothed the searing pain in her body, and misted up the future enough to help her sleep.

There might have been two weeks, or possibly a month, where she was sometimes awake with Henriette, Paulette, Rafi, or the doctor. It was hard to tell, and she didn't really care. Her right leg was definitely on the mend, and she could already bend and flex it, but the day she could move her left toe, hope surged and she hardly dared let it. She was alone, and felt a fizz in her foot and sort of knew she'd be able to do it. It hurt a bit, but not so badly. That was the day that she decided, no more laudanum. Rafi agreed wholeheartedly to put it in the cupboard, out of her reach. She did have a vague memory of him trying to lecture her about it, and this confirmed her recollection that he did not approve.

It was February, apparently, over two months since her fall. The days stretched out much longer without the drugs, and sleep came less readily, but then, something miraculous happened. Everything was a picture, and Mimi realised something that seemed significant: before the accident, she'd pushed herself in every way she knew how, tramping the streets of Paris to collect scenes to draw later, daring herself to see how far she could leap between the rooftops she knew so well, or testing the limits of what the horses would bear and the tricks she could achieve at the stables. Then the trapeze. She'd been running from something, afraid if she stopped, disaster would strike.

Now, disaster had struck, and it was her fault, no one else's. Nothing had changed. Slowing down didn't feel as terrible as she thought it would. Mimi was still in charge of Mimi and she still had herself and she was determined to make a world for herself in this room. She'd always been a keen observer, but now she saw things she'd never noticed before, even though they'd always been there. Every day, she watched how the sun travelled across the sky through her window, how the light changed, the exact spot on the wall it lit, and the intricate detail of the bare plaster, which even in its plainness was still a myriad of light and shade and delicate colour.

She watched as a spider grew, making its web on the windowpane. How the threads caught the sun. How hapless flies making a bid for freedom by flinging themselves at the light became entangled, cocooned and hopeless, like her, and were packaged up for a spider snack. Over time, the spider got fatter, the web bigger.

She trained her mind. Every visitor was fodder for her mission to really *see*. She'd always drawn street scenes, observations from being out and about, and even in her younger days, her mother had told her to slow down, that the best was often near at hand. The phrase came back to her vividly now. The only material she had for her imaginary drawings were in the confines of her little room, and she learned to notice every detail of the few people who visited and what she could see from her bed. Henriette's eyes were actually three different shades of blue, and there were times of the day where the patch of sky Mimi could see through the window was an exact match. The soft blue fleck was the morning sky, 12.30 p.m. precisely by the church bell was the cornflower shard, and the third, darker colour was at dusk at 4 p.m., as the sun gave way to the evening star.

Paulette was full of vivacity and sass when she spoke, but in repose she had a wistful, hurt demeanour. Her aggression was just her striking out before anyone could hurt her first and then she was quick and vicious as a snake. In contrast, her thick auburn hair with its copper highlights was generous and softening, and when she played the guitar, she gave all of herself to the viewer with complete abandon.

Rafi visited every day, and they talked about everything but what might happen if she couldn't walk again, about the circus and the artists she'd observed, Tif and his soft muzzle, the hustle and bustle she missed. He tried to hide how much he was worried about her, but the way his left eyelid drooped almost imperceptibly when he looked at her gave him away.

Mimi ached to capture her new observations on paper, but everything on her left side was numb. *Please, God, give me back my drawing hand.*

The building was never quiet. The two girls on the second floor sang, partied and entertained gentlemen friends with abandon, yelling cries of passion without a thought for the other residents, or themselves. But it was all part of her closed world now, a world she so eagerly drank in.

On moonlit nights, disturbed by the old widow's ravings, Mimi watched the shadows and trained her eyes to make out how dark changed the objects in the room, how the moon cast them anew. In the early hours, she lay awake, reflecting on the future. How sweet it would be, how deliciously miraculous, to walk out of here, feel the sun on her face, see the sights of Paris, be part of life once more. She couldn't help remembering the fortune teller's words, too. *You will die twice. Once in terror.* Was this that? Or was there more horror to come? But she'd said that all would be well, too. *You must endure.* Mimi made a pact with herself and God, if he existed. If she escaped her prison, she would live every single millisecond as if it were her last – please, please, please, whoever was in charge, make it so. And she would find a way to get her little girl back. She belonged with her mama. She knew it as sure as the sun rose and set, the stars drifted, and the tides ebbed and flowed. It was just a rule of the universe.

Time was not so elastic as it had been when her conscious and unconscious had merged on laudanum, so Mimi knew it was March the day she twisted around in her bed and dared to reach her right leg onto the ground. She put her weight on it, and the leg held up. Electric shocks of pain shot through her, but the pain was better than anaesthesia. Life hurt, and halle-bloody-lujah for life! Rafi was due any minute and she was determined to stay standing until he walked in the door. It hurt so much, she bit her lip till it bled, but eventually the door creaked open and she beamed.

'You look like you've just caught a zebra!' said Rafi, clapping his hands. 'Now get back in. You heard the doctor; you need to give yourself every chance.'

'This *is* every chance. I've got a leg! Oh Rafi, pick me up and swing me around, I want to feel what it's like to dance again!'

'I will do no such thing, you rebellious child. The doctor has given you express instructions. Your left leg is still fusing, and you will get straight back to bed,' he said, not managing to be very stern.

She hopped to tease him, wincing.

'Dammit, stop, you maniac!'

He lifted her into bed, as carefully as if she was made of porcelain.

'Now, stay! I'll die of a heart attack watching you play fast and loose with life!'

She crossed her heart. 'Promise. I don't want to kill you.'

'Now, I can't dance with you, but I think you might be ready for this, to celebrate.'

He pulled out a battered artist's portfolio from under the bed and opened it to reveal a pile of drawings.

'Those men you told me about, Cravat and Floppy, were devastated the night you fell. They went to great lengths to find me at my flat and asked me to give you these. They said to say, *For the girl with the green eyes and the lightning spirit.* I waited till now, so you could face it.'

It was a sketch, of her on the trapeze, twisting mid-air, hair flying. She squinted at the signature, *Pierre-Auguste Renoir.* He had her face right – the cat's eyes, high cheekbones and wide full lips – but she had a sweeter look on her face than was true to her, and her cheeks were a little too plump, like a doll's. It was an idealised version of her, as if she hadn't grown up cynical and skinny in Montmartre.

'I love it! Was this one Cravat's? It's funny, I watched them so many times from the wings, and envied their paper and pastels, I had no idea they were watching me back! Show me the next one.'

Her heart raced to think the artists had actually noticed her.

The next was drawn from a different perspective. It was more pulled back, with the emphasis on the trapeze equipment and the scene as a whole. She, as the central figure, was almost incidental, a trapeze girl, rather than actually Mimi, and though he had her hair and costume exactly, the face was just a few pencil strokes. The striking part was the way he'd rendered the spotlight, how it blazed on her, then graduated away so softly from the main beam. She'd never seen anything like it, that just a few soft pencil marks could have such an effect. It was signed *Claude Monet*.

'They're good lads,' said Rafi. 'I've met them a few times in the Lapin Agile. We stayed up till three in the morning drinking red wine, talking about that bastard Napoleon III's annexation of the suburbs. Did you know every one of us in Montmartre is paying higher taxes just to fund his damned hereditary greed and warmongering. He's a chip off the old block, that's for sure. To think how hard we fought to oust the monarchy and he's no better, and Claude agrees, and Monsieur Renoir is the most natural socialist I've ever—'

'Save your politicking for your friends, you know I think it's all a waste of time. The rich will always protect the rich, however much they pretend to be noble. What's that other picture?'

Rafi placed it on top of the others.

This one was different again. Mimi was standing in the spotlight filling the whole picture, hands outstretched to draw in the audience, the moment before she took a curtsey.

It was *her*. He'd got everything right, from the challenge in her eye, to the sensuous lips upturned in a knowing smile. It was the expression Rafi said would get her into trouble one day. He'd even got the unruly curl that always escaped her head-dress. That one detail added a carefree, rebellious air to her otherwise soignée stage persona and made her so real.

'Do you like them, you're not upset?' asked Rafi.

'I love them all, but this is the best. Who did it?'

'His name's Édouard... Édouard Manet. He's part of the group, but not like them. He's older and a toff, but his heart's in the right place. Not a bad picture, eh? He's written something on the back.'

Rafi turned it over for her.

'To the girl on the trapeze who looks me boldly in the eye and makes sparks fly. Rest, recover and shine for us again.'

Mimi read it out to Rafi, and he darkened. 'What a creep. He doesn't even know you.'

But Mimi couldn't help flushing at his words.

That night, for the first time since the accident, instead of reliving the nightmare, she fell asleep dreaming about the pictures. She might not ever get on the trapeze again, but maybe she wasn't meant to? Perhaps it had all happened to push her towards her ambition to exhibit at the Académie's annual Salon? The fortune teller had predicted an artist's palette, and although Mimi had thought it was all nonsense at the time, she could pick what she chose to believe. The old woman might have even seen charcoal smudges on her fingers. It didn't matter. The whole world out there was a feast of images and souls and stories, each made unique by her own perspective. When she got out of this room, she would draw and paint and devour the world, live and love and create and notice everything with her coals and canvases, from a speck of grime on the Montmartre pavement, to the life written on the old widow's face, to the way the light scintillated in the fountains in the squares on a summer's day. Imagine joining the coterie of artists she'd seen at the circus, who stole the world and transformed it into their own.

CHAPTER 6

Mimi had endured, more than that old fortune teller could ever imagine. The very thing that she thought would bring her Colette back had thrust her further than ever from her reach. She had less chance of making a home for her now than before the fall, and the only comfort Mimi took was that she had seemed happy with her papa, all wrapped up in her little velvet cape, giggling at his jokes. That didn't stop her whispering *Good night, sweet dreams* to Colette's doll in the yellow dress every night though. If she ever got her back, she could tell her she said good night to her every single bedtime of her life, and it would be the honest truth in a world of lies.

Drawing, Rafi, Henriette and Paulette were her lifelines, and they took it in turns to help her with her first tentative steps to build her strength, walking up and down the rue Becquerel outside her apartment. At first, the stairs were a mountain, and the street outside was a battle zone. Street hawkers, horses, men pushing carts, girls hauling sacks of fresh laundry, three wide on the pavement, were all potential obstacles. Even with her stick, there was very little sympathy for her hobbling along, making them slow their pace or getting in their way.

Gradually, the mountainous stairs became a hill and there were days when she ventured onto the street alone, without her friends' help, though she didn't tell them because they'd left her strict instructions to wait for them. But it was spring, and sometimes the lure of the soft breeze and the sun on her face after all these months of confinement was irresistible, and the sights and sounds were wonderful to collect and draw later.

Henriette and Paulette's bawdy chat had diminished in favour of something new and wonderful, too. Through Rafi, they'd met the artists who'd drawn her at the circus, and they'd already been painted several times by Renoir, Monet and the gang.

'They didn't even want anything in return, and they actually paid us,' Henriette had told her. 'I just had to stand there and try to look like I was thinking something. That was the hardest bit,' she'd screamed and they'd collapsed in giggles.

The artists gave everyone a nickname, the girls told her. Paulette was now Pixie, because of her red hair and piquant temperament, and Henriette had put those cornflower eyes to good use in bagging herself a prince. So now, Henriette was Citron – Lemon, thanks to her beau being no less than the Prince of Orange. Henriette was loopy for her boyish, debauched prince and the artists teased her for it endlessly, and like this, Pixie and Citron had even gained a little notoriety amongst the *beau monde*.

And today, the tenth of May, Mimi was invited to the private view where the portraits of her friends would be displayed. It was the first time she would have ventured out of Montmartre on her own two feet in five months and it was the most glorious, most vivid spring she'd ever encountered. Birds sang louder, buds flowered more exuberantly, and the sun shone for her alone as she walked down the rue de Richelieu towards the gallery.

When she arrived at Paul Durand-Ruel's gallery on the rue

des Petits-Champs, Mimi could hear the din of chatter and voices float like smoke on the spring air, even before she stepped through the door. It would be the first time since the circus that she would be part of a big crowd, but once she was inside, if Mimi had died and gone to heaven after her accident, this would be her paradise.

There were paintings everywhere. Not like the ordered reverence of the Louvre, but covering every inch of the panelled walls, higgledy-piggledy, jumbled together, some so high up that people had a name for it, skyed, and that was the worst place to be as you could barely make them out.

She'd never seen anything like it. At the Louvre, the scenes were always classical, where Michelangelo, Titian and Raphael created dramatic scenes of religious or mythical stories, using the models Mimi had seen dressed as shepherdesses and soldiers queuing outside the École des Beaux-Arts. That's what she'd always thought 'art' was. But here, the artists were depicting everyday scenes from Paris and the *banlieue*, the suburbs. There were men smoking at café tables, laundresses and showgirls, shabby wooden sailboats on the Seine, and scenes from the circus. Boum Boum the clown was a favourite, scowling in his worn Pierrot suit, his straggly hair and sharp features capturing the intelligent man behind the slapstick and greasepaint. This was her world, Henriette's, Rafi's and Paulette's, and these artists had noticed them, even deemed them worthy subjects for their art.

Hung prominently near the door, Paulette was framed, her wounded gaze challenging the viewer, in stark contrast to her luxuriant red locks, and there, Henriette was standing for all to see in a white slip and heels in front of a mirror, glancing provocatively over her shoulder, beautiful as a lamb, with a wolf's predatory stare.

Just being here, Mimi felt reborn, and the place was packed. Some were like the people she'd admired at the Gare Saint-

Lazare with Rafi, the men dressed in top hats and freshly laundered shirts tapping their canes on the parquet as they held forth. Women in expensive crinolines averted their eyes at the picture of Citron with her lewd stare and hung on the men's arms like rare orchids, drooping fashionably. But amongst them, shoulder to shoulder, were her kind. Henriette, now Citron, was strutting about like a queen, fanning herself with ostrich features and laughing a bit too loudly for such a genteel crowd. Paulette, Pixie, was being ferocious to some whey-faced toff who was hanging on her every word, and Renoir and Monet were prowling about making mischief in their moleskin jackets and bright silk kerchiefs.

Mimi leant on her walking stick, refusing to be cowed by such riches. She'd been happy with what she saw in her cracked mirror this morning. Her wide-set green eyes were brighter and sharper now she could see the world anew. Her best dress wasn't silk, but it was good olive-green lawn cotton and she'd nipped it in at the waist to fit her figure, which was tinier than ever after her protracted illness. Her cheekbones were more visible now, lending her a sophisticated, grown-up air. Rafi said that with her big eyes and cheekbones and full lips she was so beautiful she was almost ugly and she'd given him a playful cuff and changed the subject. Best of all, she'd walked here, all the way from Montmartre, and she could feel her body getting strong again, along with her mind, which was blazing with ideas and longing and hopes for the future so much it almost hurt.

'Our broken circus girl with nine lives, you came! Welcome to our world. How delightful to see you, and with those eyes and cheekbones and your unnatural luck, surely we must call you *le petit chaton,* kitten. I fear you'll find us dull after your flying trapeze, but we are honoured to have such an exotic creature in our humble midst. You are mended, and more splendidly beautiful for it. It's the crack that makes the china all the more precious, *n'est-ce pas?*' Monet, her floppy-haired artist

from the circus, gave her two extravagant kisses, then two more
for good measure on each cheek.

'And the dandy is all the more impressive for his depiction
of light,' replied Mimi, giving him a twirl. 'I may be cracked, but
I'm here and alive and on my own two feet and everything is
perfect.' She smiled.

'What are you doing requisitioning my circus girl?' It was
Renoir, Cravat, his friend, smiling like an amiable bear. 'Can
you do that twirl again?'

Mimi pirouetted, holding onto her walking stick to balance.

Renoir stood back and contemplated her. Not like a toff
would do, like she was a piece of meat, but admiringly, for her.
'You gave us all a bit of a fright that day. Promise not to do that
to us again?'

Mimi crossed her heart. 'Promise. I guarantee on this day,
the first day of the rest of my life. Did Rafi tell you how much
your pictures meant to me? I used to watch you from the wings
with your sketchbooks and pencils.'

'We watched you, too. There are beautiful girls in the
circus, but you have an indefinable quality that demands attention. I hope you don't mind me saying,' remarked Renoir.

'A light, a spirit, a sparkle and a toughness honed on the
streets,' added Monet with a flick of his beautiful black mane,
not really to her, but clearly hoping to get attention from the
wider gathering.

'Please excuse my friend, he's an absolute slut for attention,'
laughed Renoir. 'Rafi did tell us that you lit up when you saw
the drawings, and it made us very happy to think that our little
circus sprite managed to smile after such an awful accident.'
Renoir's eyes were wet with emotion, which gave Mimi a lump
of memory and she chased it away with a bright smile.

'I studied those drawings endlessly. You have such indi-
vidual styles and your pencil strokes come a from place that's
unique to you. You draw souls, not just faces. It fascinates me

that art can do that, illustrate your innermost thoughts, which are infinitely different from everyone else's.'

'Quite an insight from such a pretty head,' said Monet.

'You don't have to romance every girl you meet,' teased Mimi. 'Give yourself some air and speak to me as an equal before you wear yourself out.'

The pair roared. 'It's rare to be so beautiful inside and out,' said Monet. 'And I apologise if I've offended you, really. Everyone says my worst fault is to overstate everything that comes out of my great maw.'

'No offence taken. There was a third drawing, from an Édouard?' Mimi tried to sound casual, but her heart thumped. His was the drawing she felt captured her the best of all, and she knew the note he'd written with it off by heart, she'd read it so many times in her lonely convalescence. *To the girl on the trapeze who looks me boldly in the eye and makes sparks fly. Rest, recover and shine for us again.*

'He's here somewhere, but goodness knows where. He's our token toff and this is his milieu, so we leave him to it. He opens doors that we could never do. He's given up a good naval career to become a low-life artist, but somehow still manages to be society's golden boy. All these stiffs in shiny top hats with their wilting violets are down to him, and they've got deep pockets,' said Renoir. 'Come on, I'll show you some of his pictures.'

Monet melted into the crowd, and laughter and chatter seemed to bubble up wherever he stood. There was quite a bit of swooning, too, if Mimi wasn't mistaken. She could see why – the bohemian mane of hair, the roguish smile revealing unfairly straight teeth compared to the rest of humanity, the never-ending charm offensive. But he wasn't her type. In fact, she was beginning to wonder if she *had* a type; she had spent so long trying not to get herself entangled after Jean-Baptiste and her darling Colette.

Renoir just radiated warmth and gentle appreciation

towards her, and she was wonderfully comfortable in his
company. He was big and broad and expansive, and she felt tiny
and protected with him as he steered her to stand in front of one
of Édouard's works. Mimi was transfixed. The picture was of a
girl serving at a Montmartre bar, hands resting on the marble,
wearing a tightly buttoned velvet bodice, a lace collar, silk
choker and a corsage of flowers pressed to her décolletage.
There was a stemmed glass bowl piled with oranges, champagne bottles grouped haphazardly next to a collection of spirits, and soft roses in a glass. Reflected in the mirror, stretched
the width of the painting was a crowded restaurant scene punc-
tuated by smudges of light and dominated by a lavish Empire
chandelier. On closer inspection, the shapes were loose and
undefined, the highlights broad, with clearly visible brush-
strokes, but the effect was beautiful, soft, and imbued with dark
glamour. But most striking of all was the barmaid's expression.
This wasn't just a pretty illusion of a sparkling Parisian club
with a willing girl at the bar. The girl could have been any of
the laundresses cum dancers cum escorts she knew, caught in an
unguarded moment. Despite the opulence of the scene, the girl
was looking away, tired and disconsolate, at odds with her open
stance. Reflected in the mirror was the back of her head,
exposing a delicate pink earlobe hung with an innocent,
dangling pearl.

Édouard Manet, *Un Bar aux Folies-Bergère,* read the notice.
The picture made Mimi angry and nostalgic and desperate all
at once. It could easily be Maman in her younger days, before
she numbed the pain with drink.

'You look distressed,' a clipped voice cut in.

Mimi spun round so fast she dropped her stick and a man
stooped to pick it up and hand it to her. He was... golden. If the
Apollo she'd seen in the Louvre were to appear in person in
Paris now, he would be wearing the same understated silk shirt
and would look at her with this man's intense blue eyes.

Mimi took the stick and boldly met the stranger's gaze.

'Thank you. She just reminds me of someone,' said Mimi.

'You're the circus girl with the nine lives. I'm sorry if my painting upsets you,' he said, kissing her hand as if she were a lady. So this was the man who had drawn her so perfectly, whose note she'd memorised.

'In all the right ways,' Mimi replied.

He cocked his head, curious. 'How so?'

'You haven't drawn a template pretty girl tempting the boys at the bar. It's like you know her, I mean just for *her*, not just as a prop in that nightclub. There are so many ways you tell us, from her expression, to her stance, and even the man we see leering at her in the reflection in the mirror.'

After that, he must have talked to her for at least ten minutes, but she couldn't remember a word he said, she was in such a fluster, damn herself! No one like him had ever given her the time of day. He was so polished and clever, and tall and straight and sort of *glowing*, not even in an annoying way, like most toffs. She kept expecting him to melt back into the party, but he didn't until Monet and Renoir came barrelling along and amiably accused Mimi of hogging the life and soul of the party and she should release him from those cat's eyes and let him go, hadn't she given them enough of a fright already?

He allowed himself to be whisked away, but not before insisting she took his carriage back to Montmartre rather than walk on her newly repaired legs, and extracted a promise she would join the whole group along with Citron and Pixie at the Lapin Agile that night.

'Now we've found you again, we need to keep an eye on you. We witnessed it all and you belong to us now. We can't have you flinging yourself about without a safety net, can we, however breathtaking a spectacle it might be?'

A sensible night's sleep in her little room, or a chance to spend more time with this new, fascinating gang? Wasn't she the girl who'd tamed a zebra? Now here she was, at a private view in a magnificent building on the right side of Paris, a million miles away from her little room. Even better, she was out in the world, which was more shades and colours, sensations and wonders than she'd ever thought possible. How had she not seen it before?

That sly old fortune teller was right. She was reborn, and she couldn't have deserved these gifts without the horrific rite of passage she'd experienced. Whatever, Mimi still had herself, and that was enough while she could walk and breathe and everything was possible. And the closer she got to these artists, the nearer it felt to the Salon and the Académie. She wasn't quite sure how, but just like mucking out the stables at the circus had led her to the trapeze, being part of the artists' entourage would surely open up opportunities for a girl with her eye on the prize and a desperate wish to join their ranks, not just as a muse, but an artist, too? Of course she was going to the Lapin Agile. Sensible nights' sleeps weren't meant for girls like her, especially ones who had defied certain death before they'd even reached their twentieth birthday.

CHAPTER 7

Édouard's carriage was a *calèche* with velvet seats, glass windows and two horses. He handed Mimi into it as if she were a princess, checked the door was safely closed and told the coachman to take care of her, and the man saluted to her and bowed. She'd never even been on an omnibus, never mind a carriage all to herself with two whole horses to whisk her along the boulevards.

Used to stomping up the hill on her own two feet, she felt guilty when the glossy steeds began to steam on the slope to Montmartre, but when she got to the rue du Tailleur where the ragpicker children were hard at work, she couldn't resist.

'Attention, all minions. Stand back for the Queen of Montmartre.'

They screamed and waved when they saw who it was and ran after the carriage, yelling 'La Reine Mimi Bisset, make way, filthy rats,' as she waved regally to their squeals of delight. People came out of shops, cafés and factories to see what all the fuss was about, and they were more surprised to see her in a carriage with windows and two horses than the day she rode the streets bareback on a zebra. She was back in style and she even didn't care if people thought she was a dirty show-off, which beat being pitied any day.

At her tenement, she tapped the window, and the carriage came to a halt. The coachman opened the door and she gave him her hand to help her down the steps. He didn't reciprocate.

'On yer way, you've had your bit of luxury in return for whatever it was you gave him.'

So that's how it was and always would be. No matter how clever or beautiful or talented, you would always be judged by an accident of birth. Screw him.

'You're as bad as the toffs; you should be ashamed of yourself,' spat Mimi as she descended the steps painfully. Her left leg didn't bend like it used to and he stood back and watched her struggle, then let her fall onto the cobbles. He chucked her walking stick onto the ground next to her and drove off. Luckily, the butcher was on his way back from work and he helped her back to her feet.

She wished she could run after that ignorant pig of coachman and tell him he'd only stiffened her resolve. If this world didn't take her seriously, she'd make her own one that did. A picture in the Académie's Salon and all Paris at her feet should do it.

The church bells struck five and she'd promised to be at the Lapin Agile by eight o'clock; that left hours of daylight to draw by without wasting precious candles, and the minute she hobbled up the stairs, she was desperate to start. Thank God, her prayer for her drawing hand to be restored had been answered and she could hold a pencil as well as she ever had.

Renoir's pictures had started her mind racing. He loved to draw children and they were the most idealised, beautiful things: all peaches and cream, satin and bows, picnicking in sunlit gardens with wholesome, elegant mamas who resembled their little ones. They'd almost wrenched her heart in two with longing for Colette. One in particular got to her, less idealised than the others. It was an oil painting, *Mussel-Fishers at Berneval*. First of all, it was set by the sea and Mimi had always dreamed of going to the seaside on that train from the Gare Saint-Lazare. In this picture, the seascape was rugged, the sky overcast. An angular, serious young mother with a fisherwoman's basket strapped to her back kept an eye on her little children. The brother with his mop of blonde hair looked chastised by his mother's fierce look, whilst two little sisters held hands, looking out of the picture, mischievous as puppies. The youngest child, who couldn't have been much older than Colette, was adorable in her little skirt that kicked out above skinny legs and button shoes. But it was the way the older sister clutched the little girl's arm to stop her from running off that was just heartbreaking. Perhaps she was about to show her sister something in a rock pool that would delight her. Mimi would give anything to be that fierce mother protecting her little brood, and in turn to have been that protected child.

She snatched up her sketchpad and drew obsessively. Soon, the images covered the floor like confetti. Colette's profile, her plump cheek irresistible, trusting gaze looking at something – her mama perhaps – off canvas. Colette laughing, Colette holding her mama's hand, Colette with the doll she'd bought her, sitting at the circus in the front row, eyes bright... Colette in her velvet cape holding a kitten, then in her crib when she was first born. Mimi remembered every detail, from the broderie anglaise little dress, to the soft rabbit she clutched in her pristine new-born hand, fingernails perfect in miniature.

The more she drew, the more the ache eased, at least momentarily. She was part-obsessed with the images of her little girl and partly with technique. Her head crammed with ideas from Monsieur Durand-Ruel's gallery, an Aladdin's cave of subjects and styles and inspiration. When the church bell struck eight, she realised she hadn't heard it chime six or seven.

She'd be late for the Lapin Agile, and she didn't want to miss it for the world.

Plumping up her hair in the cracked mirror, she wished she had more than one best dress, but no matter. She slipped on her leather ballerina slippers, a circus money purchase that made her feel light as air, and went out into the balmy dusk of a Paris spring evening.

The Lapin Agile was buzzing. Gaslight pooled onto the cobbles under the makeshift canopy, the outside tables were packed with a bohemian crowd and the evening star was just visible in a translucent velvet sky.

'Le Chat!'

It was Monet, slightly wobbly on his feet and flushed with drink. Mimi waved back.

'Come here and cross my path to bring me luck.' He ushered an awkward-looking man with a belt made of string out of the chair next to him and gestured to it with a flourish. 'Sit your neat little derrière right there and take the weight off.'

'I think it's you who needs to sit down, my friend, you look a little unsteady,' said Mimi to the roar of the group.

He slumped in his chair and knocked back a glass. 'I've only just begun, my dear. Waitress! Two more of your finest glasses of Madeira, and add it to my account,' he said grandly.

The waitress gave Mimi and Monet the drinks and cuffed him indulgently.

'Account?' she sneered. 'Debt mountain, more like. *Mañana*, no doubt, for the settlement, as always?'

Mimi delved into her pocket for a coin. The circus had been generous. 'Here, they're on me. A cat values its independence more than anything.'

She caught Édouard's eye, who nodded admiringly.

'And like a dog who's been given a treat, I am yours now, always,' pronounced Monet, kissing her hand.

The place was jumping. Paulette was playing the guitar on

the little stage in the corner of the room. She was so petite that the big guitar made her look childlike, and Citron was sweeping about the place delighting every man with a flash of her big blue eyes and saucy jokes.

Renoir told her that the proprietor kept two tables for the artists every Wednesday night. He was an artist himself, apparently and a master pâtissier. She was in good company; everyone had a side hustle. Mimi hadn't worked out what hers was yet, but the idea that creating art could be the main event was reason enough to be here.

She could hardly hear herself speak above the din. Édouard was deep in conversation with the awkward-looking man who'd given up his seat for her. He was Cézanne, here from Aix-en-Provence, against his rich family's wishes. Another, the bookish one she'd seen with Renoir and Monet in the circus audience, was talking to an effeminate-looking man in make-up and corsets, and whatever they were discussing was pretty heated. The bookish artist was Degas, Renoir said.

The proprietor piled the table with platters of vol-au-vents, quiches and choux buns. Renoir and Monet fell on them as if they hadn't eaten for a week. Rafi was nowhere to be seen, but Mimi could see why he loved these people. The conversation turned from police censorship of literature, to the control of outdated and prejudicial juries of the Académie des Beaux-Arts, to why black bitumen paint was finished and it was all about painting *en plein air*, outside.

At one point, Monet smashed a plate on the floor to emphasise his point about capturing reflections on the Seine, and bookish Degas flared up, loudly challenging the effeminate man, the acerbic reviewer, to a duel, waving a copy of *Le Figaro* in his face.

'*The impression the Impressionists create is that of a cat walking across the keys of a piano, or a monkey with a box of paints,*' he read, furious. 'What the hell is this? Have you ever studied the look on a ballet dancer's face as she pirouettes *en pointe*? Pain! Or the texture of a tutu, grubby from nightly use, as the sun slants through it in a rehearsal room? It's everyday beauty. And *that's* what we're about. None of the overblown mythological hysterics you find in the École des Beaux-Arts. This is *now*. It's what's around us!'

The artists cheered him on.

'C-c-come, come, Monsieur Degas, why so serious? We're all just making a living, s-s-sweetie. Just a bit of f-f-fun. At your expense, I admit,' he said slyly. 'But the readers adore it, and I *was* rather pleased with the c-c-cat analogy. My apologies, gentlemen, I am unrep-p-pentant.'

The newspaper critic bowed to the assembly, slipped his jacket over his corset, picked his top hat off the peg on the wall and hurried out. Mimi had never seen anyone like him. His stutter seemed more affectation than anything, and she loved his bold cross-dressing, combining well-tailored trousers with an oyster-pink silk corset, tails and a top hat. The white foundation and red lipstick gave him a wild, pagan air and he seemed genuinely unmoved by the jeering and Degas' challenge to a duel. He had an opinion, and he wasn't afraid to voice it. She might not agree with him, but she had to admit, his article *did* sound amusing.

'Good riddance!' yelled Monet, ordering another round of drinks for the whole table on his account.

The Impressionists. So that's what this kind of painting was called, thought Mimi, absorbing everything like a sponge. The word was meant to be a slight, but it worked. Their work wasn't a faithful representation of what they saw before them; it was an ephemeral idea, a play of light and shadow, a fleeting moment in time captured.

Monet summed it up to her. 'I like to paint as a bird sings,' he said, swaying to Paulette's music.

The conversation turned to what it was to be an artist, and

who should have the right to give their life to it. Renoir said there was no other choice for him and talked of *diffuse reflection*; bookish Degas described how he was entranced by line and colour; Monet strived to capture light, painting the same object at different times of the day; and Cézanne fiddled with the string that kept his trousers up and said darkly that he wanted to treat nature in terms of the cylinder, the sphere and the cone. Mimi resolved to study what he meant by that.

'And you?' she addressed Édouard across the table. 'What brings you to this exotic table of outsiders and dreamers?'

'I love Velázquez, the way he portrays the edges of life, the ragpickers, bold street girls and magic of everyday things. He gives them the meaning they deserve.'

Mimi thought of her collection of lost and beautiful things – the sequins from the dirt, the bits of delicate, broken pottery – and understood. She had so much to give, so many ideas of how she could become one of them and paint what she saw, show people the world through her eyes, and find a way to get her little girl back.

'I would like to paint, like all of you.' The minute the words came out, she regretted it.

'What? Women aren't admitted to any of the respected schools, with good reason,' scoffed Degas.

'The woman artist is merely ridiculous, but I *am* in favour of the female singer and dancer, my little *chaton*. Look at us all, we have nothing, we suffer for our art and you have everything a woman could ever need with those pale green eyes!' purred Monet.

Mimi humoured them all and damned them all inside. Even here, these men who *saw* the likes of her, and loved them for what they were, could not countenance a woman joining their ranks.

'I see nothing wrong with a woman painter, or such ambition. Why not? It's ridiculous that those fusty old institutions,

the same ones that reject us, should decide that women could
not be just as talented as men,' said Manet.

Mimi felt she would melt at his golden words.

The night went on and grew more and more raucous.
When a knife fight broke out on the other side of the bar, Mimi
decided it was time to go. She hated big goodbyes, so she pulled
on her shawl and slipped out. The night was hot and sticky and
the stars were molten.

'Wait!'

It was Édouard.

'Ignore those posers and chancers. Women *should* have a
place amongst us artists, not just as models. If you agree to pose
for me, I'll show you how to mix paints and you can help out in
my studio, if you're serious.'

'I am. Deadly serious.' She couldn't tell even him how her
ambition burned inside her, how desperately she wanted to
learn. She wanted it so much, it hurt, and here was Édouard
offering her a chance, a way in.

'Come tomorrow, we can start straight away.'

He smelled rich, of fresh laundry and herbs, and in the
moonlight he looked as pale and perfectly hewn as a statue,
beyond her reach.

She took his card and nodded, said, 'Thank you. Tomorrow,'
and hurried away, ignoring his protests about a walk home
alone. She could handle herself better than him on the backstreets, she was sure of that, and she didn't want to be his little
piece of exotic rough. That life was behind her, with Colette,
before her fall. As the moon slicked the cobbles and she hissed
away the drunks and pickpockets, raced past the pale, blank-
faced working girls, trying not to think about Maman, she whispered into the thick night air, 'I will be an artist. I will be taken
seriously in his world.'

CHAPTER 8

Mimi had hung her best dress out on the roof terrace before she'd crept into bed last night. The damp night air was nature's laundry and the morning sun dried without bleaching; everyone round here knew the trick. Not for them the luxury of dropping off your laundry for a few days and wearing other clothes.

Now here she was, in the centre of elite Paris, clutching Édourard's card and searching for the right door. His studio was on the rue Bonaparte, right opposite the École des Beaux-Arts, and it was so grand! It was one thing wearing a different-coloured shawl and hoping no one would notice in the Lapin Agile, another arriving here in her worn dress, night laundry or not. Drawing on a lungful of Paris air, *her* air, she pinched her cheeks, and knocked on the door.

Édouard answered. She'd expected a maid, but there he was, clearly delighted to see her. Fair curls reached his broad shoulders, his shirt was splattered with paint and his loose harem pants were straight out of a Moroccan souk, the kind she'd seen in Rafi's encyclopaedia.

'Don't tell me, you walked all the way here twice as fast as anyone normal would, even though you've broken your leg in three places and have a limp.'

'The break made me stronger, and I could still beat you in a race, especially with those trousers flapping in the wind,' she laughed.

'Don't hold back. I have no doubt you could beat me in a race, but we'd make a hell of a scene on the rue Bonaparte, so just come in for now.'

His artist's studio was bigger than the room where she slept, ate, drew and cooked, but this place was for the sole purpose of creating art. High arched windows gave onto the street, flooding the room with light and framing the École des Beaux-Arts opposite. There was a piano in the corner, paintings were propped up everywhere, and covered every inch of wall space, velvet chairs dotted about haphazardly amongst easels supporting half-finished paintings, and a wood burner with glazed tiles – the kind rich people had – was stoked cosily against the cool morning.

'So this is your magic kingdom,' said Mimi.

'The magic is out there, on the streets, the cabarets, the cafés and parks.' He smiled. 'This is just my workroom and now your classroom.'

'It looks more like a palace to me,' said Mimi, admiring the chandelier.

'Sometimes it's a torture chamber. This is a fucking travesty.' He kicked an easel with a half-finished picture of a dancing girl on it, and it toppled to the ground. That expensive canvas, all those paints she would die for. Did he do the same to his models when he tired of them?

'Lucky for you that you can treat something so precious with such abandon,' said Mimi.

'The way you treated yourself at the circus?'

Mimi picked up the picture and studied it. 'She *does* have big hands for such a small figure.'

'I don't remember asking for an opinion.' His eyes glittered, hungry for her perspective despite his words.

'People other than you do have them, you know.'

'Now you're a critic? Please don't tell me you're one of those bastards.'

'The background is sort of out of sync with the central figure.'

'It's called perspective. I think we'd better get started before you tear everything in this room apart. Luckily you have insight and spirit, and that's all I need from you to begin.'

'I didn't come here to be flattered; I mean to learn.'

But she felt like one of his half-finished pieces of art, unformed and imbued with meaning.

He showed her an artist's palette, the tubes of oil paint, and the special hog's-hair brushes he used to create the wide brush-strokes he preferred.

The paints were like jewels, better than any riches. Mimi was proud of herself for buying pencils and charcoals, but now, with his help, she could hoof into an art supplier and when they mistook her for a delivery girl, she would demand ultramarine blue, burnt umber, alizarin crimson, yellow ochre, sap green and titanium white. No need to write the words down; that was for toffs. The same as the box full of treasures she kept in her room, she had a place in her brain where she collected beautiful and lost things and they were all neatly filed for when they'd come in useful.

He covered her eyes. 'Recite the colours back to me.'

She reeled off the ten colours he'd shown her, and when he released her, his eyes were wide and impressed. So, he hadn't taken her seriously until now.

He showed her how to build a background in a scene he was painting of music at the Tuileries. He painted *alla prima*, all at once, not using his artist's palette to mix colours, but creating colour and texture on the canvas, without waiting for the colours to dry one by one. Mimi couldn't imagine ever affording enough canvases to practise the technique. Surely if you got it wrong, you would have to throw that away and get a new one? But he showed her how to 'wipe', scrape away what you'd created with a palette knife, and start again. Not that Édouard started again once while she was watching. The patch of grass, with light filtering through the trees, appeared right there before her eyes as he worked. He had ten years and a formal artistic education over her. If it took her the same amount of time, her daughter would be a teenager. She could draw, there was no disputing that and she'd drawn all her life, but how would she ever learn such skill with colour without years of practice?

'There is no place for doubt. Just trust your instinct,' Édouard said, turning to her when he was satisfied.

'But there's so much to learn.'

'Technique will come, anyone can learn that, but if you can show me what the world behind your cat's eyes looks like, you're an artist. It will be fascinating to see what you can produce. In fact, I think I might be a little afraid of it.'

He gave her space and respect when he spoke to her, like he would with an equal.

The lesson came to an end, and it was her turn to keep up her side of the bargain. He showed her the Japanese screen, told her to undress and come out and sit on the chaise longue.

'I won't bite,' he said when she hesitated behind the screen.

'If you touch me, I will,' she warned. Street girls generally came off the worse with toffs; that was the first lesson you learned when you got your period in Montmartre.

'I'll be judging you in shapes and colours, nothing more. If you'd rather not...' he said gently, dropping his swagger.

'As long as we're straight,' she replied.

'You are just as much a part of creating my picture as I am. It's not your body, it's *you* I want to capture. A muse in the true sense of the word.'

'If it's just a muse you need, then all right,' said Mimi, still uncertain as to *exactly* what was required of a muse. She hoped it wasn't just a posh word to disguise very unartistic intentions. She'd met enough toffs to know that they used their big words to make what they wanted seem somehow noble, when really it was the same thing everyone else wanted.

Stepping out of her dress with only her and Édouard in the room was a risk, but she'd taken worse. Anyway, she could look after herself. She wrapped herself tightly in the throw he'd given her and sat on the edge of the chaise longue in front of the big windows.

The sun had moved, no longer pouring directly in through the windows, and he explained how flattering the diffused light would be for the portrait. He stoked the stove so she could relax, a workman at his business, like the blacksmiths at the stables. He had more rings on his fingers than men usually wore, and he looked more masculine for the femininity. With his bohemian clothes and aristocratic bearing, he didn't fit her world, or his. An artist could live outside of society. Maybe she could, too.

In that way, she *did* feel his equal; it was just circumstance that meant this studio was probably the only place where their worlds would truly merge. But now was enough, here being taught and painted in this unimaginable place. The rest would unfold, as it always did, and she wanted to absorb every second of it.

'May I?'

Édouard peeled back the throw and regarded her. She was ready to spring if he dared spoil everything by touching her.

'Ouch,' he said at the sight of the scars on her legs.

'I hate them. I was invincible before it happened,' she said, struggling to blank out Colette's look of horror in the circus tent.

'But life is all the more vivid for the pain, don't you think?'

'It was just as sweet without,' she replied.

He made sure she was comfortable on the chaise, half seated, half reclined.

'Not quite right. May I arrange you as I need?'

'As long as it's for the drawing. I'm here to learn, not as a plaything,' she said, looking him straight in the eye.

He nodded and took her hurt leg and parted it from the other, dangling it languidly off the chaise, then knelt and slipped heeled pink shoes onto her feet. He gently unfolded her arms from across her breasts and she felt like a flower turning to the sun, instead of how she should have felt – ashamed, or even violated.

'Your skin is honey and olive, like the girls on the docks in Naples. First, I'm mixing yellow and then blending red and blue, which brings me to a French girl's skin. For yours, I'm mixing in a little more blue and yellow for a darker tone.' He paused to study closer. 'Look directly at me.'

'Isn't it more proper for the girl to look away, like in the Louvre?'

'I don't paint to impress those reactionary fossils at the Académie.'

'Liar,' said Mimi.

He shrugged, grinning. 'My parents would be happy to tell their friends that their son's exhibiting somewhere respectable after he ditched a stellar naval career. Which is why I need you to look me straight in the eye with that brazen stare. Respectability is death to original thought – the first rule of art, my little *chaton*.'

The only way to hold his eye for an extended period of time, particularly such an intense glare as Édouard's, was to let her mind drift.

The clock struck several hours, the sun lowered in the sky until a dusky hue filled the studio. The quiet and peace was like a church, oiled and filled with spirits. Her mind wandered to the pictures she would paint, of Colette in sunlit gardens, the girls in the laundry shrouded in steam, the gamine, hungry cabaret girls hurrying home beneath a cruel moon.

She shifted, aching.

'Hold the pose!' he snapped.

Mimi lost track of time. It wasn't often that a girl like her had the luxury of nothing to do for hours on end and she daydreamed of an impossible life, one where she was standing in Édouard's place. When the light began to fail, he slung her the throw.

'Here, put this on and come and see.'

Kicking off the shoes, she padded barefoot to the easel, expecting to see a lewd depiction of a Montmartre girl, considering the suggestive pose he'd arranged her in, but he hadn't drawn her body at all. Instead, a pair of mocking green eyes, knowing and curious, a little wary, demanded the desire and respect of the viewer. This was not a passive every-woman, but someone completely in control of the onlooker. He'd really *seen* her.

'You asked me to undress, but you only painted my face?' murmured Mimi.

'Your mix of confidence and vulnerability was what I wanted to capture. Asking you to undress stripped away all the props, and it was just you in front of me.'

She wasn't sure who initiated the kiss. All the promises she'd made to herself disappeared, but it felt too right to worry any more. She shrugged the throw off her shoulders, and he carried her to the chaise longue.

It was dark when they were both sated, and the fire in the wood burner turned to glowing embers. He stayed and nestled them together and whispered to her that she was the most beautiful, extraordinary, determined being he had ever encountered in Paris.

He was married of course. But the studio was outside of everyday life and so transcended domestic arrangements, and this was their own painting, a world they could create on a living canvas.

They didn't leave the studio for a week. She gave him a pet name, Edo, and he painted her every day as she lay on the couch, and the air was charged until he was done and then they were tangled and warm and happy. They barely ate, and in between times, Edo gave her a canvas and paints and taught her how to build colours and layers and Mimi feasted on it.

In the evenings, he played the piano, and she danced around the studio with wild abandon, barefoot, her petite figure drowning in his shirt, chasing away shadows of the past as she pirouetted and skipped amongst the easels, and Edo would twirl her to the chaise longue and make love to her and they would sleep, exhausted and disordered.

On Monday, Mimi watched people hurry by on the street below, the hopeful models dressed up as shepherdesses and soldiers queued up at the École des Beaux-Arts and she forced herself to remember there was a real world out there. Now here she was, ensnared in a web that she knew wasn't real and couldn't last, even if it was one of her own making.

Edo joined her at the window.

'A penny for your thoughts?'

'I should go,' said Mimi, searching for the dress she hadn't worn for a week.

'Go where? I've painted you. You belong to me now.'

'Don't tease me. You have a wife and child and I—'

'Please, don't go. Give me one more night at least. I have a surprise for you tomorrow morning, something to help you forget your nightmares.'

She'd woken every night tight in his arms as she soothed herself back to sleep. So he knew.

'That's all behind me,' she lied. 'All I want now is to paint. You are helping me to forget by teaching me.'

'But what if you were high up and safe with me, seeing Paris like a bird?'

He kissed her and she couldn't leave. Tomorrow would be soon enough.

The next morning, he woke her early and led her to the screen.

Her old dress was there, freshly laundered, and it felt wrong that it wasn't by her hands. Next to it was another dress, the kind she'd seen the ladies wearing at the Gare Saint-Lazare. It was green silk, embroidered with Chinese cherry blossom, tasteful, not like the gaudy dresses the laundresses wore to the dances in Montmartre.

She put it on, twirled for Edo and flashed him a leg.

'I'll take that off you later.' He smiled.

'Why not now?' She only had to look at him to wish he was spinning her to the chaise longue and unfolding her. Everything else just felt like marking time between their melting world of skin and whispers and kisses.

'Don't half-close those green eyes at me like that. I told you, I have a surprise for my erstwhile circus girl, to replace the bad memories with good. Here, it's still early morning and you'll be cold.'

He handed her a woollen coat, fine as any she'd seen. Buttoned up, she felt like a chrysalis with her expensive dress underneath, and it was deliciously warm.

He gave her his arm, and they went out into the Paris morning, as in step as if they'd just emerged from their honeymoon.

The streets looked different on his arm, and she looked different to the streets. Men tipped their hats as they passed, servant girls averted their eyes respectfully instead of looking her up and down, and the tradesmen who might have smiled and waved, or shouted lewd comments, acted like she was a ghost from another world.

She wasn't sure she liked it. It was like she was invisible, another toff's *popette* adorning an upstanding arm. Part of her longed to hitch up her skirts and jump across the bollards like she had with Rafi.

At the Jardin de Tuileries, Edo told her to cover her eyes. A roar blasted the air and heat billowed into her face. Edo steered her closer to the sound.

'Now!' he said, and she uncovered her eyes.

In front of her was the biggest basket she had ever seen, attached to a balloon, decorated like a Russian jewelled egg in symmetrical patterns of blues and pinks and greens. It was magnificent and beastly at the same time. The heat and gas roared, and the balloon strained at its tethers, drying out the chilly morning air.

He swung her round in circles. 'I bring you Paris. I wanted to take you somewhere high up, but where you could feel safe. You're not afraid?'

'Never!' Which was not true. But no one had ever wanted to make her feel safe, not since her mother had given up on life.

'You can just admire it from the ground if you prefer.'

'And miss the greatest lesson in perspective that was ever laid at my feet? Admiring from afar is unworthy of the great Mintaka.'

'To hell with all mortals,' yelled Edo as he lifted her into the basket. 'Ready?'

'Just keep holding me.'

'I can't give you everything, not even the whole of me, but I give you the best of me. I hope you can believe that. I know without you telling me how often life has failed you and how many times you have clawed your way out, but this is the beginning. I don't want us to only exist in my studio.'

Us? After one week? If she allowed herself to admit it, she *had* daydreamed of a life with this talented man from another world, away from society, painting and making love with no one to disturb them. Why not take the gift?

'The canvas and the sky are ours; what more could a girl from Montmartre ask for?' Mimi smiled. But the balloon would have to come back down to earth again. It was a fleeting thought that disappeared as soon as they rose above the trees and the early-morning sun gilded the horizon in cyan and yellow.

It was cold up high, and they huddled together with the whole of Paris to themselves as the pilot steered them above the Seine, a sparkling viridian serpent. The blue-grey Haussmann boulevards cut across the city in neat lines, broken by the medieval winding streets that still remained. Notre-Dame was a child's toy and the Butte of Montmartre looked out over it all, dotted with windmills and churches, and gashed by the gypsum mines.

'Sap green, virgin blue, dove grey,' shouted Edo to the cold air.

'Toffs and hookers, showgirls and ladies, sequins and feathers and murderous thieves,' Mimi whispered into his mouth as he kissed her, and the pilot discreetly averted his eyes.

Somewhere down in the grimy streets was hardship and strife and her little Colette strolling the boulevards with her papa. One day she would show her daughter this Paris, high up and dreamlike. But now, this moment, safe with Edo above society, sadness and hypocrisy, was all that mattered.

CHAPTER 9

Mimi wasn't a fool, though. True to her word, after the balloon alighted safely and he'd whirled her out of the basket onto her own two feet, she left Edo and walked home to Montmartre. She had to, even though he begged her not to go. Like a new melody, what was between them was always in the air, and they only had to meet to make it real. Happy, unlikely fate.

Too happy. She might be only twenty, but she wasn't stupid enough to think it could last, and she was glad she knew enough not to get pregnant again. Edo had been careful too, which made her like him even more. Despite that, a wonderful, dreamy week was enough, even when the streets looked greyer at the thought of never seeing him again.

As soon as she got home, Mimi counted out some of the circus money, rolled it into the pocket of her new dress and went to the art shop on the boulevard Montmartre, feverish with a different kind of desire.

She was the only woman buying and the shopkeeper was more suspicious than impressed by her new-found expertise. To hell with him. She asked him to wrap the few basic colours she could afford and have them delivered, along with a precious canvas, to the Empress Emilia Alexandrina Bissetto, top flat, rue Becquerel.

The man raised his eyebrows. 'I don't like to send my delivery boy there.'

'Send it straight away, and make sure you have your boy come all the way to the top,' she said as she swept out.

That was the best she'd felt since the accident.

When the boy delivered, she gave him a whole franc and he thrust it deep in his pocket, hotfooting it in case she changed her mind. Good for him.

Unwrapping the paints was strange and intoxicating. The metal tubes were so neat and perfect, the glossy colours doming promisingly when she unscrewed the lids. Until now, her life had been black and white. What worlds could she create with these new things? Propping up the pristine canvas on the windowsill and oozing paint onto the new brush, she hardly dared make her first mark and spoil the newness of it. How to express her longing in the line of Colette's dimpled cheek? The tenderness of the soft curl at the nape of her neck as she bent, fascinated, by a ladybird on a blade of grass? How did you draw the warmth of a tiny hand as it held her mama's with the entitlement of a daughter sure of her mother's protection?

The first stroke was a curve of colour, unguent and seductive. Mimi dipped the brush in turpentine, a heady smell that filled her little room, and tried another colour, a cadmium yellow that reminded her of the morning sun from her balloon ride. It matched her optimism, but not the exact colour she needed. She worked on blending, controlling the paint to adhere to the vision she had in her head, and didn't stop until the daylight disappeared and her candle burned too low to waste.

Rising early to make her painting day as long as possible, Mimi worked day and night on her one canvas, lost in the possibilities the paint gave her. No creation lasted more than an hour. With only one canvas, she had to let her creations go for the sake of advancement and the minute they were finished, she scraped and started again. Everything passed, good or bad, but painting meant you could choose what you wanted to keep forever once you mastered it.

Some of her paintings were just details, things she needed to perfect in her new medium: an eye, a veined hand, a rotting peach she'd found under the market stall on the boulevard Montmartre. She didn't stop until she began to understand how to depict light and shade, planes and form and, most important of all, her own way of expressing what the subject meant to her. Then she scraped again, ready for her next attempt. A week, maybe two passed in this way. Time was inconsequential; she forgot to eat.

Paris was hers, and she stole everything she needed just by looking, and kept it for later: the meat on a butcher's slab, the professional smile the girls faked to greet their gentlemen callers in the downstairs apartment, the washing strung up on the *bateaux-lavoirs*, the brim of tears and hate in the eye of a ragpicker-boy beaten by his master. She was obsessed with observing every detail, fretting that she'd never live long enough to portray everything she needed to. Every face had something to say, the drabbest dress its unique texture and colour, a leaf a thousand shades of green, every street a dizzying kaleidoscope of ideas and hues.

When Paulette arrived at her door with a black eye, sobbing and cursing men, reality punched a hole in her world of dreams.

'Hush, what happened?' soothed Mimi. She kept her voice calm, but her fury at their world was dismally familiar.

'I said no, and he took what he wanted anyway. Dirty pervert. I'll kill him,' she said shakily.

Mimi held her tight. Paulette was tiny, just a bag of bones. There was no way she could kill a man, but Mimi would do it for her.

'He didn't...'

'No. He just wanted to hurt me in my tenderest parts.' She lifted her skirt and revealed dark congealed blood on her pale thighs.

'Bastard!' Mimi exclaimed, holding her tighter. Thank God, there'd be no baby. 'Here,' she said, leading Paulette to her bed. 'Forget him, it's your best revenge. Lie there and we'll get you cleaned off and make you comfortable.'

Mimi flung open the windows and slammed the pots and pans to banish him as she boiled water for Paulette, singing Maman's childhood lullaby to calm her. Inside, she was raging, but she'd felt this outrage so many times that her anger was a disease, a slow, dull ache.

Paulette washed herself, using endless buckets of soap and water to clean him away while they joked about his piteous drooling at the sight of her and how he couldn't get it up. It was their only way to get back at him. There would be no recompense for Paulette. The injustice was humiliating, disgusting. Mimi vowed, along with Paulette, to never depend on a man and always reach for the light. He would not win, and they shook on it. Mimi wiped away Paulette's tears, and she settled into weary resignation, which was worst of all. Eventually she fell asleep while Mimi fiercely guarded her. This world did not belong to them, but she would make it hers no matter how the odds stacked up against her kind.

Mimi forced herself to stay awake so she'd be there if Paulette stirred. Her friend was pale with sleep, like a baby, but she could still make out her lurid black eye in the half-light. It was so many different colours, as many as the myriad little injustices they suffered every single day just for being born a woman in this time and this place, with no parents, no prospects, no money. And what did the world do? Despised them for it, called them whores, degenerates and sluts. But as sure as Paulette's body would heal the bruise, Mimi would use everything she had to claw her way out and when she did, she'd show the world what happened in the backstreets while society looked the other way. There was beauty in the dirt, just the same as everywhere else, and the artists she'd met – Edo, Renoir, Monet – saw it too.

While Paulette slept, Mimi kept painting. First, she painted the man who hurt Paulette, an imagined amalgam of all the men who'd wronged her or her friends, riddled with the diseased anger she felt, his melting flesh the colour of Paulette's bruise. It was ugly and brutal, and when she finished, she scraped it clean and purged her brushes with disinfecting turpentine. Next, she described Paulette with fuller cheeks and a gilded smile. She scraped it and started again, this time Paulette with her guitar, happy on stage at the Lapin Agile. After that, at the laundry shrouded in steam, laughing with Henriette. She worked through the night and built a different world for her friend on canvas.

When Paulette left, her scars healed at least on the outside, Mimi drew Paris from above, the way she'd seen it from the balloon. Nothing but lines and forms and the sparkling Seine, free of slums and injustice. But that wasn't Mimi's Paris. Amongst the grime was love and lust and glamour and endeavour and all the possibilities in the world and they were hers for the taking.

It was only when the church bells rang the Sunday summons that she realised at least another week must have passed and she'd mastered the slippery, wayward paints and bent them to her will a little more. The precious tubes of oil were depleting, and as they emptied, she was filled with thoughts of her and Edo, a picture demanding to be finished. His look of kindness at her delight in the balloon, the way he followed her with his eyes as she padded around his studio, the intensity with which he built the colours on his paintings and made disparate shapes and colours into people and places, the last rays streaming in the big windows as they talked about nothing, not wanting the day to end.

When a package arrived addressed to *Le Chat*, the handwriting assured and beautiful, Mimi tore it open, knowing it was from him. Inside was the shawl Edo had given her while she was modelling. At his studio, it had seemed like just another prop. Now, in her sparse little room, it looked exquisite: ivory, with *chinoiserie* embroidered flowers. She buried her face in it and smelt his cologne, the scent of grass and something fresh, like citrus, mixed with paint and turpentine. Did he feel the same as her? A note slipped out and fell to the floor. Scooping it up, she raced over the words. *It's an empty rag without you. Come back. I miss you.* She had to fight it. Art and Colette, nothing else. Edo and the gang might be her ticket to the Académie and the Salon, but she didn't want to depend on any one man, or be let down again in the way Colette's father had abandoned her.

Apart from Rafi, of course. He still used their old signal of three quiet raps and a jaunty kick, from the days she sneaked him in from the cold street, and she flew to the door, still wrapped in Edo's throw.

Rafi scowled. 'That thing would buy supper for an entire orphanage. So it's true that you're his latest muse?'

Mimi tutted. 'Rafi, can't you stop your bleeding heart just for one minute? You know me better, and we had a bargain. I posed for him, and he taught me about painting, that's all. I want to learn and what he's doing is so different from anything we've seen in the Louvre or the École des Beaux-Arts. It's so fresh and new.'

If Rafi knew about the chaise longue, or dancing in Edo's shirt, or the balloon, he would think the worst and break the spell. Mimi let the shawl fall to cover Edo's note.

'Please be careful that your lust for life doesn't get you into trouble, that's all, after all you've been through.'

Rafi picked up her sketchpad and leafed through.

'You have paper now? At least your walls are spared, and these are good. Is the little girl Colette?' Rafi scrutinised her. 'Is this what you've been holed up doing all this time?' He put the sketchpad down and touched her arm gently. 'We've been through this a million times. She's better off where she is. Try to forget.'

Mimi nodded. No point in the argument, but she was never going to stop, or forget.

'I came to show you this,' said Rafi, a rare sparkle in his eye as he dug into his satchel. He threw a copy of *Le Correspondant* newspaper on the table. 'Look!'

He'd taught her to read and write in this little room and she read his name, Raphael St Pierre.

'They're calling me a Naturalist. It's meant to be an insult, but it's what I mean to be.'

Mimi read the poem. It was as insightful and real as an Impressionist painting, far removed from the Romantic verse she'd read in his library of poetry books.

Naturalist. Impressionist. Mimi rolled the words around in her head. The old regimes were shifting at the edges and she and Rafi were a part of it. She was as proud of him as if he were her real brother and said so, kissing him on the forehead.

'Get the hell off me,' he said, laughing, but a shadow crossed his face.

Mimi wished him gone. He made her feel uncomfortable and confused and guilty all at once. It was claustrophobic. Perhaps they knew each other too well. She didn't want to belong to any man, but she wanted Rafi in her life. She wanted him, but she didn't; it was all so mixed up, and clearly he was, too, judging by his face when she called him her brother. Why couldn't they just be friends, like they'd always been since they were kids?

As soon as he left, she put Edo's note under her pillow and

painted feverishly through the night. When she woke, the sun was already high in the sky and the congealed paintbrush was still in her hand.

Mechanically, she padded to the sink and dipped the brush in turpentine ready to start again, when another package arrived from Edo. This time, it was his paint-spattered shirt. *I can't bear to see this without you in it, so you might as well have it*, read the note.

She painted in it from then on, imagining a studio of her own, where he could visit, but didn't send a note back. Better to feel the pain now. The next three days brought more deliveries. On Thursday, it was peonies. She didn't think he'd been listening when she described the peonies she'd picked to put on Maman's pauper's coffin. She stuffed the flowers into her washing jug and smiled at such care, and her resolve wavered. She always just took what she wanted. Why not him? But she liked him too much. And in her experience, as soon as you started liking someone too much, you got hurt.

Emerald earrings came on Thursday, *to match your eyes*, said the note, and that made it easier. Too expensive, too much like a transaction. On Friday came a full artist's set in a wooden box, with every colour she could dream of, along with a clutch of sable brushes. *Learn to build the colours as I showed you, alla prima, and show me your thoughts. Everything is mere appearance, the pleasures of a passing hour, a midsummer night's dream. Only painting, the reflection of a reflection, can record some of the glitter of the mirage. I ask nothing more of you. I understand now, no one owns a cat. I will take only what you offer.*

It was impossible to resist. Barely a day had gone by when she didn't think about their week together. There was a bond between them, body and mind, that she'd refused to acknowledge for fear of being hurt, or of him somehow wanting to possess her. But here, in black and white, he told her he understood not only that she could not belong to anyone, but that her burning, overriding ambition was to become an artist, and he would help her.

She threw on the shawl and ran all the way to the rue Bonaparte. When he saw her at his door, flushed and smiling, he didn't ask where she'd been or what she'd been thinking.

Another week, maybe two, passed in their studio cocoon and neither of them cared what day it was. He filled the studio with peonies and she danced on the scented air for him. They made no promises, and here in the studio, there was no future or past.

The only counterpoint to their days was the delivery boy, who intermittently brought what they needed. Oysters and Muscadet; fresh bread, Abbaye de Belloc cheese and Burgundy wine; oils, canvases, and hog's-hair brushes for her lessons.

Edo couldn't paint any more without his muse, his street cat from Montmartre. She'd crossed his path and enchanted him with her lightning eyes, quick wit and elusive step. Mimi was smitten, too. She'd think about the rest another time.

'Let's go out on the town. There's a gathering at the Folies Bergère tonight. We'll be like an old married couple, except we'll be in love.'

'If you promise not to mention that word again, I'll come,' said Mimi, holding out the vermilion red he needed to finish the detail of her in the *chinoiserie* shawl.

'Love?'

'Marriage. I never want to belong to a man.'

He ran his fingers through his hair in relief, a nervous tic she'd noticed. There, he'd said the word love. She felt it, too, though she hardly dared.

The Folies Bergère was packed, and the cabaret was in full swing when Edo and Mimi arrived, arm in arm, stepping out together in all their finery. Edo had an uncanny eye for the most sumptuous and exquisite silks, poplins and chiffons for his models and spent hours rummaging at couturiers for the perfect piece. Tonight, she was wearing one of his finds, a dress created just for her in peacock shot silk, which changed colour as it caught the light, like her fortunes, he said.

'They'll all be jealous of my tamed kitten,' Edo said when Mimi asked him if he cared about his reputation. 'They're only wealthy by luck and gentile robbery, but your riches are natural. A wild pearl is always more beautiful than a cultured one,' he told her.

They joined a raucous table of Renoir, Monet, Degas and the rest of the gang. Rafi was there too, deep in conversation with a glowering Cézanne. Rafi nodded coldly in her direction when she waved, and she felt a little ashamed of her new dress. Well, he was wrong about it.

Monet was already drunk. He stood to salute them, slopping his wine. 'The golden prince and his exotic showgirl.'

'Not nearly as handsome as my kind bear and his dissolute partner-in-crime,' Mimi said, kissing Renoir and Monet on both cheeks. 'Do you two ever do anything but party?'

'We try not to,' declared Monet.

'Bollocks. Your studio's a hovel, but who'd have thought such reprobates could paint like you two? That kind of talent doesn't appear by mistake,' said Edo.

'Wait till you see our floating studio on the river at Chatou. The air's much sweeter there,' said Renoir.

'Mimi and I would be delighted to accept.'

'I don't remember inviting you.'

'Then that was a gross error on your part,' said Edo, squeezing Mimi's hand. She wasn't sure she liked his assumption that she would be with him, but it was also irresistible. Chatou might as well have been Moscow for all the unfamiliar colour and adventure it represented.

'We're going next month, and bring your swimming clothes,' said Monet, like anyone could just take off to a floating studio whenever they chose. 'The train gets you there in the blink of an eye and the swimming's heaven.'

'What if I can't swim?' said Mimi.

'Don't be ridiculous. If you can fly on a trapeze, you can swim.'

The vast auditorium was buzzing, a sea of shiny top hats, muslins, silks and feathers. Women peered through opera glasses to see the cabaret and assess their rivals; men filled the air with cigar smoke and debated noisily. Chandeliers like crystal waterfalls glittered overhead and the serving girls looked almost as fine as the punters, except their hands were red-raw and their dresses worn in places. She noticed that it was an unwritten mark of superiority to choose more muted colours, to wear fewer feathers and jewels than the working girls.

'Daahling, how absoluto ravishing to encountenance you here.' It was Henriette, with her wan prince glued to her side. She'd taken to using words that befitted her new status – the longer the better – but she never quite got them right.

Mimi hugged her friend tight. 'Look how beautiful you are!' Her cornflower eyes were sparkling, her cheeks plump and rosy. 'You're a lucky man,' she said to her prince.

He nodded, drunk, and they wafted into the crowd, Henriette leading the way.

'Lucky? She's a trollop. He already looks like she's given him syphilis, the poor man,' said a woman on the next table, wielding her opera glasses at Mimi like a lethal weapon.

'Better syphilis from her than being turned to stone by you,' countered Mimi.

'Edo, really, I thought you had better taste,' said the woman, ignoring Mimi.

She jumped up to give her what for, but before she could say anything, Rafi was ushering her away.

'You don't need to,' he said, steering her through the crowds towards the stage.

Yes I bloody do, thought Mimi, fuming at everything that sour, tight-lipped harridan represented. The superiority, the cutting her dead with a 'you're beneath my contempt' flare of her oversized nostrils, the diminishing of all the lightness and fun of her evening with Edo and her friends with an undeserved put-down. The only thing that woman had to recommend her was an accident of birth, but in Paris that still trumped everything good that any of Mimi's kind had to offer. It wasn't right. It was people like her that meant Colette didn't have both parents with her to protect and love her.

The orchestra struck up, and the dancing girls arrived. Mimi recognised some of them from the florists and hat shops in Clichy and they hoofed up a raucous cancan. They were magnificent – gaudy, exuberant and brazen, dancing away their cares in the limelight, and Mimi knew how deep and raw their cares would be. They'd all lived a thousand lives compared to the likes of Edo's so-called friend.

From above the stage, a girl swung out on a trapeze, right over the audience.

'She's using it as a glorified swing. No finesse,' tutted Mimi.

'Good, I hope she's holding on tight,' replied Rafi.

But Mimi had an idea. 'Wait here a moment, I'm going to powder my nose.'

'La-di-da,' teased Rafi.

Backstage, she found Paulette, who played and sang regularly at the Folies. They hugged. Paulette smelled pickled, and Mimi's heart went out to her. She knew that distinct sweet/sour odour from her mother.

Paulette introduced her to the Master of Ceremonies, who loved her idea. They rustled her up a costume and the wardrobe mistress promised to take care of her expensive peacock silk dress.

Up in the rafters, she took a deep breath as the trapeze girl handed her the bar.

'You're sure?'

Her guts twisted, but she managed a smile. Plus, it wasn't really a trapeze, not like the one at the circus. It was just a glorified swing, and it was worth it to show those snooty bastards who had guts and skill and life inside them.

'The magnificent Mintaka, Paris's Dark Star of the Heavens. A miracle manifest, back from the dead, right here, in our humble concert hall. Her comeback per-for-mance for your delight and delectationnn!'

Mimi rolled her eyes. This man certainly loved his purple prose. She braced, then flew out across the hall, trembling. Searching the crowd, she spotted Edo's friend, who was gaping up at her like a fish. That gave her all the strength she needed. Flipping upside down, she gripped the bar with her legs to the gasp of the crowd, pushed back for momentum and swooped. Judging it just right, Mimi swiped the gaping woman's opera glasses right out of her hand, flipped back up to seated, mock-surveyed the crowd with the stolen binoculars and flashed Edo an exaggerated wink.

The place exploded. Monet leapt on the table, stamping his foot to the music; Renoir crossed himself and screwed his eyes shut. Edo got down on his knees and genuflected to his flying goddess, to the delight of everyone in the club. Only Rafi looked away.

With her feet back on steady ground in the rafters, Mimi was triumphant, heart thumping loud and clear, every nerve fizzing.

Backstage, Rafi was waiting, hands rammed in his pockets, furious. 'What the hell were you doing?'

'Being magnificent,' said Edo, walking through the door and spinning her round. He kissed her and didn't care who saw. The dancing girls whistled and catcalled. Rafi disappeared. 'I'm taking you home with me, right now,' whispered Edo.

Of course he was. She'd just proved to him, and herself, how a little daring and panache could explode the invisible class divide. Everyone had their worth, rich or poor, and no one could make her feel differently.

Slipping out of the backstage door, Edo flagged down a cabriolet and helped her in. With the hood down, they watched the stars bloom through misty clouds as they sped through the boulevards, a generous buttery moon lighting their way through an endless Paris sky.

CHAPTER 10

Mimi's escapades at the Folies made her the toast of the café-concert crowd. In Montmartre, she was recognised on the streets by people who had previously turned their noses up at the sight of her. Now, men tipped their hats, and girls looked her up and down enviously. It was almost like being on Edo's arm, only this time it was for *her*, not for who she was with. Citron told her that *flâneurs* on the grand Haussmann boulevards gossiped about how they'd met her once, or witnessed her fall at the circus, regardless of whether or not it was true. Citron told everyone she'd known Mimi since they were two *gossins* grubbing around on the streets of Montmartre, and how even then Mimi leapt between the rooftops and knocked the breath out of everyone watching.

Edo's star was rising on both sides of Paris. He fascinated society with his outrageous entourage, though the Académie still rejected him, and in the backstreets, he was admired for his empathy and glamour. Mimi was the darling of her new artist friends and every florist, couturier and laundress on the wrong side of Paris dreamed of being her.

She had a new job, too, at the Folies. It was on her terms,

just once a week, and with top billing, enough to keep her in food, paints and canvases. She could almost thank the binocular lady for driving her back to the trapeze to avenge her snobbery. However, the management agreed she danced a splendid cancan, and as the money rolled in, her trick of kicking a top hat off a lustful toff on the low point of the trapeze, then spinning it back in place on the return with impressive accuracy was legendary. It was child's play compared to the circus, and she loved flying across all those top hats and tiaras between the glittering chandeliers. It made her feel like an avenging angel.

There was a boisterous camaraderie between the girls backstage, and they got used to her sketching furiously between acts, filling her notebook with their raucous laughter, brags, heartaches and scars. She sketched society too, from the wings, watching the unwritten codes and secret interactions that they thought set them apart from lesser mortals: a tap of a silver cane, a tight tilt of the head, a chaste pearl earring to match an ivory silk evening gown.

Et voilà! Without so much as a grope from the punters, she was self-sufficient. Mimi: 1, Society's Expectations: 0, and they could all go to hell. And she met Edo as an equal, taking lessons from him, and anything else was given freely by them both. When they could, they gave everything. Her life was dancing, painting and Edo and their time was precious, snatched between his family and both their work.

Mimi couldn't remember a June in Paris like this one. The sun flooded the backstreets, so high it reached the darkest corners. The street children played with their makeshift toys cobbled together from sticks and balls of rags, the light and warmth late enough in the day to let them be children after their work. Mimi ventured further afield, into the parts of Montmartre that were still country lanes, and the hedgerows were filled with daisies, foxgloves and poppies. Grubby children hopscotched amongst the shacks, scattering the chickens in the vegetable patches, and the leaves on the trees were as lush and pristine as the new summer.

As she strolled, she dreamed. When Maman was her age, twenty, Mimi was already four years old and she was left alone for whole nights, praying for Maman's footsteps on the stairs. When Maman did return, she looked haunted and exhausted, and it scared Mimi. But at least she did return as best she could, thought Mimi with an ache for her *maman*, and her daughter. As for her *grand-mère*, she'd died young, and Maman never spoke about her.

Walking back to town, and up the wide boulevards under the plane trees towards Edo's studio, Mimi congratulated herself on breaking the cycle. What if this Bisset girl became a famous artist? It would give dignity, sense and worth to their suffering. And the next girl along the line, her innocent, untouched Colette, wouldn't even have to think about it, please God.

Flâneurs paraded in fine wool ecru sack coats, tipping their straw boaters to the pretty girls in floaty cotton morning dresses. Mimi looked down at her shot-silk dress and understood. In this part of town, there were a whole set of rules to a game she didn't know but that she was determined to learn. Her dress wasn't right for a summer's day, it was evening wear, and for a moment she wished herself in their silk shoes, floating along without a care in a Worth dress, a wide-brimmed hat shielding untroubled eyes.

She quickened her step. Never mind all that, because tomorrow, she would be on a train with Edo to visit Renoir and Monet's floating studio, taking off in a hullabaloo of steam and grit out of Paris.

Her heart always raced a little faster when she reached the rue Bonaparte. Shutting the studio door behind her was like shutting out her past and facing her future head-on. It wasn't just about him, though he was all she ever thought about; it was the tubes of paints, the wooden boxes full of fixatives and brushes and colours, the easels and the souls and places on the canvases. Edo explained his process while he painted, and she loved listening to him. There was a science to it, a whole new language, and words like ferrule, chroma, cobalt, cadmium, oxide, copal and dammar were satisfyingly commonplace to her now. Every time she heard a new word, she logged it in her imaginary box of treasures to bring out and study in her garret at her leisure.

'Don't worry about the background, concentrate on the tones,' Edo said as she curled up on the sofa, to watch him work. His long hair was tucked behind his ears, and he was carelessly ruining another shirt with spatters of colour, but his painting hand was as precise as a dancer's and she loved seeing the shapes become people and places. Often, she found herself idly imagining the worlds they occupied, who they were married to, the homes they lived in, their hopes and dreams. 'Trust the process, start with the large shapes, then add in layers of detail. Your drawings are brilliant likenesses, but that's not enough. You're painting a soul.'

He painted hers and caught it, fleeting and light as air.

Everything should have been perfect that day, with Edo at her side and her dream trip to the countryside, but something was unsettling her, and she couldn't quite work out why.

Her eye kept being drawn to a new painting of a woman with dark hair, propped against the wall. She looked well-to-do, like one of the floaty girls from the boulevards, but there was a sensuous, neurotic curve to her lips and her dark eyes looked intelligent and sad. It was the dress that bothered Mimi, and the way she was sitting, slightly dishevelled, leaning back on the sofa, looking wistfully away.

Edo always painted Mimi naked, looking straight at the viewer, brazen and bold. She liked that's how he saw her, it's how she was, but this woman was afforded more respect somehow and there was an unrequited air about the composition.

That night when they fell into bed, Edo made her feel as salty and succulent as an oyster and dark and sweet as a fig. He held her close, all night, but she couldn't sleep. The picture of that girl was watching them with her wistful eyes.

In the morning, while they ate breakfast, Mimi couldn't shake off her presence and Edo's eyes strayed towards the painting every now and then. They'd never made any promises to one another, but this was a horrible feeling: leaden, urgent and burning all at the same time. No, it was a useless emotion and she did her best to diminish it and shoo it into the shadows – the long, lazy mornings with Edo were precious and she was wasting time. He always insisted on setting out fine china on a white tablecloth, like a luxurious still life, and the smell of coffee and buttery croissants was deliciously wholesome after their dark, heady nights. They'd chat about nothing and every-thing and linger to luxuriate in each other's company. Was this what it was like to be respectably married?

Edo saluted out of the big window to the École des Beaux-Arts opposite.

'Those bastards will accept me one day,' he growled.

'Me too,' said Mimi, standing to attention.

'Don't be ridiculous,' said Edo teasingly. But he meant it. Even though he'd said women could be artists when they'd first met, and he'd been generous in teaching her, he clearly never imagined she should aspire to the lofty heights of the Académie.

Mimi bustled to the stove to cover her disappointment and brought the coffee to the table. He looked up over his copy of *l'Avenir National* and grinned.

'You know that a gyroscope can help with navigation?' Edo read the science column avidly every day.

'Funnily enough, no.'

'It means you can navigate using the rotation of the earth. Imagine what that means.'

'I'm trying, but not very hard,' she laughed, but she wondered if the dark-haired woman would know what he meant.

'It means you can find true north based on the axis of the Earth's rotation, instead of just magnetic north. It's truly amazing, like you.'

'Don't try to charm me into talking about it; we've got a train to catch.'

Mimi tried to sound casual. A trip on the train, her first time ever leaving Paris, and there was no way she was going to miss it.

Her blue dress was trimmed with red, and the white ruffled collar was the height of fashion. A morning dress, like the ones she'd seen on the boulevards. Amazing how easy it was to pass if you had a keen eye and some money to make it happen. At the Gare Saint-Lazare, she blended in with the ladies she and Rafi had watched and envied only a few months ago. As Edo helped her step up onto the carriage, she needed an extra push to get through the door because of the size of her crinoline. *Never give up on your dreams*, thought Mimi triumphantly.

They had their own carriage, with padded velvet benches and little lamps with ruched shades. Mimi flung open the window and perched on the edge of the bench, taking everything in, while Edo lounged with his paper, smiling at her enthusiasm.

'That's the Butte of Montmartre. It all goes by so fast! How many kilometres is it to Chatou, how long does it take? It's like all those houses and lives are in miniature and the slums are disappearing and turning into countryside. All that misery, when just a few miles west, it's so open and lush.'

'That misery is life and striving and possibility. It made you, for goodness' sake. The countryside is lovely, but I wouldn't swap it for Paris in a million years.'

There was no use in arguing. He would never know what it was like to grow up where she had, and at this point, she was running as far in the opposite direction as she could, and she didn't intend to stop.

Chatou train station was just a building and a platform, not nearly as grand as Gare Saint-Lazare, but the air was sweet and innocent compared to Paris's smog. A day trip, just for fun. The likes of her didn't take whole days out like this, but she did, now.

In the cabriolet, the driver geed the horses and they picked up speed. Mimi tore off her hat, turned her face to the sun and let the wind take her hair from its pins. Edo held her hand and pointed out the streets and pastel-coloured houses. When they reached the river, Monet and Renoir were lying on a rug wearing white singlets and straw boaters. The fields on the other side of the river stretched away wheat-gold and viridian green.

'The perfect couple for a golden afternoon,' said Monet, embracing them both theatrically.

'You look beautiful, like a summer breeze,' said Renoir, laughing at her windblown locks. 'I trust you found the train journey to your liking?'

'As good as a magic carpet. I don't know how I'll keep all those pictures in my head, but luckily I've brought my sketchbook.'

Did she see mockery pass between the men?

'You won't need that old thing today. There's swimming and lunch on the deck at the Maison Fournaise and we expect to be entertained by your quick tongue and limelight smile. We can't have you frowning down at a sketchbook like an old man, my dear.'

'Though I've seen her drawings and she does make very

good likenesses,' stuttered sweet Renoir, sensing her disappointment.

'There's no need to be kind, but thank you. If I want to sketch, I shall. I can't spend every waking moment making tableaux for you to paint. My soul will disappear if I give it away too much.'

But she knew she wouldn't sketch today. How could she, in front of these masters of their craft?

Renoir and Monet linked each of Mimi's arms.

'Come on, we promised you a floating studio, and you shall have one!' said Monet. 'Edo, you must let us escort her, you can't keep her all to yourself. Isn't it enough that you're the only man she'll allow to paint her?'

'Nothing is ever enough when it comes to my Mimi. But go ahead and show her your floating absinthe den; I'll be watching from the bank, and she'll be my focal point. It'll make a nice change from your moonlike face staring out like you've discovered Shangri-La.'

Monet shook his mop flirtatiously. 'You know how happy it makes me to be out on the water. The light—'

'I know, my friend, and you capture it like no one else I know. I'm envious, that's all.'

'What's this, a mutual appreciation society? No one allows or releases me, not even Edo, but I'm dying to see it. Come on.'

Mimi strode down the riverbank with the boys. Monet hopped onto his boat and handed her in. She sat on the little padded bench. How amazing that just one step away from the riverbank could transport you into another world. Being on the water, surrounded and rocked by it as the sun played on the ripples, was sublime. She could see why he loved it here.

Monet had rigged up a makeshift canopy and set up a spindly wooden chair in front of an easel. A wooden travel paintbox was open on a rickety table, and there was a half-finished painting propped up on the easel.

The painting caught everything in bold, luminous lines. Punts bumped up against each other, girls stood on the jetty in bloomers ready to take the plunge, laughing, hair streaming, whilst men stood in groups shooting the breeze, or swimming and ducking each other. The way that he'd captured the water was astounding. Thick, almost crude strokes of blues, whites, greens and browns came together to miraculously create the scintillating luminescence of the ripples as they ruffled the surface of the deep river.

'The water's playing with the light and sending it back to the sky in diffused colours, like your painting,' said Mimi.

'Eloquently put,' replied Monet, looking at her as if he'd really seen her for the first time. 'What do you think, Renoir? Do you think a baptism is in order?'

'Absolutely. She was mistress of the skies, now she must be the spirit of the river.'

'You mean swim? I can't, I never learned.' She looked over to the riverbank where Edo was leaning back on his elbows, watching.

'Nonsense, darling. Everyone can swim if they have to. At least the water will hold you up if you fall,' said Monet wickedly. 'I dare you.'

It was the first time she'd laughed about what happened at the circus.

'Anyway, it's not deep here, you can stand up, and we're here to fish you out if you need us to. All you need to do is move your hands and legs like this and not panic.' Renoir made a face like a fish and showed her the pushing movement with his arms.

The girls on the jetty were having a high time, it was a baking hot day, and just trailing her hand in the silky water was cool and seductive. Why not? Had her body ever let her down?

'All right. I have never refused a dare. But if I die, my life is in your hands.'

The boys crossed themselves gravely as she unbuttoned her

morning dress and let it fall. Monet watched admiringly, and Renoir turned away to preserve her modesty. He should know she didn't hold with any ridiculous coquetry. They were all human, and she liked her body, so why shouldn't they? Besides, she'd posed for Edo enough times and understood how an artist could appreciate and study her body dispassionately.

Sitting on the edge of the boat in her petticoat, she blew a kiss to Edo, who was sitting up, hands raised in question, and slipped in. It was colder than she'd imagined, and Renoir was wrong about touching the ground. Her head went under, and she panicked for a second, until she came up spluttering to the surface, her feet thankfully finding the ground in the shallow water. Renoir was already on the edge of the boat, throwing his jacket off, but she kept her head, tried the pushing stroke that he'd shown her but kept to the shallows. She circled the boat, laughing at the shock and sheer wonder of being in another element.

Renoir knelt and held out his hand. 'Here, I'll help you back in.'

'Not yet!' said Mimi and the boat pulled on its anchor, the rope tautening as it floated away from her.

'Stay close to the bank, away from the currents in the middle!' yelled Renoir.

Mimi spread her arms and watched the water filter through her fingers, making fluid shapes.

Boats floated by, breaking the water and scattering the light, and on the banks the flowers swayed. Maman had made it her business to know the names of the flowers she loved, and she'd spent hours teaching her in better days. There were bee orchids, purple teasel, pink mallow, yarrow like lacy parasols, misty yellow *jacobée* and grasses hanging their seed heads languidly over the river under the willows. Swifts screeched overhead and skimmed the water on sleek wings.

Mimi lifted her feet, which were sinking in the mud, and a

current caught her and carried her so quickly that within seconds she could barely see the boat. Something wrapped itself around her leg, and she panicked and thrashed and the weeds tangled her more, locking her in their dark grip. Yellow lilies like evil eyes watched dispassionately, devouring the sun, while the dogged river poured over her like treacle. She stopped thrashing and concentrated on untangling herself, but every time she moved, it was worse. Her heart beat in her ears and the swifts screeched like banshees and she trembled violently with cold, sculling to keep her head high. Thank God, Monet appeared, breaking the water with a muscular front crawl, dived under and ripped away the weeds. He got her on her back and pulled her against the current to the bank. Edo was there, shouting, with Renoir close behind, and they laid her out on the grass, coughing and spluttering and laughing.

'You do realise you're not invincible, don't you?' said Edo, with an edge of shaken anger.

'Just as well I spotted those yellow lilies and saw you there. You looked quite beautiful, like one of the flowers, until I saw you struggling. I should have known, cats never take to water,' teased Monet.

She was shaking violently now. Why had she not learnt yet that her confidence didn't always pay off, that things could take a dark turn if you took too many risks? One minute you were in a sunlit eddy, the next...

'Take everything off, you'll catch a fever,' said Edo, unbuttoning her petticoat, but she pushed him away.

'Stop! People will see.'

Monet held his hand up. 'My dear, there is no one around this far down the river, and we sketch from life models every week. We're practically like doctors, we've seen it all so many times before. I suggest you obey, and warm up.'

Renoir looked away once more to spare her modesty, and she allowed Edo to undress her and dry her off with his jacket.

He wrapped her in the picnic blanket. They sat for a while to recover themselves, and in the river the yellow lilies spread their shadowy leaves to lift up their livid blooms to the light. They stayed awhile, and the incident was something and nothing. The boys made light of it, saying that they'd been watching her every move, knowing she couldn't swim, and as she warmed up, she looked back at the lilies, and realised how close she'd been to the bank all the time. She watched the clouds scud, and her hair dried into waves, and Renoir brought her the dress she'd left on the boat so she could join them at the luncheon party, where they planned to tell tales of Monet as Achelous, the river god.

The lunch at the Maison Fournaise was on a deck jutting out over the water and it was packed with the artists' friends. There were artists, muses, actresses, buyers, poets, writers and bureaucrats and the conversation was loud and bawdy. Mimi joined in with the best of them, loving having an audience, and they in turn loved her. When the conversation lulled, she leaned back on the railings and surveyed the scene. Light dappled the beautiful crowd, picking out highlights on the girls' flowered bonnets, glinting on the silver salvers piled with peaches and swollen black grapes. The rumpled tablecloth was strewn with crumbs and the wine bottles and glasses distorted and mellowed the late-afternoon light.

'You are baptised, and emerge Queen of Montmartre!' Monet had declared expansively. Was it possible to cleanse yourself of your past, of misery and deprivation? It felt like it was, like she had really been baptised into a new beginning as she snuggled sleepily into Edo on the train home, the world rushing by as if it wasn't real. Perhaps she'd even be like the dark-haired woman in Edo's picture, with her floaty boulevard-girl posh dress, someone people respected, someone who could provide her daughter with a good home.

'I'll walk home from here,' she said to Edo at the Gare Saint-Lazare.

She didn't explain when he looked askance at her. Today had been too nice. He'd followed her with her eyes, full of desire all day, proud when she held the crowd at the luncheon party. But it was important not to get attached to anything too good.

That night, she fell asleep remembering the way the water had cradled and rocked her, and longed to have her hand on Colette's crib, to be the river that would envelop and support her, take her gently downstream on life's journey through torrents and storms. Her wide-eyed little mermaid, dark curls caught in the sun.

CHAPTER 11

Mimi stretched the linen canvas across the frame and secured it tight. The ritual of stretching and priming the canvas was immensely satisfying, a combination of dexterity and dominion, the blank canvas a unique creation of her own making. After her first foray into the art shop on boulevard Montmartre, she'd learned that no artist of any repute used shop-bought canvases. While she worked, she smiled to herself each time she remembered a glance between her and Edo, a secret joke, a stolen kiss as the river rolled by.

She applied the gesso and set it aside to let it dry, then grounded a primed canvas with a pale, golden tint. Propping a mirror in front of her, she drew a self-portrait in sharpened willow charcoal. She looked at herself and imagined Edo, to see what he saw. Her features softened, her eyes glowed and the ghost of a smile turned up the corners of her mouth.

Careful, she said to her reflection.

There were two paintings she had to create, and a week, maybe two, crept past almost unnoticed before she stepped back and contemplated them, satisfied. The first, epic in scale, was her, emerging from the river in a white dress. Edo was Jean the Baptist, and Monet and Renoir were acolytes, holding up white sheets, ankle-deep in the cleansing river. Mimi didn't believe in God, but churches were peace and power at the same time, and Jesus understood the ecstasy and agony of people brought up on the streets.

A new beginning, said Mimi to the mirror. In this picture, she wasn't a *grisette* from Montmartre playing to the crowd. She was the central figure, serious and optimistic, emerging into a new world. That the other artists were bit players in her picture was significant. It was only on canvas that she could take such prominence amongst men. Maman would have said it was blasphemy, but what pity did God take on her? It didn't matter; it would never be shown anyway. It was still only a drawing, but her vision was there, ready to take the colour and shapes she'd seen at her outing, her own perspective.

The second picture was a finished piece in oils, and much smaller, the size of a handkerchief. It was a painting of a mother cradling a child in christening robes above a stone church font. The young mother looked adoringly down at her baby's pristine face, the rest of the world shut out in their circled gaze. A haze of votive candles lit the backdrop, rendering smudged haloes of hope with their flames.

When Colette was baptised by her new family, Mimi had sneaked into the shadows at the back of the church and watched the congregation of fine citizens accept Colette into their society in a way that she could never hope to be. Her daughter had screamed blue murder the entire time, and it had taken everything she had to stop herself from snatching her out of Jean-Baptiste's arms and soothing her like only a mama could.

Her Madonna and child painting was good enough to be the first picture she would dare to show Edo. After her baptism in the river, she felt a new confidence, and a more crystallised ambition, a clearer path to what she wanted: the impossible dream of being accepted by the Académie against all the odds, and a Salon exhibition. And with that, her daughter home with her where she belonged.

She'd held off telling Edo about Colette. She wasn't ready to trust him with that, yet. Remembering how Colette's new family had acted like she was a dirty secret when she gave her away, how could she risk him thinking the same and ruining everything? But now, maybe with this picture, he'd understand how she felt.

At the studio, Edo had covered the floor with Japanese fans. Japan was part of Edo's magpie eye for anything new, and his collection of woodblocks and paintings that depicted life in papery, flat scenes of cherry blossom and block colour were his prized finds from the exhibitions that were now all the rage in fashionable Paris.

'You'll look stunning in these,' he said excitedly.

'*In* them? They'll barely cover my modesty.'

'Why would you want to cover anything up?' said Edo, fluttering his eyelashes and flourishing two of the fans in front of his face.

'Stop,' she said. 'I came here to show you something.'

'That's what I meant,' he teased.

She almost didn't want to show him, but she needed him to understand. *It's good, your best yet*, she told herself as she propped up her painting on an easel.

'It's certainly competent. In fact, very pretty.' He scrutinised it more closely. 'It's you... and is that you as a baby? She looks like you.'

Mimi had spent so long trying to bury it, she couldn't say the words.

'It's good, it really says something. How many girls of your age from Montmartre take their babies alone to get baptised?

The candles make it hopeful, but we all know that the situation is desperate.'

'Who cares what society thinks? There's nothing lovelier than a mother and child, and the desperation makes it all the more precious. Surely nothing else matters?'

'Apart from the folly it takes to put herself, and the poor child, into that position. It's life, and I have every sympathy, but any girl with a bit of nous knows it's an impossible situation. Look at you, you're far too clever for all that. But the composition is good, the chroma could be—'

Mimi snatched the canvas off the easel. 'I'm glad you like it. It's nothing, really.'

Edo regarded her. 'Now I've offended you. It's good, very good, my little cat, and you've absorbed every single word I've told you, and every lesson I haven't. You get so caught up in the process when you're curled up on that sofa, watching with your curious eyes. But you do know you can never be exhibited? It's even illegal for women to attend life classes, and that's a crucial part of artistic education. You'll always be excluded from any worthwhile commissions or exhibitions, not least the Académie. It's just impossible, I'm afraid. I'm sorry, but I don't make the rules and I can't lie to you.'

'Don't give me that rubbish about the Académie and rules; I thought you hated all that.'

'I do, but they still make the rules.' Edo turned to face the École des Beaux-Arts building opposite and bowed. The habit irritated her more than ever this time. 'It will come tumbling down one day, but not in our lifetime. And you're right, I intend to kick a brick or two off, but it's still the route to acceptance and any kind of fortune, like it or not. And I have the means. We're different...' He trailed off.

She could howl at the injustice, and how could he possibly understand? What had she been thinking? That a man would solve everything for her? That all the emotion she'd invested in her baptism painting would somehow pave the way for her to tell him about her Colette, and that he'd sympathise? That her careful application of all the techniques he'd shown her would impress him and change his mind about the possibility of her exhibiting at the Salon alongside the others? He was kind, and more open-minded than most toffs she'd met, but still, at the heart of it, he wasn't brave enough to support the ambitions that the rest of society would scorn in horror.

'Let me show you something,' said Edo gently.

He uncovered a painting of her. It was the one he'd begun on the first day she'd posed for him at the studio. She was naked on the chaise longue, wearing the silk shoes he'd given her, lying on the Chinese shawl. Pixie was the maid, leaning over to offer her flowers from an imagined admirer. There was a peony in her hair, and a red ribbon around her neck, still challenging the viewer as he'd captured her expression on the first day. A black cat with green eyes looked curiously on, an allegory to her. It was so lifelike as to be brazen, shocking and wonderful, so unlike the 'acceptable' religious or mythical allegories taught at the Académie. This girl was modern, real, and in charge of everything about the picture.

'It's going to be hanged at the private view tomorrow, but I wanted you to see it in advance. You *are* an artist, to have given me this, just by being you. I couldn't have painted it without you. I'm calling it *Venus*.'

Venus. Rafi had told her about the Greeks and Romans. She was the goddess of love and fertility. But Edo's picture wasn't an idealised portrayal of femininity. It was real and harsh and true. He thought he knew her, had portrayed her essence in this picture, but a huge part of her was missing, and he had no idea.

That night, after Edo went to sleep, Mimi lit a candle and studied the picture of Colette's baptism once more. Hadn't the fortune teller mentioned an artist's palette and a river, told her she'd have two lives? Surely this was it? She couldn't stop painting, whatever anyone, even Edo, might think. It was in her and she just had to do it. She didn't believe in hocus-pocus, or destiny; leaving things to some nebulous being wasn't her style. But even she had to admit that it was a lucky guess, the kind of luck you didn't come across very often.

Everyone who was anyone in their world was at the private view at Durand-Ruel's gallery. Mimi and Edo lingered in the doorway to take it all in. Paintings crammed every wall and it was a feast of styles and outlandish, groundbreaking work.

Citron was there as always with her wan prince, pretending to be interested in the art, furtively glancing sideways every time someone walked in to make sure she wasn't missing out. Pixie was on the arm of an angry-looking toff, appearing unusually cowed for her sparky friend. She made a mental note to take Pixie for a good square meal and a friendly ear after their shift at the Folies.

Mimi unlinked Edo's arm and slipped through the hubbub to the back of the room to study the works in peace. This was where she found Degas skulking in the shadows next to his paintings, looking cynically on at the crowds.

'Ah, Edo's Venus and muse. Shouldn't you be out there, lapping up the attention?'

'I'm trying to avoid them so I can actually look at the paintings. I could spend days in here looking at all the details and techniques. Is this yours?'

Degas nodded dismissively. There was something haughty and asexual about him, and she was clearly beneath his attention as a fleshy woman at an exhibition, rather than under control on a canvas. No matter, she wasn't here to be flattered, and his painting made up for his rudeness. At first glance, it was a pastel picture called *The Dance Class*, pretty little dancers in tulle tutus rehearsing in a practice room.

But it was so much more interesting than that. The girls were the *petits rats* she knew so well from the streets. The central character, looking at the dominant dance teacher leaning on his big stick, was a sharp-faced little thing, full of sass and backchat, ambitious and ruthless. And it wasn't drawn in pastels, it was painted in oils, used to such light effect as to be capturing a gossamer moment in time that would pass in the next second.

Next to Degas' painting was one from Monet, a wintery scene. A single magpie perched on a rickety fence at the end of a snowy lane, pale winter sunlight catching the landscape behind it.

Edo stepped beside her and saluted the magpie superstitiously. 'My lord, send greetings to your lady.'

Everyone she knew in Montmartre had a saying to ward off the bad luck of seeing a single magpie, but she'd never heard this one.

'I wouldn't expect a man of science like you to salute a single magpie like a peasant,' teased Mimi.

'You can't be too careful, *n'est-ce pas*? Especially at an exhibition showing *Venus*, which is, in my opinion, one of my best works.'

It was true that *Venus* was getting a lot of attention, not all of it good. One woman had even fainted, attracting a tutting, fanning little fuss of dissenters around her. What sanitised cotton-wool cocoon had she been babied in all her life? Mimi was secretly pleased at the shock it was causing. What the hell difference was there between her on a chaise longue, and one of those idealised, naked goddesses by Botticelli?

A crowd had gathered around it since the fainting, and at the centre of it was the fey man she'd met at the Lapin Agile. She'd since learned he was the eminent art critic Albert Wolff, who wrote for *Le Figaro* newspaper under the name Masque de Fer, The Iron Mask. He clearly loved a crowd.

'Some people are content to laugh at such things. But it makes me sick at heart. These self-styled artists call themselves "intransigents". They take canvas, paint and brushes, splash on a few daubs of colour here and there at random, then sign the result,' he intoned to a rapt gathering.

The person standing right next to him, nodding censoriously in a shiny top hat, made Mimi's heart stop. It was Jean-Baptiste, Colette's father, shaking his head disgustedly at her, the brazen hussy in the picture.

Encouraged by his audience, Wolff really hit his stride. 'We come to be elevated, not to be debased by gazing upon an odalisque with a cat, a common prostitute inviting us to sample her questionable charms. Someone tell these people that trees are not purple, sky the colour of butter. Dirty three-quarters of a canvas with black and white, rub the rest with yellow, dot it with red and blue blobs at random, and you will have an *impression* of spring before which the initiates will swoon in ecstasy.'

Men laughed behind their hands; women looked sideways at Edo's beautiful picture, which he'd imbued with realism, daring and everyday beauty.

Edo strode off fuming, pretending not to care. And instead of chucking him out, Durand-Ruel encouraged Wolff, revelling in the notoriety the scandal would bring the gallery. Amidst it all, Mimi wanted the ground to swallow her up.

She realised now that it couldn't be her staring out of the picture. Not if she wanted to get Colette back. The whole of Paris would be scandalised, and the picture would ruin any hope she had of ever becoming a respectable mother. She slunk back into the shadows, feeling exactly as she had the day of Colette's baptism, like a dirty pariah.

Reeling away from the fracas, she found herself staring at a painting that she couldn't have seen at a worse moment. It was called *Le Berceau – The Cradle*. A mother gazed into the cradle of her sleeping child, the net pulled between her baby and the viewer as if protecting her. God, it hurt so much to look, but she was drawn to the painting's skill and luminous beauty, and its composition was as skilful as any she'd seen. The mother's gaze, her arm, the child's arm, and the baby's closed eyes formed a diagonal link between mother and child, whilst the cradle net cocooned the two together even further, adding to the intimacy and sense of protection.

She searched for the artist's name. Berthe Morisot. A woman! Exactly what Edo had said wasn't possible.

'I think it's beautiful,' said a familiar voice.

'Darling Renoir, it is. The way she's rendered the net—'

'I mean the picture of you. I saw that scoundrel Wolff sounding off, and you scurrying away to hide yourself like a pearl in a clam. Edo is a master, and you the ultimate muse.'

'You think I give a damn about that razor-tongued old hack?' lied Mimi. 'I'm happy to leave him to gather his little acid band of bores and sycophants around him. All I care about is tearing their hypocrisy right down to the ground.'

'You have sharp claws, Le Chat, which is why we all adore you,' said Renoir affectionately.

'Is she here, this Berthe Morisot? I thought women couldn't exhibit?'

'This one has special dispensation.'

'From whom?'

'Edo, of course, you know he pulls all our strings. He's the only respectable one amongst us, so he gets to say what and who is acceptable to his sensitive band of toffs with deep pockets. That's why you're here; he has very good taste.'

'Flattery will get you everywhere.' Mimi smiled, trying to keep the shake out of her voice. Only last night Edo had as good as squashed any hope she had of ever being taken seriously as an artist, and now, hanging next to the rest, was a woman's work that he'd helped get on the walls. How could he? 'I'd love to meet her,' said Mimi. She had to know who she was.

Renoir pointed across the room to a woman studying a picture. He steered Mimi over to her.

'Berthe, I'd like you to meet someone.'

Berthe spun round and Mimi's world shifted. She was looking at the dark-haired woman from the picture in Edo's studio. She was thin and very pale, with big black eyes like a china doll's. The way she was dressed, like the boulevard girls, in simple but exquisitely tailored voile, made Mimi feel brash, even though she was wearing her brand new, stylish clothes.

'Edo's Venus! I'm honoured. It's his best work, and it must be thanks to you. You are just as captivating in the flesh.'

Mimi should hate her, but when she smiled, Berthe's delicate face was kind and empathetic.

'I saw your painting, *The Cradle*, and wanted to meet you,' blurted Mimi, flustered.

'Oh that. It's all they'd let me show. I have better paintings at home, but a mother and baby is the only thing judged appropriate for a mere woman.' She rolled her eyes conspiratorially at Mimi.

'A man could never put such understanding and love into the subject, which is the most important in the world. It's magic. The composition and tenderness showcase your talents beyond any doubt, it's plain for everyone to see,' said Mimi hotly.

Berthe cocked her pretty head to one side to assess Mimi, fascinated. 'How so?'

Mimi analysed the composition as she saw it, guessed at how the layers were built, the canvas and materials she'd used. If Berthe was surprised at this street girl's knowledge, she never once showed it, but listened gravely to every word, and Mimi couldn't stop talking about her favourite subject. To illustrate a point she was making about highlights, Mimi invited Berthe to study Monet's magpie picture.

Berthe saluted the picture. 'My lord, send greetings to your lady,' she said enigmatically.

'That's not the usual magpie oath,' said Mimi, feeling like someone had walked over her grave.

'Silly, isn't it. But I *have* to say it. My sister and I made it up when we were little.'

So Edo was party to this intimate saying, made up between two beautiful, privileged, talented sisters. Mimi's instincts had been right about the picture, and Edo's admiration for this woman. Worse, the world, including even her rebellious Edo, fierce champion of the working-class girl, deemed this society beauty to be worthy of an exhibition in a way that she never would be. She felt sick.

In a blur, she found Edo. 'Can we go now?'

She had to fight it, know that Edo was hers, not Berthe's. It was the opposite of what she should do as he was the cause of her unhappiness, but she felt so floored that all she wanted was Edo to comfort her. And it wasn't just him, it was the whole bloody world she was fighting, trying to punch through the status quo that no one would even think to question.

'My little cat, you look like you've seen a ghost! I should have challenged that bastard sham Wolff to a fucking duel. How dare he criticise the Queen of Montmartre? Let's get out of here.'

He took Mimi dancing. He didn't deserve it, but she was too proud to be angry with him, and dancing was her way of forgetting. She whirled the day's cares away on her new silk slippers. Edo was attentive, the tallest, most handsome man in the room with his sparkling muse. But it was no more real than the fleeting moments caught and pinned like butterflies on the canvases of Durand-Ruel's private view.

CHAPTER 12

Back at the studio, they fell into bed and Edo unbuttoned her gown. Mimi could dance and pretend with him, but not this. She pushed him away.

'That picture, *The Repose*. I met her today. She's very beautiful, and clever.'

Edo sat up and glanced at the picture and a haunted look clouded his face for a moment. Her stomach lurched.

'Berthe? Bonkers, and charming, yes. She's just an old family friend.'

'That's not how she seems in the picture. There's something unfinished about it, unattainable and wistful.'

'That's Berthe,' said Edo. 'Her mother always says that she never chooses anything that's within her reach, and she's right.' He took her hand. 'What's bothering you? You haven't been your usual difficult self since you showed me your painting. I feel like I've opened some sort of Pandora's box.'

He had no idea that she'd been living in Pandora's box since the day she was born. Death, disease, addiction, alcoholism, injustice had swirled around her all her life, but at least one good outcome was that it had made her strong. She was going to leave it all behind, whatever it took, and break the cycle for her and her daughter, give them both what they wanted in life.

'It can't be me in your Venus painting, despite it being the thing I'm proudest of in my life so far.'

Edo jumped up. 'You of all people, bothered what people think? What the fuck do you care? It's what I love about you! You're free, whereas we're all restrained by our background to behave in a certain way.'

'I'm not free,' said Mimi. She just couldn't say why. 'And you're restrained by your background? Don't you think any of us would kill to have a tenth of the privilege and opportunity you've had? You're as bad as the rest of them. I thought you understood. I won't be young and beautiful forever, and then where do you think I'll be? Back in the gutter, or worse, drunk and dying on the streets, a dirty, salutary lesson to the great and good.'

She'd wanted him so badly, to overcome her feelings about Berthe and the Académie and her thwarted dreams. She thought she'd find a way, but now she didn't know what the hell she was doing here. Mimi flew to the door and Edo ran after her.

'Please, don't go. You always elude me; you're as unpin-downable as air. I'm a bloody idiot for saying what I did – it's just you have this devil-may-care attitude about you. I should have realised it's just your way of fighting the undertow so you don't get dragged under.'

She spun round. 'I'll never have what she has. My pictures will never hang next to yours and all because I was born in a hovel in Montmartre. No matter how clever, or brave or talented. I might as well be a different species to you and her.'

She hated herself for her bitterness, but there was something about Berthe that brought out the worst in her. Maman always said that green eyes meant jealousy. It was a mean, hope-less emotion, but she couldn't shake it, and her ambitions seemed so insurmountable, thrown into stark relief by Berthe's inherited riches. It wasn't just money, it was her cachet and acceptance by everyone she met, just by being Berthe Morisot. And Edo was clearly captivated by her. An acceptable love, not just a toff and his mistress. Stupid, stupid her to have got herself into this. She almost wished she was still running round Paris with Rafi, blissfully ignorant in rags, just accepting her lot in life.

'You *are* a different species, and that's why you'll never end up in the gutter. Look how many lives you've lived already and you're only twenty. You'll surpass the lot of us with your spirit. Please, let me make it up to you. Stay.'

It wasn't his fault. He didn't know the full story, and he was trying to understand, in his way. She'd known since she was a child that it was Mimi against the world. Everyone was alone when it came to it, especially if they wanted to kick against the unwritten rules. She'd always told herself she'd run to the light, and at this moment, he *was* the light. His world of art and rebellion was one she wanted to join, and he championed her in so many ways within the limits of her position. And the way her looked at her, with such admiration and wanting, was molten honey.

They sat in front of the wood burner, drinking coffee and talking as the moon crept across the sky. Edo told her about his family, how his father would not accept him after he left the Navy, how his mother helped him in secret, how much he would support his own son in whatever he wished to do or be. Mimi told him more about her mother, her sad and painful demise, the nights she'd stayed awake, terrified that this would be the night she wouldn't come home. She told him everything, nearly, but not the thing that mattered most to her, Colette. And she didn't return to the subject of the Académie Salon, and how desperately she wanted to be accepted, like Berthe.

'I can't tell you why, but you have to use a different model for *Venus*. You can paint over me. I've seen you scrape and restart a million times.'

'But it's my best work ever and no one else looks at me like that. Let me think about it, Le Chat. I rather liked the idea of all those respectable wallflowers fainting at the sight of you, but only with your permission. You know the ancients believed that a picture could steal your soul? Is that how you feel?'

And my heart, thought Mimi.

She left him there in front of the fire to curl up on the bed, exhausted.

When she woke, the sun was already high and streaming through the windows. Edo was sitting on the bed watching her.

She smiled sleepily. 'Good morning, you.'

'I have a surprise for you,' said Edo.

She slipped on his paint-spattered shirt and let him lead her by the hand to an easel.

'I've been working on it all night,' he said.

It was his picture of the girl at the bar at the Folies Bergère. In the top left-hand corner, Edo had added a detail, a pair of insouciant legs dangling from a trapeze, wearing green ballet slippers.

'See, it's you, but I'm not stealing your soul by making a likeness of you.'

'You've made my legs a little fat,' teased Mimi, but inside she was singing at his thoughtfulness.

'I'll keep the cat in my Venus picture, too, to remember my inspiration, but I'm going to rename it *Olympia*. I couldn't paint you over and keep the name – that belongs to you.'

She hesitated.

'I can't change the world, but I can make one for you here, in my painting, if you'd let me.'

It's not enough, thought Mimi, but for now why not seize the day? What she felt for Edo was a kind of love, but until he could accept her for the whole of her, including Colette, she could never give herself completely. But then, any life she was living was a half-life without her daughter, and this one, in the studio with Edo, was the best she'd had so far. And their nights were irresistible, and gave her a power and magic that couldn't be analysed, it just was.

She let him carry her to the bed and take his shirt off her. She abandoned herself to her body, devouring him like a flame sucked oxygen to give herself fuel and burn away her sorrows. She'd take her chances and think about the rest another time.

It was his turn to sleep and when he woke, she made sure she was the one there, waiting when he opened his eyes.

'You're still here.'

'You asked me to stay, but I'm going tonight.' She was in far too deep to stay, and he knew better than to beg.

'Go on, disappear and reappear as you please. I will take what you can give, I've always told you that. But I want to help. Let me paint you one last time. I'll make you respectable, if that's what you need. Look.'

Edo picked a book up off the floor and opened it where he'd marked the page. It was a picture entitled *Las majas en el balcón* by Francisco Goya.

'I want to recreate this, it's so clear in my mind. There's a balcony at Berthe's mother's house, room enough for three people to be clearly visible. I'll set up outside and you'll be a central figure, a grand lady at her balcony, dressed in style.'

'Like Berthe?' said Mimi sarcastically. It was beneath her, and she immediately regretted it.

'Like *you*. You can be anything you want to be.'

Apart from an artist.

'But these are obviously courtesans,' said Mimi.

'My picture will be of modern Parisians at the balcony of their grand house, inspired by Goya's picture. It will be a commentary on women, how things are changing, how they are half in the domestic realm and half taking their place in the world. It's perfect for you, my independent cat, who belongs to no one.'

I belong to Colette, Mimi longed to say, but she just nodded and fought her green eyes about the idea of posing alongside Berthe. She *was* jealous, but Berthe fascinated her, with her deep intelligent eyes and obvious talent. This painting could be perfect for her plans. A painting of Mimi as a lady, next to a society beauty who was also lauded as an artist could only be to her advantage. To succeed, she had to put aside base feelings that would get in her way, and she had to admit that, despite everything, Edo was doing the best he could by her. It wasn't his fault that he didn't know about Colette, yet.

'You're more honourable than I ever thought when I risked taking my clothes off for you to paint me.'

'Stop it, you're making me sound unbelievably boring,' said Edo, throwing her on the bed and stripping off.

CHAPTER 13

Mimi took a step back from her baptism allegory painting where she was standing in the river, surrounded by her artist friends. Her back ached, her eyes were sore, and her hands were raw with cleaning her brushes and starting again. It was a travesty and the bodies were all wrong. She might have all the colours she ever needed in perfect little metal tubes, have stretched the canvas in her favourite linen, primed and grounded it with newly acquired knowledge, understood how to mix the flesh tones and paint luminous highlights on the river, but something was missing. Her memory was good, and her vision for the painting was vivid, but a woman wasn't allowed live models, and without the anatomical practice it gave you, it would never be a masterpiece. And she wanted to create a masterpiece, to be noticed by the people that mattered, to be accepted in the highest echelons, to prove to the art world she was worthy of it, while simultaneously smashing it apart for all its rules and conservatism. It *was* possible to do both. She'd seen Edo do it. Because of his birth and standing, they outwardly scoffed at him for his outrageous ways, but secretly admired him for his daring.

You could do that if you came from the right place. If you didn't, you were just beneath contempt, worse if you were a woman.

Mimi looked around her little room. It was only a few steps from the narrow bed to the sink with the dripping tap. A few more to the cupboard where she kept her clothes, barely big enough for the full skirts she could afford now. The old widow downstairs was shouting to high heaven, startling her caged birds, who were squawking an alarm in place of their usual songbird chirrups. Nothing was quite right, she couldn't think straight with all the racket going on and she hadn't seen Edo in weeks.

Since she'd met Berthe, she was consumed with jealousy of her hold over him, whilst her body ached for him. Love – or was it obsession? – took away your powers, but also gave you new ones. She'd learnt so much with him, about art, how to 'pass' in his world through manners and clothes and speech. He'd broken secret codes for her, and given her the key. And nights with him made her feel alive in a way that Jean-Baptiste never had in the five minutes he took. She and Edo delighted in each other, explored the dark, intimate recesses of body and mind in a warm glow of enchantment, filled each other with a deep thirst which could only be sated by the other. He set her on fire in every sense. She was in as deep as the river in her picture, and if she wasn't careful, she'd be swept from the sunlit eddies that she controlled and out to sea. It could mean adventure, or storms, or both, but everything was so mixed up.

She might not have seen Edo for weeks, but she knew he was there whenever she wanted him. *Just disappear and reappear whenever you want*, he'd told her, and she wondered if he had any idea of how much that meant to her. She didn't want to belong to any man, but that didn't mean she didn't want to love one.

Her heart jumped at three quiet raps and a kick on the door.

It was Rafi's childhood knock, still their secret code. She checked herself in the cracked mirror, brushed down her painting smock and flung open the door, kissing Rafi on both cheeks.

'I thought you'd abandoned me!'

'No, it's definitely the other way round, Mademoiselle Bisset, you're far too busy being the toast of Paris. What are you doing holed up in here with that huge canvas? It's almost as big as your cupboard.'

'Trying and failing,' said Mimi.

Rafi dumped his satchel by the door and studied her half-finished painting.

'I always knew you could draw, but this is something else. Is that Edo raising up his arms about to baptise you? And those scoundrels Monet and Renoir holding the sheets? And the central figure – you? – looks so serious and hungry.' He hugged her tight. 'Don't pretend, your drawings always tell me the truth.'

Edo would never say that, thought Mimi, remembering her Madonna and child picture.

Rafi bent closer to study it, pushing his cap back off his head. 'This has the makings of a really competent work.'

'Competent? I want to be a master.'

'Then stop being a mistress.'

'I've already told you, Edo's helping me, that's all.' Mimi slumped on the bed and looked at the picture. 'What's missing is live models. I can't do a painting on this scale without them, and who's going to come to this rabbit hutch, to model for the likes of me?'

'My Mimi would never say that. My Mimi thinks of ways out, not reasons why not. The men you're mixing with have been doing this for years... in Edo's case, for over a decade. Competent is beyond the wildest dreams of anyone other than you. Give it another year and who knows where you'll be?' Rafi chucked a newspaper on the bed next to her, folded onto an inside page. 'See if this cheers you up.'

Mimi picked it up, ran her finger over the headline, *Édouard Manet's Venus, a review by Raphael St Pierre.*

'Scorned and admired in equal measure, Monsieur Édouard Manet shows us life how it really is, an uncomfortable truth-too-far for many who see themselves as the gatekeepers of decency, whilst secretly enjoying the delights of everything Paris has to offer.

'Manet's *Venus* elevates a young woman of questionable birth into a living, breathing being. Not for him the passive gaze of a mythical goddess. Venus is Parisian, bright and knowing, and has her own plans for the implied encounter. This woman occupies a world of her own making, and challenges the viewer to argue otherwise.

'Monsieur Manet's insouciant portrayal of a fleeting moment seemingly rendered in quick brushstrokes belies a masterful skill as a draftsman, an all-seeing eye for composition and, most of all, the ability to capture the essence of his sitter through his painting. He conveys her, and a commentary on Parisian life, right now, in real time. Academicians may rail at the lack of edifying religious or mythical allegory, rage at a loss of tradition, rue the dearth of conventional beauty, but no matter, they are the past, and Monsieur Manet is the future. *Venus* is fresh, insightful and invigorating, a brilliant commentary on our times and a salute to a brave new world. Brava, Monsieur Manet and his modern, audacious muse.'

'So you *do* understand.'

'Yes I do,' he said sadly. 'Just don't let this change you. It would be very easy to be swept away in modelling and dancing and dresses and grand houses. And who could blame you? But you're not Citron, or Pixie, or even Le Chat. That's their version of you. Make sure you keep your own version.'

Mimi didn't tell him about Colette's father's disgust, or that

Edo had agreed to paint over her. He'd only tell her to try to forget.

When Rafi left, she missed him. He was the closest she had to family, apart from Colette. The newspaper article showed her something else, too. He was prepared to embrace, even praise, a rival for her sake. Proud as she was of him, she couldn't help feeling a bit disappointed that he so readily accepted the idea of her and Edo. At the same time, she realised that there was maybe even a little rebelliousness in her relationship with Edo Manet, a breaking away from things past, including Rafi.

The Montmartre church struck ten, and she was meeting Edo at the Tuileries at eleven. She guiltily pushed Rafi out of her mind. It was the first time she was seeing Edo for weeks and they were going walking on the streets of Paris together to collect ideas for his work. Edo took her to the *grands boulevards* and pointed out the people he knew, told her stories of their secret liaisons and curious habits as they politely lifted their shiny top hats to her. In return, Mimi showed him Montmartre, took him to the gypsy camp where Jean Lagrène led his band of guitarists and fiddlers, introduced him to the local characters whose lives played out on the streets. It didn't matter whether they were parading in silks and diamonds, or swaggering in rags and glass jewels; all life was there to see on the streets, and she and Edo revelled in it.

Mimi paused in front of her little wardrobe in preparation for her rendezvous with Edo. They were going to Edo's mother's house on the rue de Saint-Pétersbourg for his balcony painting. His mother was away, but Berthe Morisot would be there, and she wasn't about to have anyone look down their nose at her. She picked the most expensive dress she'd ever bought, the light satin one with fashionable emerald stripes, a heart-shaped bodice and modest long sleeves, perfect for a toff summer's day. It took an age to do up all the little hooks and buttons – ladies' maids must spend half their time just doing that, never mind anything else – then she reached up to the top shelf for the matching parasol Edo had bought her to twirl against the hot Parisian summer. Hastily piling her hair up under her bonnet, she ran down the four flights of stairs, lifting her skirts away from the grime. It was hard work being a lady.

Outside, the sun was bright, but she wouldn't put the parasol up until she reached the rue de Rivoli. In Montmartre where everyone knew her, the parasol would be too much of a la-di-da statement and you didn't rub people's noses in it round here.

At the Tuileries, the sandy white gravel was blinding and the uniform hugeness of the Tuileries Palace with its verdigris statues, gilded balconies and hundreds of opulent windows was almost like a snub to the dirty people like her who came from the winding backstreets. But today Mimi flicked up her parasol and blended right in.

She was early, so she strolled through the arch and towards the ponds, taking gulps of the fresh, clean air. Children sailed wooden boats, giggling and teetering on the edge guarded by nannies and indulgent parents. In a different life, she would have bought Colette her own little boat, and they would come here as often as her heart desired. Before she could turn away, a fat hand grabbed her arm.

It was a plump young woman, with rosy cheeks and kind blue eyes, out of breath and nervous.

'I followed you all the way. Pixie told me I'd find you here today, I hope you don't mind.' She curtsied, and Mimi remembered of course she would curtsey, with her dressed the way she was, like one of the classy boulevard girls.

'What is it? Do you need money?' said Mimi.

'Begging your pardon, Mademoiselle, I'm not here for the money. It's your little girl, Colette. I loved her like my own, and I can't bear to see it.'

Mimi's world shifted. The ponds were black poison, her

breath thick as tar. She grabbed the young girl and shook her. 'What do you mean? Where is she?'

The girl pulled herself free. 'You're her mother and you have a right to know.'

'*Bordel de merde*, you're frightening me!'

'I'm sorry for it, but you're a grand lady now, and maybe you can do something about it. I was her wet nurse and she was such a bright-eyed, lively little thing, right from the start.'

'If she's ill I have to see her.'

'She's well, and no one could break her spirit, however hard they try. She's a fighter, but why should a mite like that have to fight? Do you think you could pretend not to know her if you met her? She's here, but I can't do it unless you promise.'

'Just take me to her now; you can trust me.'

They hurried towards the trees as fast as suspicion allowed. The maid's name was Agnes, she told Mimi. Colette was a real handful, always running away, little fingers in everything, and backchat was her speciality. Jean-Baptiste adored his daughter, but he was sickly, and his dominion over the household was waning. His sister had dismissed Agnes for her mollycoddling ways, and she now had sole care of her and she resented Colette like a cuckoo in the nest. Sometimes, she shut Colette in the nursery for days on end, and there were times when she struck her so hard, she'd break her skin. But she wouldn't cry in front of her adopted *maman*. Her holding back the tears would break your heart.

Agnes stopped short. 'There!'

A child with olive skin and dark curls was hanging upside down in a tree, taunting her nurse. She was a little elf, all fire and fun and rebelliousness. God, she was beautiful, and so much like her. Mimi would have given anything for her to recognise her *maman* and run to her at that moment.

'Come down now, you're worse than an urchin.' The nurse's voice carried over the lawns.

'I won't!'

'Maman will punish you like last time.'

'I wish *she* wasn't my mama!'

'Wicked child!'

Colette swung upright and dangled her legs, humming.

'You'll fall and break your neck and it'll be a relief for all concerned,' harrumphed the nurse. Mimi understood Colette's look of hurt chased by defiance all too well.

Agnes feigned a chance encounter with the nurse and introduced Mimi as her new mistress.

'Do you think it's right to speak such words to a child in your care?' said Mimi to the maid.

'Begging your pardon, ma'am, she's such a wayward child, she exhausts us all, isn't that the case, Agnes? Like the mistress said, you indulged her too far and now you're dismissed, look what I have to deal with.'

'Never mind, at least she's got spirit. Hello, Colette,' Agnes called up to her.

Colette's eyes lit up and she waved. 'Agnes, see how high I am?'

'I'd rather not look,' she said indulgently.

'Shouldn't you be off?' said the nurse to Agnes. 'Mistress said you weren't to see her again.'

'It's not illegal to be in the Tuileries, is it? I'll be off now anyway. I'll see you back at the house, Mistress,' Agnes said to Mimi, blushing at her lie about being Mimi's maid.

Mimi hugged her and whispered thank you, slipping a coin in her pocket.

Agnes melted away, clearly at the limits of her nerves with the encounter.

The nurse sized Mimi up and looked impressed.

'I always find kindness is the best policy at such a tender age,' said Mimi, churning inside. Eight months was a long time in a child's life. The last time she'd seen her was at the circus and she was five years old now, a defiant, confused sprite in the tree, desperate for someone to understand.

'Give her an inch and she'll take a mile, that one, ma'am. Leave her to me.'

'Let me see if I can persuade her to come down. I was quite a tree climber in my youth.'

'A fine lady like you? No, please. She'll come down in time, and get a good hiding for the trouble, don't you worry.'

But Mimi had already hitched up her skirts and was halfway up to Colette.

'You can't catch me!' said Colette, sticking out her tongue as Mimi found a branch to perch on near her daughter.

'We're like birds in a tree,' cajoled Mimi.

How was it possible that she was here, sitting next to her little angel? She was adorable and perfect, and hers, and it was torture not to hug her and tell her that Maman would make things right for her.

'You're very pretty,' said Colette.

'So are you.' The words caught in her throat. She'd know her anywhere. Her own pale green eyes looked back at her, Grand-mère's full mouth, her papa's curly hair. She belonged with her.

'I'm not coming down, I'm a bloody nuisance.'

'You're just braver than them, that's all.' *And they hate you for it*, thought Mimi.

Colette pointed at the maid. 'I don't want her to tell Mama.'

'Why not?'

'She'll shut me in, to learn.' Colette blinked away hot tears with a defiant shake of her head.

'Learn what?'

'I'm a common upstart. But I won't say it.'

'That's good. You shouldn't. Always be kind and nice, but everyone is the same, no one is better or worse than anyone else.'

White lie number one to her innocent little baby. The world didn't work like that. It was all Mimi could do not to snatch her to her, bury her head in her curls, and tell her everything would be all right.

Colette folded her arms. 'They can't get me here. None of them can climb.'

'But hold on, or you'll fall.' Mimi's heart was in her mouth, but she didn't dare reach out.

'I never fall.'

'How fast can you run?'

'Very.'

'If you come down, I'll give you a race; I bet I can beat you. I'm really fast too.'

Colette was already picking her way down the tree, light-footed as a cat, and Mimi felt ridiculously proud of her brave, sure-footed daughter.

The nurse was apoplectic. 'Just look at you, and you've torn your dress, you little scut.'

Colette clutched her skirt and saw the tear with a look of absolute terror.

What the hell did they do to her to make her so afraid? Agnes had said they shut her away for days on end. At least Mimi had always had the freedom of the streets, and that freedom was what saved her. If Colette was anything like Mimi, there couldn't be a worse punishment, and no doubt Jean-Baptiste's sister had already worked that out.

'You may well look like that. Your mama will be furious; wait till I tell her and then there'll be what for.'

'And I suppose that you'll be in trouble too for letting her tear her skirt? Here, you can get her a new one, and no one will be any the wiser.'

Mimi delved into her purse for some coins, willing her hand not to shake as she held them out.

The nurse hesitated.

'Let me, a good deed for the day to help a hard-working nursemaid. She reminds me of me when I was her age, and it makes me happy to be able to help. You'll be doing me a favour if you take it.'

The nurse looked at her curiously. Perhaps even her dull eyes had begun to see some sort of resemblance.

'I'll take it, thank you, ma'am. But it'll teach her the wrong lesson.'

'From what I gather, she has already had enough lessons to last a lifetime. Please allow me this kindness.' *Please, God, or I won't sleep for a week.*

'What about our race?' said Colette, ignoring the nurse's protests to stop bothering people with incessant demands.

'Come on, I'll give you a head start to the pond, count to three,' said Mimi. 'One, two, three!'

Colette raced, going as fast as she possibly could, curls streaming, giggling as Mimi pretended to be exhausted by the speed.

'Beat me,' laughed Mimi as they reached the pond.

'Easy,' said Colette. 'To the trees!'

'Now that's enough,' said the nurse, catching them up with a painful grip on her little girl's arm. 'Stop bothering this poor lady. Time to go home.'

The most natural thing in the world would have been to scoop Colette up and spin her round, but if Mimi ever wanted to see her again, she had to leave.

The nurse pursed her lips and nodded at Mimi. '*Au revoir, Mademoiselle.*'

Mimi blew a kiss at Colette, who returned one enthusiastically.

'I could beat you any time,' she said as she was dragged away.

'You could beat anyone,' replied Mimi to her back. She

stood and watched her go, running two steps for the nurse's one, dragged too fast for her little legs. Birds screeched in the trees, the sun was so hot it hurt, mothers clutched their children's trusting hands without a care, precious facsimiles of themselves with fledgling worlds in their eyes. Mimi should never have let Colette go.

CHAPTER 14

The Tuileries clock struck the hour, and Edo was waiting under the arch as she hurried to meet him, aching for her daughter. Perhaps if she hadn't dressed up like a lady to meet him here, the encounter with Colette would not have happened so easily. She braced herself with a smile and shook out her parasol to hide her tears.

'I'm honoured you brought my parasol, even though you once refused it.'

'You should be. Come on, I need to walk forever.'

'What are you running away from now? You haven't been the same since you showed me your painting. Let me help. I worry about you, all alone in your room in Montmartre. Have you thought about the apartment? I have money to spare, and you have none. Please let me help you.'

'It's nothing you can help with. And the answer is still no, but thank you.'

'Let's walk; at least I can try to distract you. See that couple over there?' Edo pointed to a richly dressed couple who were prancing their way through the Tuileries like a couple of dressage horses. 'He's up to his eyes in gambling debts and she has visions. Only last week she swore she saw an angel hovering over the opera house.'

'Maybe she did,' said Mimi. Was he being respectful of her privacy, or trying to avoid anything too difficult? Edo's paintings were visceral, he faced down his critics like a lion and his keen eye never glossed over Parisian life on canvas. But he kept real life in neat, ordered boxes. She in one, his wife in another and who knows who else in others? Perhaps she did, too.

It was all she could do to make it to his mother's house on rue de Saint-Pétersbourg without collapsing, but this was the picture he'd promised would make her respectable and it was more important than ever. Would a portrait of her as a lady, rather than a whore, begin to change the way society saw her? Would Colette's father forget Venus, and replace her with a more acceptable image?

She couldn't think what else she could do. Every time she sat for a painting, she learned more about her craft, and artists were accepted by society. Without it, the best she could hope for was a gentleman funder or a life scrubbing laundry, anaesthetising herself with absinthe. How would society regard an artist mother and her illegitimate daughter? There were no precedents she knew of. The harsh truth was that despite her cruel circumstances, society would still consider Colette to be lucky to be living in a wealthy family, and the veil of respectability was as thin as the delicate thread of her new satin dress, but as hard to break into as a fortress.

Edo's family house was palatial. She could fit three of her Montmartre rooms into the entrance hall alone. She imagined Colette tiptoeing across the cold marble floor of somewhere equally cavernous and unfriendly, ushered along by her nursemaid.

Edo occupied the space with ease, welcomed by his old family servants, delighted by a rare visit from the prodigal son.

Introduced as Lady Camille Bisset, today's model who had

kindly agreed to pose for Edo's latest painting on the balcony, Mimi felt like she'd entered enemy territory. The servants went along with it, curtseying and offering to take her gloves and parasol, but she knew enough to spot their sideways glances and pursed lips. At this precise moment, she'd give anything to be cackling along with Pixie and Citron, roaring at the lewd jokes and lounging around her little room, or alone with Edo in his studio where they were equals in a world of their own making. Everything about this place was designed to show off superior taste, and intimidate anyone who didn't belong, and here she was, colluding in it.

Edo showed her up the sweeping staircase into a breath-taking suite. Five sets of floor-to-ceiling windows spanned the width of the room, each with its own Juliet balcony looking out onto the wide avenue. Persian rugs covered the marble floors, gilt mirrors reflected the light that poured in through the windows and three chandeliers gave off prisms that danced like Degas' ballerinas.

Berthe Morisot was sitting in the corner in a white dress, reading. When the servant announced them, she held up a hand, and turned over two more pages before she put the book down to greet them. She looked up with tears in her big dark eyes.

'I just want to scream at her for her own destruction! Darling Mimi, how lovely to see you. Have you read *Madame Bovary*? I don't know how a man could write about a woman with such understanding.'

Mimi shook her head. She'd never read a book in her life. Who had the time for such things when you had to eat and clean and work?

Berthe kissed Mimi on both cheeks. 'When I've finished, I'll lend it to you,' she said kindly. 'Edo, *bonjour*. I hope you don't mind me making myself at home before your arrival?'

He kissed her hand like she was made of china, and Berthe rolled her eyes at Mimi.

'No need for such formalities, Edo, how long have we known each other?'

It was a fleeting exchange, but so charged. His obvious desire, Berthe's attempt to spare Mimi's feelings.

Mimi steeled herself. Edo owed her nothing, Berthe was nothing but kind to her, and she was here to sit, that was all. Compared to this, though, the trapeze was easy.

'Now, the light is perfect and we'll be a good few hours, so do you mind if we start? I've got every detail planned, so I hope you're happy to be bossed,' said Edo.

'Will this do?' Berthe was in a white walking dress, ankle-length, classically simple and nipped in to show off her wasp's waist.

'Of course, impeccable taste as always,' said Edo. 'And for Le Chat, the *pièce de résistance*.'

He opened a dress box to reveal the frothiest, finest, white lawn cotton, pressed and folded no doubt by someone like her. It was the first dress he'd ever bought for her to pose in – the first time she'd pose for him actually wearing clothes. She should be delighted, but he wouldn't presume to tell Berthe what to wear, or give her a nickname like all the other muses. Mimi had already thought of one for her, though: Fatale, as in Femme Fatale. There was a drama about Berthe, an underlying sadness, and her dark eyes could kill Edo with longing.

'Go on, take it out,' said Edo, obviously disappointed at her reaction.

Mimi lifted it out of the box and held it up against her.

'Perfect,' he said, assessing the length. 'What do you think, Berthe?'

'Like a wedding dress,' she said, smiling at Mimi. Her perfect teeth were almost too small for her mouth, like a child's.

'And why not? I'd marry you if I wasn't already taken,' he

said gallantly. Mimi wasn't sure if the comment was meant for her or Berthe, whether he was already taken by his wife, or his beautiful friend.

A maid helped her into the dress. With layers of gossamer striped white cotton, trimmed with ruffles and wide pagoda sleeves, it was the height of summer fashion, as light and airy as Edo's apartment.

When she emerged, Edo was impatient to arrange them on the balcony, meticulously placing them to create his vision inspired by his beloved Goya.

'I'd like you sitting, half in and half out. You are to represent the Parisiennes who are emerging from domesticity and taking their place in the world.'

He gave her a fan and asked her to look away, down onto the street.

Berthe stood next to her, holding a parasol. This time, Berthe was the one looking straight at the viewer, and Mimi couldn't help thinking that Edo had arranged it like that to give himself an excuse to lose himself in her dark eyes.

Edo asked for complete silence and for Mimi to think of something sad. It wasn't hard. Now she knew for certain Colette needed her and that she wasn't actually better off, even with all that money, what was she going to do? Kidnap her and install her in her miserable little room in Montmartre? She couldn't afford school, or nice clothes, and she couldn't leave her when she had to work at the Folies, which was the most decent way she could think of to earn money. She wanted Colette to be Berthe in the balcony picture, not Mimi. Someone the servants wouldn't look at sideways, who was meant to feel ashamed in a place like this. But the truth was, Colette was already a bit like her, half in and half out. Colette was living in a beautiful, respectable home, but they were treating her like dirt.

But she'd spoken to her daughter, and she was so like her. What an angel and what spirit! And Agnes had said her papa adored her, at least. That made Mimi happy, it was something she'd never had, and it made her decision to give her away easier to bear.

'You're smiling!' yelled Edo. 'I told you to look sad!'

'How can he expect our Mimi, who's like lightning, to look mournful?' laughed Berthe.

She meant to be kind, but lightning is always followed by a storm; had Berthe not thought about that?

CHAPTER 15

Mimi slept fitfully that night, haunted by Colette's scream, her fall, her little girl's defiant declaration that she was a bloody nuisance. So when the clock struck 3 a.m. and there was an urgent rap on the door, she was already wide awake.

'Who is it?' she called, throwing on a gown.

'It's me, Agnes, from the Tuileries.'

Mimi's heart throbbed in her ears as she flew to the door.

'What the hell is wrong; is it Colette?'

Agnes stepped inside, looking shocked at the size and plainness of her little room.

'No, Mademoiselle, it's Jean-Baptiste. He's dying, we don't think he'll last the night, and he's asked to see you. I am to take you to him, but please hurry!'

Mimi dressed, hands trembling at the hooks and buttons on her new dress. *Putain, too many of these!*

Agnes helped. 'Less haste, more speed. We'll get you sorted and I've a carriage waiting outside. He paid for it. He's a good man, Mademoiselle, and I'm sorry for him.'

In the carriage, Mimi fired questions at Agnes like a mad thing. No, Colette didn't know her papa was dying, he'd adored his little girl, called for Mimi incessantly, much to his sister's chagrin. So that was the reason for today's encounter. Even though she'd been dismissed by his sister, he knew he could trust her, and he'd despatched Agnes to find her, and report back. She'd told Jean-Baptiste what a fine lady she was, and how kind she'd been to Colette and now he wouldn't take the last rites until she came. Yes, it was that bad, the priest had been summoned.

Mimi rapped on the carriage window. The cabbie was driving like it was a bloody Sunday promenade.

'Faster! A man is dying, for God's sake!'

The cabbie whipped the horses and the carriage jolted into a gallop, bumping over the cobbles and forcing Mimi and Agnes to cling to each other to steady themselves.

Agnes whispered prayers under her breath over and over again, *Please, God, please, God, let us get there in time*, while Mimi's mind raced. She thought she'd never see him, or Colette, again. How could she have been foolish enough to think that, when they'd made something so precious together, when the golden thread that connected her to Colette would never be broken?

The carriage juddered to a halt in front of an elegant villa on the Left Bank. She'd never known where he lived.

Pressing a coin into the coachman's palm, Agnes ushered Mimi to the door, opened it herself and led her up the marble staircase. Mimi had expected to see servants running back and forth, the house in uproar with the master dying in their midst, but it was eerily quiet and empty. A fat priest held open the bedroom door, crossed himself in distaste as they passed, and there was Jean-Baptiste lying still, covers pulled tightly up to his chin, like he was already a corpse. Agnes slipped away, and Mimi stifled a gasp. She'd forgotten how young he was, only a year older than her. All the authority and shine his superior status and money in life had conferred upon him was gone. He was so pale and thin, on the edge of life and death, staring into the next life, muttering as if he was willing himself to stay alive for her arrival. His eyes lit up when he saw her, but he couldn't lift his head off the pillow. She ran to his side, found his freezing hand under the covers.

'You're a sight for sore eyes,' he breathed.

'I'm here,' she said, forgiving him everything.

'She's a facsimile of you,' he said with a proud smile.

'I saw her today, in the park. She's a beautiful little imp. You did well.'

'Not well enough. I'm dying. I can't protect her any more. I should have stayed with you.'

'I am fine, and I will find a way to protect Colette in your place. Be at peace, Jean-Baptiste. We were young and stupid.'

His eyes closed. He was just a boy, really. She kissed his hand and he smiled.

'I've left a will. My sister is bitter; I can't trust her. I dismissed them all, ready for your arrival. Agnes is on her way to the notary now. I've left you money, and entrusted Colette to you. Do you accept?'

'With all my heart, Jean-Baptiste.'

Mimi's heart beat faster than a train; such joy out of such tragedy wasn't right, but she felt it.

'I wanted to watch her grow,' he said, a tear springing and spilling down his face.

'I'll watch her for you.'

He closed his eyes and she knew she had witnessed him leaving. A change in the air, a sweet peacefulness, a kind of magic only birth and death brings, a connection to something more than we could know, a levelling of the stakes.

'Godspeed,' whispered Mimi, kissing his forehead.

When she stood, she saw the priest standing in the shadows. She hadn't heard him come in. They locked eyes for a moment, then she left.

A woman jumped back from the door when she opened it. She looked like Jean-Baptiste, the same eyes, the same way of flaring her nostrils at an awkward situation. She'd been eavesdropping. It must be his sister, Colette's adopted *maman*, Marie-Thérèse.

'I'm sorry,' said Mimi.

The woman looked away wordlessly with an expression of utter contempt and disappeared into the gloom of Jean-Baptiste's room.

The funeral was two days later. Mimi bought a thick veil for the occasion and stood back respectfully. No one would know who she was, and it was better that way. She didn't want to cause undue stress to the family, but neither did she want to miss the chance to say goodbye to Jean-Baptiste, and pay last respects to Colette's papa. What an awful, tragic mess.

Jean-Baptiste had been a popular bon viveur in his short life, and the funeral cortège was huge, so it was easy to slip in unnoticed and walk in step with the funeral drum.

There were no black plumes on the horses, and the coffin carriage was almost as plain as a pauper's. Mimi cursed his sister. Jean-Baptiste would have wanted a grander send-off in front of his elegant friends. He cared too much about appearances, but didn't all toffs? Appearances were what stopped the right things happening, including a mother and father caring for a child together. In this context, it was all utterly stupid and pointless. Poor Jean-Baptiste. At least he'd made amends in the end, but it was strange that no letter from a notary was delivered, no notification of the will that Jean-Baptiste had mentioned. Mimi had no idea how it all worked, she hadn't had a lot to do with lawyers in her life, but she looked forward to negotiations with the family when the time was right. She'd waited this long; she could wait a little longer to be reunited with her daughter. And she'd thought about it in the interceding days, after she'd got over the shock of it all. How life could turn a corner in a day and knock you sideways, and not always for the worse. Colette had lost her father; how would she feel about leaving his family altogether? There may have to be a transition period, and she had all the time in the world for whatever was right.

At the church, Mimi hung back, a solitary figure once more, as she had been for Colette's baptism. She could just see her daughter sitting stock-still, very upright, next to Jean-Baptiste's sister. Her adopted *maman* didn't once put her arm around her, or comfort her, though Mimi tried to make it so through sheer force of will. How could she leave her to suffer like that?

Marie-Thérèse and Colette led the procession back down the aisle. Colette was ashen, solemn, not a trace of the little girl she'd seen climbing trees only a few days ago in the Tuileries. Mimi knew what it was to lose a papa. She'd tell her that one day.

Marie-Thérèse saw Mimi, excused herself from the procession and beckoned her to a silent part of the church away from the crowds.

'What the hell are you doing here?' she hissed.

'I had to say goodbye, I'm sorry if I've disturbed—'

'Your brat's exactly like you, and nothing like him. Now I see where she gets all her sass and—'

'I won't have this conversation here. But if you harm one hair on her sweet little head, I'll—'

'What, now you care? You abandoned her and ruined him. What are your grubby little fingers after now? This is not the time or place, but come and see me tomorrow at the house and we'll have this out.'

Marie-Thérèse swept back into the crowd, heaving false sobs. Mimi was furious, and grief-stricken, and terrified of this woman all at once. Outside, the rain was heaving down in sheets and as soon as she was around the corner, out of sight, she tore off her hat to feel the rain on her face. What the hell was going on?

The next morning, Mimi picked out a day dress, which made her look exactly like the boulevard girls in their tasteful clothes, and rushed as early as decently possible to Jean-Baptiste's villa. She'd hardly slept for two nights, so she pinched her cheeks before she knocked on the door.

The nurse from the Tuileries answered the door and this time didn't bother to bob a curtsey to her, now she knew that Mimi was just passing as a lady. In fact, she didn't bother to disguise her contempt.

'She's waiting for you in there,' muttered the nurse, jerking her head towards a door without properly showing her the way.

Marie-Thérèse stood, hands clasped in front of her.

'I won't ask you to sit; this should be very quick.'

'Maybe Jean-Baptiste didn't tell you about the will?'

'What will? That boy wasn't capable of anything but drinking and womanising. And now look what the cat's brought in.'

'If you tell me the name of your lawyer, I'll go there myself. He had Agnes despatch it the night he died. I'm sorry, and I understand if you're angry, but he was very clear. He said he wanted to pass the care of Colette to me, that he'd left some money for us.'

'If it's money you're after, forget it. He squandered the lot on gambling debts. All he left us was your brat, and penury.'

So poor Jean-Baptiste had let her down again, even in death. This woman didn't care about Colette, she already knew that, and now it was up to her. Mimi took a moment. All toffs really cared about was money. It was the only thing that set them apart, aside from their imagined extra refinements, and Marie-

Thérèse was clearly skint. In her world, Mimi was used to the buying and selling of people by other names – maids, prostitutes, labourers – who worked for next to nothing in return for a roof over their heads and enough food to keep them alive. There was no reason why Marie-Thérèse wouldn't be the same, and no point in pussyfooting around.

Mimi looked her straight in the eye. 'I don't care about the money, but I swore that I would take Colette and look after her. I'm her mother and I should never have given her up. You can see she's mine in every way and I promise I will make her happy. I'll buy her from you. Just name your terms.'

Marie-Thérèse slumped into a chair with her head in her hands for what seemed an age.

'Listen, I'm sorry, I've been harsh with you; it's all been so quick, and he's left us with nothing, I can hardly think straight. He was right, she's so like you; he talked about you a lot and how he did you wrong. It was all I could do to advise him what a foolish course it would be on his part to beg you to come back and turn his back on decent society.'

Well, that was a sudden change of tack. Bullseye. The old harridan clearly knew how to put on a good show when she needed to, she'd give her that.

'Let us make a pact. I can't let Jean-Baptiste's little girl go until I know she's going to be kept in the kind of accommodation she's become accustomed to. I can see the passion you have for her, and for Jean-Baptiste's will, even if it never existed. I have to admit, I heard what he said at the door, and it broke my heart.'

Mimi doubted she had anything that passed for a heart, but she bit her lip. She'd play any game she needed to. 'What is your pact? I'll do anything.'

'Show me that you are living in suitable accommodation, and distasteful as it is, I have no choice but to accept a sum of money for her transfer to you. Let's say ten thousand francs. It's cost us more than that to give her everything that Jean-Baptiste wanted to, from circus trips, to ponies and governesses. He couldn't afford any of it, but we did everything her heart desired, and that would go some way towards recompense for your foolishness. There's also a small matter of five thousand francs settled on her next June, on her sixth birthday, which is in ten months' time. That would come to me should I keep her in my care, an amount not to be sneezed at. You'll find you won't see Colette until you can fulfil my terms, so don't try anything stupid. Obviously you'll need time to get that sort of money. I'll give you until next March, seven months, over half a year. Should you raise the sum, that gives us enough time to arrange things before her next birthday. Any inkling that you've communicated our deal with anyone will make it null and void. This family's had enough scandal at its door.'

Ten thousand francs? It was impossible. What was going on in this bitter woman's head? It wasn't just about the money; she wanted to punish her in some way. Did she want to push her into prostitution? But she'd already missed too many of Colette's birthdays, and she didn't intend to miss another.

'I could never put my hands on that kind of money. It's unreasonable and against your dead brother's express wishes.'

'Your kind can get money if you need to. I'll leave it up to you as to how. However, I am not completely without a heart. We may be from different worlds, but I understand family bonds, and she is of no use to me, apart from as a maid or a ward to sell off. Don't protest! I am merely telling you the truth of the matter.'

This woman was as bad as the madams who ran the brothels, buying and selling girls, but at least they were honest about it. Jean-Baptiste's sister was trying to make it look like a fair deal. The only way Mimi could get that kind of money was as a courtesan, and what kind of mother would that make her? It was everything she'd strived to avoid all her life.

'How can I be sure you won't renege on the deal? I want it in a contract, overseen by your notary, the one Jean-Baptiste told me about.'

'You are sharper than you look. Very well.'

Marie-Thérèse scribbled down an address and gave it to her.

'Meet me here tomorrow at 12 p.m. sharp. I'll have him draw up the terms and witness it. That way, we are both protected. If you are anything like Colette, you'd turn around and stab me in the back if there were not strict measures in place to prevent it.'

How could a five-year-old child possibly get the better of her? Marie-Thérèse was spiteful and bitter, and she was playing a strange game with her. Mimi wasn't afraid of much, but this woman gave her the creeps.

Marie-Thérèse said she couldn't think straight, but how could anyone come to such a conclusion in a heartbeat like that? She didn't trust her, Jean-Baptiste had told her not to, but she had no choice but to agree. Marie-Thérèse held all the cards, including her daughter.

Mimi left, reeling. God, she wished Maman was alive, or that she had a papa to confide in. She couldn't tell Rafi; he'd just tell her to leave it be. Pixie and Citron wouldn't understand. Relinquished babies were ten a penny where they came from, and most knew they just had to accept their fate and hope their babies would grow up in a better place than them.

But Mimi knew what she had to do. Edo wanted to install her in an apartment, to visit her whenever he pleased. It was a respectable offer – she worked as his muse, he needed her to create his art, so it wasn't like Citron and her prince. She'd been proud and thought the trapeze, or dancing at the Folies, or her beloved art could get her where she wanted to be, but it was the best the likes of her could hope for. Other girls would kill for an offer like that. An apartment on the Left Bank, money to spare.

Money could buy you anything, even respectability. She'd seen famous mistresses gain a certain status in society and, along with that, seen their children thrive.

Edo was right, things were changing. Laundresses became shop girls, shop girls lived on the same grand boulevards as the women they dressed, the women they dressed could be whores or ladies and nowadays it was hard to tell. Hadn't Berthe said she was wearing a wedding dress? Maybe for once Mimi should let someone help. Edo had only ever been kind and she needed help desperately for Colette's sake. Edo's money could buy her the status she needed, and after that, all Colette needed was love, and she had that in spades. It would mean sacrificing her independence, but the trapeze was a disaster, and she was no closer to the Académie and the Salon and she needed money fast. There was no choice any more. She wasn't that sixteen-year-old child who'd given away her daughter; she was twenty now, old enough to do something about it. Who knew how long her youth would last? If you came from where she did, an apartment from a toff was success. And if he loved her, he'd understand and help her find the money she needed.

CHAPTER 16

Mimi flung open the windows. On the rue des Batignolles, the air was sweet, and the avenue was wide enough that the sun greeted you every morning. A wrought-iron balcony underlined the view of plane trees and elegant houses, and carriages trotted by stuffed with ladies and gents dressed in acres of silk and fine wool. Some lucky couturier could retire on just one bloody carriage load.

Reflected in the gilt mirror was a young woman in *déshabille*, one Mademoiselle Mimi Bisset. The hungry look she was used to seeing in her cracked mirror in Montmartre was replaced with a full-length image of a beautiful lady with a serene glow whose olive skin shone against her white slip and embroidered kimono.

The main salon was big enough to sing a whole verse of 'Le Papillon et la Fleur' as you danced from one side of the room to the other, which Mimi did every morning. It was the lullaby she sang to Colette when she was a tiny baby in her first exquisite days in the world, just the two of them. Being here made her feel closer to the day she'd bring Colette home. She just needed time to find the right moment to tell Edo her plan.

Edo himself had overseen the furnishing of the high-ceilinged, white-panelled salon, with elegant furniture uphol-stered in jewel-coloured damasks, a marble console, a grand piano that Colette might one day learn on, and more mirrors than the Folies. And the salon wasn't even the only room. There was a bedroom with a feather bed and a dressing table with a whole hairbrush set, backed with mother-of-pearl. On the other side of the salon was a kitchen with a range hung with big polished copper pots, and the dresser was crammed with enough fine crockery, cutlery and serving dishes to feed a whole brood of hungry children, never mind just Colette.

Mimi floated across the polished parquet floor and stoked the fire, which didn't even smoke, and toasted herself against the morning chill, wiggling her toes just for the hell of it. It wasn't right to have the window open *and* the fire going, but she hadn't quite got over the fact that she just could, and stuff the cost of coal. Besides, it kept her maid in employment, laying fires and sweeping out. As a kind of offering to whoever was in charge of fate, she'd paid the gangmaster of the ragpickers for a young girl to help. She wished she could have bought them all from that bastard.

Mimi sipped her coffee out of a cup so fine you could see the liquid through the china. *A painter can express whatever he wants with fruits, flowers or clouds*, Edo had told her, and he was right. Now she was installed in his apartment, they'd agreed that he'd no longer paint her. They didn't want to flaunt their assignation to anyone, but that didn't mean he couldn't show her how he felt about her on canvas, or that she wasn't still his inspiration. She'd only been here two months, and the walls were already hung with testimonies of his love for her in a series of still lifes of peonies for romance, prosperity and a happy marriage.

Edo couldn't marry her, but the pictures were their secret. Some of the peonies were arranged in graceful vases, painted in

harmonious pastel hues to symbolise languid days together in
the grand salon, reading and talking and dreaming. The one
where petals had fallen and scattered on the table was inspired
by Mimi's slip discarded on the floor next to the feather bed.
Sunshine-bitter lemons, ripe peaches, dark figs and succulent
oysters were their nights together. He visited her at every opportunity he could, and when she knew he was coming, she
dismissed her maid so that they could undress each other at the
door and make love wherever they chose to: in a shaft of
sunlight by the big windows, the kitchen table where they
scraped aside whatever was on it, plates and pots clattering to
the ground, or tenderly in the big soft bed, luxuriating in the
sweet peacefulness and waking in each other's arms to the
sound of church bells, street hawkers and gently falling summer
rain.

Like the opium dens she'd seen in Pigalle, it was an ivory
tower of the sweetest illusion. She hadn't drawn or painted
since she'd arrived here, and she hadn't told him about Colette,
but there was a moment for that which hadn't yet arrived and
was too important to squander. Besides, the pact came with a
price of ten thousand francs, and it was no small sum to ask of
him. Colette was living with that horrible woman, but Mimi
had waited this long, and she trusted her to keep her safe and
healthy, if not happy, with that amount of money at stake. It was
crucial that everything was aligned and she was terrified that it
might all go awry if she was too hasty. She was in a very precar-
ious position, completely beholden to Edo, more than he would
ever know.

And Edo came to escape. He didn't like to see easels or
charcoals and paint when he visited. *Just you and me, away
from everyday cares. Our own work of living art.* And it was
perfect. All her life she'd been cold, or hungry, desperate, poor,
always reaching for the light. And here *was* the light, and

Colette was within her reach. Every day she checked in her dressing table for the contract she'd signed at the notary's.

'Most unusual,' he'd said sniffily as he'd dipped a pen in the inkwell and handed it for her to sign.

'You understand the delicacy of the matter? I must ensure the child is going to a suitable home, and of course I love her very much. The money will be some sort of recompense for the ignominy I have suffered to protect my brother and his child from scandal.'

The notary didn't look convinced, but was happy to draw up the contract and take the cheque. The contract was the most precious thing Mimi had ever owned. Whatever machinations Marie-Thérèse was planning, this was assurance. It didn't matter about their status in life, the law was the law, and she had it in black and white that her daughter would be returned to her.

She had to hold her nerve and believe that Colette would float around in gossamer threads, luxuriate in front of the blazing fire, sit by the open windows and feel the tender breeze on her face, see music at the Tuileries dressed in silk and walk the boulevards in leather slippers – she'd be one of those girls she'd envied in their floaty day dresses. Mimi wasn't a fool. She knew everything had to be paid for, somehow, and that maybe she was paying with her ambition, but any sacrifice was worth making for Colette. Didn't Mimi have nine lives? And by her calculation, this was only number five. Her childhood, motherhood, the circus, the world of artists and cabarets and now Edo and the apartment. Next, her, Edo and Colette.

Even the church bells sounded kinder here, fuller and richer. When the Église Sainte-Marie des Batignolles struck 11 a.m., she ran to the door to open it for Pixie, still not dressed.

'Fuck me, is that what you wear in bed? Just that dressing gown would buy me my own laundry! You've landed on your feet here, my friend.'

Pixie pushed past her. She reeked of booze and the night was clearly only just ending for her. She was still wearing her black stockings and gaudy red dress from the cancan and, judging by the way it was all skew-whiff, it had no doubt been wrenched up against some stinking alley wall, and she hadn't even bothered to straighten it afterwards.

Mimi followed her into the salon and watched Pixie throw herself onto the sofa and kick off her shoes.

'Not a bad place for a working girl to put her feet up for a while.'

Pixie gave her a forced smile, but there were tears in her eyes.

'I'll get us some tea, and you look like you could do to eat.' Mimi rang the bell for the maid.

'What the hell is that thing for, your pet dog?' said Pixie, running her finger over the damask cushion and sucking in her breath.

'Remember that little girl we used to pass in the ragpicker gang, the one with the rosebud mouth and dead eyes?' said Mimi.

The maid came in, bobbed a curtsey and took the order for tea.

'Bloody hell, it's her.' Pixie staggered over and gave Mimi a big, alcoholic hug. 'Good to see you haven't forgotten your own, you social-climbing little whore.'

Pixie meant it to be a compliment, but it stung.

'I don't care about all that. I love Edo and he loves me.'

'Yeah and the rest is just fringe benefits. You enjoy, girl. Haven't we known each other forever? I don't care why you're here.'

'Pixie... I want Colette back. She's used to big houses, so I need this. I'm going to bring her here to live with me and she won't have a clue about the lives we've lived. She'll just play on swings in the sunlight and have enough to eat and go on holiday to the seaside and grow up to choose whatever she wants.'

Pixie took her hands and looked into her eyes. 'You really mean it, don't you? Good luck to you, but I wouldn't be your friend if I didn't say it won't happen. Dream on, but this Edo or whoever he is won't want a brat living here.'

Pixie coughed and blood bloomed on the dirty handkerchief she pulled out of her bodice to catch it.

'That's not good, you're ill. Here, have some tea and relax. Let me get you a throw.'

Pixie took a sip of tea, but her hand was shaking so violently she lost half of it on the floor. 'Nah, that? The alcohol will purge it. I don't suppose you could pour me a teensy bit of cognac to steady the shakes?'

'Isn't it a bit early?'

'What are you, rationing it? It's not like you haven't got bloody everything you need in this gilded whorehole.'

'Pixie, what's happening to you? Why don't you tuck up in my bed and get some sleep. You look half dead.'

Pixie let the tears come. 'It's the only way I can relax. Please give me a drink, and I'll be a good girl, I promise.'

Mimi reluctantly poured her a measure of cognac and Pixie lay back on the sofa, relieved.

'Tell me everything,' said Mimi.

'Tell you what? That everything's fine, I've got a nice steady job in a hat shop and met a kind man who wants to marry me and love and cherish me happily ever after? That doesn't happen to the likes of us. You've tried your hardest to escape, but even you're only one step away from a man's complete power over you. Don't look at me like that. I don't want sympathy, I just want to forget.' She held out the glass. 'Get me another, will you?'

'No. You're killing yourself. You *do* have options. You don't have to take the first thing that life throws at you.'

But Pixie was already snoring.

Mimi covered her with the softest blanket she could find, and for the first time in months, picked up her sketchbook and drew her friend, sleeping peacefully, her feet sticking out of the bottom of the blanket, still in their black stockings.

Then she drew her dancing a frenzied cancan, then playing her sweet melodies on the guitar in the Lapin Agile, and at the laundry fresh-faced and glistening from the steam. She could weep for her friend's hopelessness.

Mimi was still there, sketchpad in hand, when Pixie woke up, squinting in the afternoon light.

'Afternoon.' Mimi smiled.

'Good to see you drawing again,' said Pixie, propping up on an expensive silk cushion.

'And good to see you sober.'

'Not for long, please God.'

'That's not even funny any more. You've got to stop destroying yourself.'

'Don't be such a stick-in-the-mud, little miss high and mighty with all your fine clobber. Come on, are you going to show me around or not?'

Pixie must have the constitution of an ox, thought Mimi, as they skipped around the apartment together. They smashed a plate off the dresser, just because they could, ate bread and Camembert and the last of the summer strawberries out of the pantry, then Mimi flung open the wardrobe doors and told Pixie to take anything she wanted.

They dressed up in every new dress she owned, and giggled like the spoilt princesses they'd dreamed of being as children and hugged and chatted about nothing. Pixie wouldn't be coaxed to tell her what was eating her up, and Mimi couldn't bear to make her serious and bitter again. At least she'd slept and eaten, and her new maid had even drawn a bath for her and put it by the fire. She and Pixie blew bubbles into the flames and that's how it was for them, these pearlescent bubbles, delicate and beautiful, catching the daylight till they were destroyed too soon. Somehow she'd fly higher and escape, and take her broken friends with her if she could.

Pixie left in Mimi's best crimson ball gown, her flame-coloured hair glowing bravely in the evening sun, and took a part of Mimi's heart with her. She hadn't been able to save her mother, and now Pixie had the same pall around her. Please, God, let her save herself.

CHAPTER 17

Pixie was wrong. Edo loved her, as much as he could in this messed-up world, and Mimi was pretty sure that given time he would accept her daughter. How could he not love Colette as much as she did? It was autumn now, and as the leaves on the plane trees outside her balcony window turned russet and flew about in the swirling winds, Edo had confided more and more in her. He'd made his wife pregnant out of wedlock, and he'd married her to give his son a home. He didn't love her, but he'd done the right thing, and he adored his son more than anything in the world. Surely it was just a little leap for him to understand her own predicament? She'd have to find the moment, it just never seemed to be quite the right one, and if he rejected Colette, she wasn't sure what she would do. While she was biding her time, everything was still possible.

He lavished her with everything she wanted, and he might be a toff, but he had the soul of an artist and he saw things differently.

Mimi picked up the mask they'd chosen together, from Worth, the most fashionable couturier in Paris. He loved choosing dresses with her, and tonight's was pale green, to match her eyes. The mask was in the shape of a cat, sewn with glass and sequin embellishments to complement her dress.

When the carriage arrived, she ran to the window and there it was, lamps lit, driver smart as a soldier, with Edo blowing kisses to her from inside.

Her maid pinned a silk peony in her hair and Mimi swept down the marble staircase. Edo loved dressing up for occasions, and the masked ball at the opera house was the occasion of the season. He was relaxed, burnished, and immaculate with a top hat, cane and fine wool cloak. They were quite the golden couple. Surely he would make a wonderful godfather for Colette?

'How delightful to be picked up by the most handsome man in Paris.'

'And you look beautiful in your new gown, though I loved you just as much in that cotton dress you wore to my studio and threw off so defiantly that first night.'

He kissed her and held her hand, and neither of them could stop smiling as they whisked through the Paris night. When they arrived at the opera house, the place was packed to the rafters.

'The Duke and Duchess of Les Pivoines,' the doorman announced from Edo's card.

The Duke and Duchess of the Peonies. Mimi laughed, delighted at his cleverness. In art, peonies represented beauty, rarity and impossibility, and at this ball, they were achieving the impossible with her walking into respectable society on his arm. Thanks to their masks, no one would know who they were. In this *demi-monde*, they could be together, and Mimi wished she could stay at this point, walking into this place, with men bowing and women straining to see who they were, the most beautiful, stylish, talented couple in the room.

A sea of top hats mixed with feathers and flowers and tiaras, ball gowns and evening dress were interspersed with serving

girls in stripy stockings and white aprons, or dressed as harlequins, or circus girls. Stretching high up into the gods, every
balcony was packed, some populated with gents and their showgirls, stockinged legs dangling through the railings, others
peopled with haughty-looking women checking out the compe-
tition with opera glasses, their attentive gentlemen sipping
champagne from crystal coupes.

Chatter filled the space like a heat haze, fans flickered,
jesters and tumblers mingled with the crowds and the orchestra
pumped out fast waltzes and polkas.

Their little clique was instantly recognisable, and Mimi and
Edo gravitated to them, pushing through the throng. Monet's
dark hair was longer than any of the other men's and he'd
shunned the typical top hat and tails for a velvet jacket and
floppy cravat, his mask more like a bandit's than a Venetian's.
And Renoir, dishevelled in his bohemian way with a crumpled
but endearing spotty cravat, was staring from behind a clown's
mask at a beautiful waitress with tumbling red locks. Degas
stood slightly aloof from the proceedings in a tight waistcoat
and elegant tails, and Cézanne glowered from behind his plain
mask, looking awkward and uncomfortable in his newly bought
evening dress.

Monet put his fingers to his lips as they approached. 'No
one breathe a word, but I know these people. Let the ball begin!
Your light shines even brighter with your mysterious mask, Le
Chat,' he said, kissing her on both cheeks and warmly shaking
Edo's hand.

'And you, Monsieur, could pass as a lord if you didn't spend
your whole time trying to flatter ladies in such a gaudy way.'

'Your cruelty is so alluring that I forgive you.'

'You actually don't know how to stop, do you?' laughed
Mimi.

'Waiter! Bring the lady champagne; perhaps that will
mellow her a little!' He played to the crowd, then kissed her

hand. 'Seriously, I adore seeing you and Edo together; you make each other glow. I'm very happy for you.'

'Thank you, my dear friend. And really, you don't need to get me champagne; I worry that you can't afford it. It costs more than a month of a shop girl's wages in this place and no one's selling any pictures at the moment, least of all you,' she whispered to him.

'Oh, since when did you get so boringly sensible? Let a boy from the gutter enjoy an evening at the opera, won't you?'

She smiled, and took the overflowing champagne coupe. 'Then thank you, my dear friend.' They clinked glasses.

A woman sheathed in violet silk which showed off her slim figure in a fishtail style approached her. She held a black beaded mask over her eyes with a pale, delicate hand which trembled with the effort, but Mimi would recognise those intelligent, watchful eyes anywhere. Berthe Morisot.

'Darling, you've captivated every man in the room, and rightly so. You are radiant tonight,' she whispered.

Why did her rival have to be so *nice*?

'Now, you're not to run away from me like a skittish cat; I want to propose something to you.'

'You know a cat's curiosity is its downfall, but irresistible nevertheless,' laughed Mimi to cover her discomfort.

'I hear you've stopped painting and there are barely enough of us females to go around at the Salons to start with. Darling, forgive me for prying, Edo is a great friend, but I know he doesn't like you to paint at your new apartment. So, I'd like to put my studio at your disposal. It's none of his business if you want to pick up a paintbrush and do whatever you like if it's with me, and I would love the artistic company, so you'd be doing me a favour.'

Mimi could have wept.

'Really? Edo has been so generous, but I've missed it so much. It's not that he doesn't want me to, it's just that he comes to me for a rest and...' It sounded so wrong when she tried to explain it to a toff.

Berthe put her finger on her lips. 'Shh, not one more word. We are friends, and you don't need to explain a thing to me. I'm doing this for entirely selfish reasons; it's actually quite lonely being me, the only girl at the feast, as it were.'

Berthe made it easy for her to grab the invitation with both hands before she was whisked off by a tall man in a top hat, one of Berthe's many admirers.

Renoir asked Mimi to dance, and he whirled her around the floor reverently, as if she were a china doll. A wild polka with Monet made the peony fall out of her hair and get trampled, but Edo was her favourite dance partner. They just fitted, and she liked how they must look, him sophisticated and suave, her petite and light-footed spinning together under the lights in a world they had invented. She missed Rafi being there, he was hardly ever at any of the places she went to any more, but if he'd seen her and Edo together tonight, he would have understood that she was in love with him and he her, as far as it was possible in the circumstances.

'Let's get out of here,' said Edo. 'I want to show you something.'

'I'll just say goodbye while you call the carriage,' said Mimi.

'No, let's just slip out and walk. Who needs jesters and tumblers and showgirls when we've got the whole of Paris to entertain us?'

She grabbed her cloak and pulled it around her against the open air, and they left the mêlée. The cold snatched the festive feel from the evening and had them huddled together and her Paris felt unfriendly and bleak all of a sudden. It was at these times, without the distraction of parties and the glamour of the *demi-monde*, that the pull for Colette was strongest. It seemed so hopeless out here in the cold streets. What was she thinking?

'I dragged you out too early. You looked so happy and care-free in there. Do you want to go back?'

'No, but the reality is, it's only in those places we can really be together in public, and only then in a mask. Everything else is a sham and I don't like accepting money and an apartment from you; it makes us too unequal.'

She needed him as a father to Colette, as well as an escort for her, his muse.

Edo's step faltered. 'I can't change society and fix all its hypocrisy. I can paint how I feel, and I paint as I see, in the moment, and that's how I am with you. There is no past, or present, or future, but just now, and who in all reality can ask for more than that? I've tried to show you in a million different ways how I feel about you through my painting because it's hard for me to find the words. I've always been taught to hide my feelings, to look the other way from poverty and hardship, to look down on it. Let me show you something to try to explain.'

They hurried in silence down the boulevard Haussmann, then turned at the place de la Republique until they were facing a grand building. *Musée des Arts et Métiers*, Mimi read in stone letters.

Edo reached into his waistcoat and took out a key, which fitted a side gate and creaked it open. Inside the courtyard, the nightwatchman recognised Edo and doffed his hat.

'Evening, sir,' he said, giving Mimi a sly glance. 'Looking for the place to yourself?'

'If you'd do the honours, I'd be grateful,' said Edo. 'My cousin has a keen interest in science and her family wouldn't approve of such unwomanly vices.'

'Begging your pardon, Mademoiselle,' said the man, embarrassed. 'Didn't realise you were acquainted.'

So just with one social marker, she was acceptable. What idiots people were.

He let them in through the main door and gave them a lantern.

'Come on,' said Edo.

He clearly knew his way around this place – a museum for science and inventions – and he whisked her past looming machines and glass cases full of incomprehensible and fascinating-looking contraptions until they came to a cavernous marble hall.

'There,' said Edo.

Suspended on piano wire attached to the domed ceiling was a brass sphere which moved of its own accord. Beneath it was a circle of glass, and Mimi counted twelve metal pins in an even circle, which the sphere narrowly missed.

With Edo at her side in this beautiful silent hall, the sphere swung silently back and forth, and it was mesmerising. Mimi hardly dared breathe for fear of disturbing the movement until the sphere knocked over a pin and made her jump. Edo clasped her hand.

'What's moving it?' Mimi whispered.

'It's Foucault's pendulum and it's turning imperceptibly, which is why it knocked over the pin, but it's not the pendulum that's turning, it's the earth itself. Galileo knew it from stargazing and he was forced to deny it in front of the Inquisition. But some truths can't be stamped out, however much society would like to. The pendulum is an irrefutable law of the universe, proof that the Earth itself is turning. Hanging it from your little flat in Montmartre, or the Tuileries Palace ballroom, would make no difference; life force is what makes it move. If we were together officially nobody would accept us, and we'd begin to hate each other for it. But that doesn't stop an irrefutable truth, that I love you and think you are the most captivating creature I have ever met. It's you and everything you represent that inspires me, and my best work is because of you.

It's you who is paying me by agreeing to the apartment, and allowing me to visit whenever I please.'

They strolled back to the apartment, slowly, watching the stars cross the sky, witnessing the world turning. But every day, and every night, every celestial cycle of moon and star rise, sunset and dawn, was another missed moment with her daughter. Still, Mimi couldn't bring herself to tell Edo. She wasn't quite ready to break the spell, and despite all his talk of pendulums and love, she wasn't sure if Edo would accept the reality of an illegitimate child. A mistress and a muse was acceptable in his world, but nothing more. Another irrefutable truth.

CHAPTER 18

Berthe's house was even grander than Edo's mother's house on the Rue de Saint-Pétersbourg. It must have been five stories high, and as many rooms wide, more of a mansion than a normal house or apartment.

Mimi had worn her plainest dress and a practical wool coat for the occasion, knowing that she'd be painting and using thinners and turps, but she wished she'd sacrificed one of her grander dresses to the occasion. She gave the knocker a sharp rap.

The maid opened the door, looked her up and down, but didn't invite her in.

'Your model's here, ma'am,' called the maid.

'I'm actually an artist, here to visit Mademoiselle Morisot, and it's very rude of you not to invite me in,' corrected Mimi, pushing inside.

The maid pursed her lips and bobbed a reluctant curtsey. 'Begging your pardon, miss.'

'It *is* possible for the likes of us to change places, you know, you just have to dream,' said Mimi.

The girl blushed. 'I've been here since I was a kid; I'm not sure I'd know how to any more,' said the maid, retreating at such unthinkable thoughts.

She's right, it's more frightening to dream than to stay where you are, but that's what makes it so exciting, thought Mimi.

'Mimi, let me look at you! You're like a butterfly in its chrysalis in that old coat. Such a tiny waist and a dazzling peacock-green gaze.' Berthe beamed as she swept down the stairs.

'And you look like a black swan, all melancholic drama, waiting to spread your wings, even though they're clipped.'

'That's a little *too* insightful for my liking. Come on, I'll take you through to the studio,' said Berthe.

An older woman who must be Berthe's mother was standing at the top of the stairs, looking concerned.

'Don't mind her, she disapproves of *everything* I do. It's just worry, really; all she wants me to do is eat and get married.'

Berthe did look dangerously thin for someone so rich. There wasn't an ounce of plumpness in her cheeks, which emphasised her big brown eyes, and her prominent cheekbones gave her intelligent face a tormented air.

Berthe whisked Mimi through the house and into the most beautiful garden. Mimi couldn't name most of the flowers, none of them were the wild ones her mother had taught her, but they were planted so harmoniously, and the autumn wasps were so drowsy and content, that it made her feel nostalgic for something she'd never had. She'd build a garden for Colette like this one day.

At the bottom of the garden was a building, like an orangery. It was stone-built with windows the entire width of it. Inside was a wonderland. Easels, paints, tables set up with still-life tableaux, vases of flowers, pots of paintbrushes in every size and shape, cupboards and drawers overflowing with as many paints as Mimi could dream of in a lifetime. Light diffused through the windows just right, not too bright, and birds chirruped in the garden.

'I thought your parents didn't approve,' said Mimi.

'They did when I was younger. They thought it was charming and had this built for me. Now I'm serious about it and consorting with revolutionaries like Edo and Monet and Renoir, they're kicking themselves for indulging me. Ridiculous that they have a say over anything any longer; I'm a grown woman now.'

Mimi looked around at this artist's paradise. How easy it was to dismiss such inconceivable luxuries for the likes of Berthe.

'I'd give anything to have parents, never mind this,' said Mimi.

'Now I must sound like a spoilt brat. The least I can do is give you all the space you need here. Please, use it even when I'm not around.'

'Really? I'd love to, but what about your mother and the disapproving maid?'

'I'll talk them round, and I'll give you a key to the side gate so you don't need to run the gauntlet every time you want to pick up a paintbrush. Here.' Berthe led Mimi to an easel set up with a fresh canvas and paintbox. 'Please, take whatever you need. I'd love to watch you work; Edo tells me you're quite a draftswoman.'

Mimi chased away a stab of jealousy. So they met outside of Mimi's world, and even talked about her. She called him Edo, too. The picture of the dishevelled *Repose* picture of her in Edo's studio flashed through her mind. He'd caught Berthe exactly. There was something so intense and alluring about her intelligence and drama, but a longing, too, as Berthe's features crinkled in fragile concentration.

But the garden studio and Berthe's attentiveness soon made her forget. How wonderful it was to be mixing paints again, preparing colours in 'nuts' on the palette, blending skin tones and chromas ready for application from expensively pigmented globs of glistening promise. Then the myriad brushes, from the mongoose round, to ivory flat, to the broad bristles that all produced different textures. She discovered varying sizes of palette knives, thinners and primers, which all added sophistication and nuance to a painting. Instead of the feverish obsession in her Montmartre garret, playing with all the finishes and effects in this oasis was like being a child again.

Berthe painted too, finishing a portrait of a red-haired girl sitting on a veranda, drawing on a sunlit day with a flower-filled, wild garden in the background. The girl's hair was tied in a cornflower-blue ribbon which looked achingly soft and beautiful against her burnished red hair. Her head was turned away from the viewer in concentration, and the girl looked so peaceful and carefree and absorbed in her idle task, it made Mimi feel sick with longing.

'You like it?' asked Berthe when she saw Mimi staring.

'It's beautiful. I'm not sure I could ever have your lightness of touch; the oils are so thick, they don't always do what I mean them to.'

'Oh rubbish, you've got your own style. Don't even look at anyone else, just trust your heart. I've got a game for you that I play on myself when I'm having a day of doubts. Pick a theme and draw three variations on it. I'll set my pocket watch, and you can only take fifteen minutes for each painting. Don't worry about wasting paint or paper, just don't even think,' said Berthe, eyes sparkling with the challenge.

Mimi sketched on each of the three pieces of paper in charcoal, fixed the lines with India ink, then helped herself to the brushes and paints and thinners and abandoned herself to the colours and finishes.

She was barely conscious of what she was doing, and it seemed like no time had passed when Berthe called time. Mimi stood back and regarded three still lifes of roses in a jar. The first was a black rose in full bloom, and an accompanying bud, edged with delicate pink. In the second, the delicate pink rose had grown and blown, its fine petals dried and browned, and alongside it was another bud, a vigorous peach colour, almost bursting to open. In the third and final picture, the vigorous rose was just open, a perfect fresh and new bloom reaching for the sun, and a bud, just the same colour, was hiding beneath the parent's petals.

Berthe looked at her curiously. 'These are from the heart, I just know it. What do they mean?'

'It's three generations. The black rose is my grandmother – I always think of her as exotic and rare. I never knew her, so I can imagine whatever I like. The pink rose is Maman, the vigorous one me...'

'And the final bud, clinging to its beautiful *maman*?'

'The next generation, as yet unformed.'

Berthe gave her a penetrating stare, but Mimi gave it right back. She wasn't about to reveal all her secrets to Berthe like some exotic *grisette* she could pin to her canvas. She had Rafi and Pixie and Citron for confidences, and she refused to be just another curiosity from the wrong side of Paris.

'Your drawing is excellent,' said Berthe politely, clearly not wanting to pry. 'Where did you learn to be so precise?'

'By driving Maman crazy with coal, pencil stubs, anything I could find, and drawing on her walls.'

'So it seems we both scared our poor *mamans* with our passion for the craft, but I have had so many more advantages than you. I had copying lessons at the Louvre, tutors as soon as I was old enough. Your talent is raw, and all the better for it,' said Berthe.

'But I want to be good enough to exhibit at the Salon. I know they don't allow women, at least not ones like me, but there's got to be a first time for everyone.'

'Then you and I share an ambition,' said Berthe warmly. 'There is nothing I want more.'

Berthe's pictures were of mothers and children. Idyllic, light-filled, ephemeral scenes, moments of simple joy caught in gardens and breezy beaches. Not sentimental, but fleeting and light. They were as good as anything Mimi had seen at the Paris Salons.

She left Berthe's full of ideas and when the wind blew up and it looked like rain, she quickened her pace on the Avenue de l'Opéra. In a whirlwind of russet leaves, a leaflet landed at her feet and she picked it up: *Cirque d'Hiver.* So it was back in town, spreading out its magic at the bottom of the Butte like a magician's cloak. Almost a whole year since she'd caught her zebra and he'd set in motion a transformation to her fortunes. Only last year, she'd been just another *grisette* at the laundry looking for something, but she didn't know what. And now here she was, lifting her silk skirts away from the pavement grime, hurrying home to an opulent apartment in Batignolles, a toff in love with her, and she with him, in a way. Not the wholesome, slightly dull love of a marriage between equals, but something different. Edo was handsome and talented and saw Paris, her world, for all its dark glamour and tragedy. And he let her share his world, to an extent – in the places where their lives came together in a carnival of ideas, colour and exuberance where the rules didn't count. In the Lapin Agile, or the Opéra, the dance halls and under the lantern-lit trees of Montmartre, toff-republicans became rabid socialists, scuts from the streets became poets, and cancan girls held aristocrats in the palms of their hands to do with as they wished. But the reality was that when the party was over, everyone went obediently back to their stations and the toffs were none the worse for their forays into the underground. Maybe a pilfered wallet, or a dose of the clap, but they would never allow the two worlds to merge. They had too much to lose, and her kind had already lost.

Mimi folded the circus leaflet and put it in her pocket. If anyone could find a way, it was her. If there was a chink she could slip through, shoulders back, head high, and claim her Colette, she'd bloody well find it. Rules were made to be broken, even ones that were thousands of years in the making. She had to tell Edo about Colette. There would never be a good time, and she just couldn't live with the lies any longer.

Her maid answered the door before she could dig in her pocket for the key.

'Monsieur is here,' she said, blushing.

Mimi kissed her on both cheeks, catching her breath. 'Here, take the afternoon off, go and see your *maman*.' She smiled, giving the maid a coin.

She grabbed her shawl and left.

Edo was waiting for her with an easel covered with a cloth.

'What are you hiding under there?' said Mimi, kissing him on both cheeks and pulling off her gloves.

'A surprise,' said Edo, 'but first, tell me all about your afternoon with Mademoiselle Morisot.'

'It was paradise, Edo. We just played with all the effects you can achieve with different brushes and thinners, and she was so generous with her time and knowledge.'

'And did she look well? I worry that she's too thin, or that she's unhappy.'

'I think she's probably both. There's an underlying sadness about her, even though she's got everything in the world she could ever want. You'd never know it from her pictures, though, which are so carefree and light. I'm going to go every week and—'

'Did she mention me? I'd love to be a fly on the wall in that sunlit studio with you two sharing secrets.'

'We talked about gesso and pigments and the best canvases, our inspirations...'

'And what did Berthe say inspires her?'

What about knowing what inspired Mimi? She chased away the thought as unworthy of her. Even though he practically owned her now, she didn't own him.

'Her sister and children, domestic settings. At least that's what I deduced from her half-finished work.'

'Do you think that's because she's not yet married? There must be a certain longing to have those things for herself, do you think?'

'Or perhaps she's just painting what's deemed acceptable,' replied Mimi, disappointed that Edo wasn't interested in hearing about her own experiences on her glorious afternoon. 'Are you going to show me what's on that easel?' she said, to change the subject.

'It's for you. To show you that you can be anything you want to be.'

Edo uncovered the painting. It was *Le Balcon*, finished. Mimi was seated in her white dress, holding her fan, looking away, wearing her red choker, with a peony in full bloom, planted in an elaborate pot next to her. This wasn't a defiant *grisette* looking out at the viewer, it was a grand lady, melancholically dreaming about something far away.

Mimi remembered she'd sat for the picture the first time she'd seen Colette at the Tuileries. Edo had caught her mood exactly.

Berthe was standing next to her, about to pull off her kidskin gloves, holding an umbrella as if she'd just arrived, facing the viewer, but looking beyond them. Edo had got her, too, the sensuous, almost cruel curve of her red lips, the curls stopping just short of dramatic eyebrows, the sad brown eyes and doll-like face. Was it possible to be in love with two people at once?

There was no interaction between the two figures whatsoever. It was like two separate portraits painted side by side. Caught behind a bright green wrought-iron balcony, the figures were also cut off from the viewer, both unattainable and living in their own worlds.

'I've never seen anything like it. It's like the Goya picture you showed me, but there's something so modern about it. The greens and the separation of the figures, the flat colours. I was sad that day, and that's there, too.'

'You look the same today. I know I asked you to look sad that day, but you already looked stricken. You're either a brilliant actress, or there's something terribly wrong. I'm worried about you.'

Did she really wear her heart on her sleeve so obviously?

'It's something to do with your irrefutable truth,' she confessed.

'That I love you?'

'That you love me, but not the whole of me.'

'We're together as much as anyone can be and who cares about the rest?'

Mimi steeled herself. He loved her, he'd given her a beautiful home, and painted a picture of her filled with respect and insight. It was his way of telling her she could be anything, including a grand lady. Surely a man with such intuition and generosity in his art was big enough to understand, despite his upbringing? Everything he'd done in his life had kicked against the society he came from. She turned to face him.

'Because the rest is a daughter I can't live without.'

Edo stood up, covered up the picture again. It was a strange gesture, and the silence was horrible.

'Who's the father?' Edo said coldly.

'You don't know him. He's a toff, like you, and I gave her away because I thought she'd be better off, but she's not. I see her in the Tuileries and she's so like me. She climbs trees and is wild as an imp, but her new family hate her for it.'

Mimi told him the whole story about Jean-Baptiste, the overwhelming love she had for her daughter, about her plan for

Colette to come and live with her in the apartment, how they could be a family of sorts. She wouldn't expect him to be a father, more an uncle or a godfather, and that she'd be the happiest person alive and how Colette was suffering where she was and how her daughter desperately needed her *maman*. He listened silently. He let her talk and talk; it all flooded out, including Marie-Thérèse's cold-hearted plan to as good as sell her daughter back to her. It was such a relief to tell him everything.

'If I were you, I'd forget her and leave her exactly where she is,' he said.

Mimi reeled, her head spinning with betrayal. How could he be so cruel? How dare he live by such double standards like the bloody rest of them?

'Then you're a hypocrite. You have a son, born to you in very similar circumstances.'

'But I had the decency to marry her,' said Edo. 'I can't have two families and you should see sense.'

'Sense! There *is* no sense. She's my daughter and I need her with me. The only reason she's not is because of some stupid unwritten rules I don't understand. You like having me here, waiting whenever you need me, and you've defied society with your art, but when it comes to it, when it really matters, you're a bloody hypocrite and a coward like the rest of them.'

'And you're a cliché like the rest of them. I thought you were different. I thought you were smart, but you got yourself pregnant with some fly-by-night dilettante with more money than sense. How could you have been so careless and got yourself into this mess?'

Mimi wanted to scream and shout, but maybe he just needed time to absorb things, to really understand, so she explained.

'I thought I loved Jean-Baptiste, and he loved me. The only

mistake I've made is to believe another toff and his "love", which will only go so far as mummy and daddy's money allows.'

'Jean-Baptiste. What's his surname?' said Edo, turning white.

'Beauregard.'

'I know the Beauregards very well. My mother was at his funeral. You're right, Marie-Thérèse is a piece of work.' Edo stood, hands behind his back, face set. 'I can't get involved, Mimi. It would be social suicide.'

'Then you're not the person I thought you were. I never want to see you again.' Acid tears streaked her face, her heart congealed and somehow her legs took her to the bedroom, where she fumbled in the dresser for the key to her hovel in Montmartre.

He didn't follow her, though every fibre of her body cried out for him. She found the key, which smeared her hand in brown rust, thrust it in her pocket and took out a bag to pack her dresses. She only took the ones that she'd bought with her own money; he could bloody well keep the rest, including the white muslin one he'd given her for *Le Balcon*. Wedding dress indeed. He'd no sooner marry the likes of her than cut off his own hand, however much he loved her. That was the worst of it. She realised at that moment that she loved him, and he loved her, but that wasn't enough on the rue des Batignolles. It wasn't enough that your daughter was a miraculous facsimile of you, and you had talent and ambition and dreams big enough to fill the whole of the Paris sky. What mattered in Edo's world was who your parents were, that you understood the rules. When is a diamond or a pearl appropriate? Silk or lawn cotton? Which bloody fork to use first, and where you were born. It was endless and incomprehensible. By those standards, she was dirt.

Out in the hallway, she saw Edo standing looking out of the window in the beautiful living room, his back turned.

'You're a coward and a snob,' she said to his back. 'You

pretend to understand with your street scenes and bar girls and portraying things how they really are, but only with a paint-brush in your uncalloused hand. When it comes to messy real life, you retreat back into your gilded cage. You can stay in your elegant trap for all I care. I'll live a thousand lives for your one pale imitation.'

He didn't even turn around, but she knew him. He was dying inside, but he couldn't do it, not even for her. His reputa-tion was worth more than his own happiness.

She slammed the door on him, her imagined life of art and ease, of bringing Colette to live with her in an elegant apart-ment, on the protection and love of a toff with an eye for beauty in the dirt. As she paced through Pigalle, she hitched her skirts so she could run faster than her beating heart and hissed away the drunks leering at her bare ankles. She felt like she was in a game of snakes and ladders, and she'd just slid down the longest, most poisonous snake on the board.

CHAPTER 19

'What you doing on your own two feet?' shouted a kid as Mimi passed the ragpicker children on the rue du Tailleur.

'Where's your fancy carriage? Did he dump you?' shouted his mate.

She managed an affectionate cuff round his lug and a 'More like the other way round.' She'd heard so many girls say it round here that she *did* feel like a cliché. A sad, worn-out shell, stripped of foolish dreams she should never have had in the first place.

She trudged up the creaking stairs to her old room and as she dug into her pocket for the rusty key, she realised the door was open. Inside, Pixie was passed out on her bed fully clothed, snoring loudly. She'd forgotten she'd told Pixie to use her room any time as an escape, and the place was filthy and littered with bottles. The leaking tap was dripping brown water, Pixie's guitar was neglected in the corner, and dusty cobwebs added to the air of utter squalor.

Mimi poked her. 'Pixie, wake up!'

Pixie shot up with a start, alert for danger, reeking of booze.

'Fuck me, you gave me a fright. Look what the cat dragged in.'

She picked up a bottle off the floor and drained the dregs. Mimi took it off her.

'You've had too much already.'

'Not enough, more like. Chucked you out, has he?'

There was a gloat about her Mimi didn't like.

'I left.'

'He seemed pretty sweet on that drama queen, Berthe Morisot, at the last exhibition. Couldn't take his eyes off her, like a fucking puppy dog.'

'Stop, for God's sake, Pixie. What are you trying to do?'

She subsided. 'Sorry, you look like death. I'm just angry for you, that's all. You should know they're all the same.'

Mimi collapsed on the bed next to her.

'You're right. I told him about Colette. It's the last thing in the world he wants, and it's all *I* want.'

'So you came back here to give her a better life?'

'I came back here because I can't live a lie.'

'Well, I hope your principles serve you well. You can't eat truth.'

Mimi pointed to the bottles on the floor. 'Have you got any more of that stuff hidden away anywhere? I could do with forgetting just for tonight.'

'If you've got a franc, I can get some,' said Pixie, her addict's eyes glowing and desperate. Mimi had seen this look a thousand times from her childhood bed and it made her feel scared and unsafe.

'Here.' She gave Pixie one of the last francs from her purse. 'Careful on the stairs!'

But Pixie was steady as a barmaid. It was the same with Maman; she could always keep it together as much as she needed to get a fix. Funny how it was always the strongest, cleverest, most charismatic ones. Maybe they were the only souls who could hack the pain and debilitation of being permanently pissed.

Waiting for Pixie to return, Mimi realised something was missing. The old lady downstairs was quiet as a mouse, and her birds had stopped singing. However much she'd wished her to shut up in the past, the silence was eerie.

It must have been half an hour before Pixie returned proudly wielding a bottle of absinthe.

'All I could do to prise the change out of his sticky little hands,' said Pixie, chucking the grubby centimes onto the table. That would have to last Mimi all week, until she got herself a job. She'd think about that tomorrow.

Pixie wiped out a couple of dirty glasses and poured the green stuff in. They didn't have matches or sugar, like when she'd had it with Juliet at the circus, so when Mimi knocked it back, it was as bitter as her heart, but she felt the raw edges begin to numb. Good.

Four or five later, and she and Pixie were cuddled up dizzy and dazed. Not happy exactly, but her troubles were a dull throb waiting for her to wake and feel the full force another time. Now Mimi understood Pixie. If the only way you could eat was to open your legs to every low life that needed somewhere wet to put it, absinthe was the sweetest medicine.

Careful, said her imagined papa's voice from somewhere in the room. She chose to ignore him; he'd abandoned her too long ago.

When Mimi woke the next morning, Pixie was still passed out. Asleep, her skin was marble, and she was so innocent and childlike curled up on her little bed. Pixie was only nineteen, a year younger than Mimi. *Please, God, she'll get over this nightmare.*

Mimi lay there for a moment as her split with Edo, Jean-Baptiste's death and dying wish, her little Colette and her gaoler Marie-Thérèse came crashing back over her like a wave. She'd

give anything to wind the clock back a few days, to when everything seemed possible. Her head throbbed, and she could have
drunk a lake, but she didn't trust the brown water from the
leaking tap.

Careful not to wake Pixie, she crept over to the stove to boil
some water, but remembered, no matches. God knows how
Pixie had survived here all these weeks.

Creeping down the stairs, she knocked on the old lady's
door, but a man answered instead, and looked her up and down.

'Is Widow Brombert here?' asked Mimi.

'Sorry, love, she's no longer with us. It must be a few months
ago that she went. I'm afraid she was found some time after she
passed away, apparently, and with no one to tend to the birds...'

Another lonely death in this godforsaken hole. Poor old
thing. Mimi whispered a silent prayer for her.

The man lent her the matches, and she went back upstairs
to boil up the water. One foot in front of the other, she told
herself, no need to think any further.

Pixie didn't wake up the entire day, and Mimi didn't have
the heart to do anything but just lie there and stare at the ceiling
and try not to remember.

Pixie got up that evening, brushed herself down and left.
Two weeks later, she hadn't returned, and Mimi's pile of
centimes were now one centime. The little stash of coins, her
dresses, paintbox and canvases were all she had in the world.
She'd left everything else, even an allocation of money that Edo
had given her to live on and begged her to take, at the rue des
Batignolles. At least she wasn't a whore. Not yet anyway,
because she was hungry enough to be one.

The autumn sun streamed through her dirty window and
the church bells struck midday. Edo had made no attempt to
contact her, and she'd barely left the room, apart from the odd
shopping trip to eke out her meagre funds on food. She knew
what to spend it on – a large bag of dried beans, millet, turnips,

onions. Apart from that, she hid from herself and the world. She knew people round here; they'd gloat at her fall, see her as just another piece of fluff blowing around Pigalle on the prevailing winds to land wherever fate took her. She didn't blame them; a life of hardship made you bitter. Being confined to her room by the leaden black cloud pressing her down and wringing her out was worse than when she fell from the trapeze. At least then she'd *wanted* to get up. Breaking limbs was easy compared to this. It was like something was broken inside her head and it made her listless, exhausted and entirely without hope. In the end, it was the same outcome: she couldn't move.

The walls were still covered in her drawings and friezes, her whole short life daubed right there, packed with observations, ideas and memories. Hidden in her wardrobe, the doll in the yellow dress that she'd saved for Colette was still in her box of beautiful, broken things. All of it was useless, just broken dreams, the whole bloody mess just another sad story among a multitude of them.

When the church bells struck midday again the next day, she'd hardly noticed twenty-four hours go by, and hunger gnawed even harder at her stomach. At least it was a feeling. She considered her options, and came to the same conclusion she had every day since Edo, that there weren't many. She couldn't bear to go back to the Folies, or to any of the dance halls to offer herself up as a dancing girl who could do tricks on a swing. She couldn't risk bumping into Edo and the crowd; it was all just too humiliating and painful. To think that she'd let herself love him, and allowed herself to imagine she might be an artist! The laundry was the only thing she could do in order to eat. After that, the final option was whoring.

She hated the laundry, but it was honest, and they always needed girls. And if she worked hard enough, she could lie low, save money and buy herself some time, and the strength to think.

As she walked slowly down the boulevard Montmartre, she shivered at an autumnal bite in the air and remembered her wild zebra careering madly straight at her, and how a different Mimi had caught and tamed him. It was almost a year to the day.

At the laundry, the concierge shuffled out of her glass office with a small cake of soap. 'Ah, Mademoiselle Bisset. I told you you'd be back, and I'm never wrong,' she said triumphantly. 'I hope he left you with soap money at least. I already told you I'm not a charity.'

Mimi held out the centime and the concierge bit the soap in half with her teeth, spat a gob that narrowly missed Mimi's boots and took her last coin.

'Here, and I'm being generous. Second one down on the left's got more work than she can finish today. Ask nicely, and mind you drop your airs and graces. I can see those hands haven't done a day's work since you flounced out of here last year, but you never forget how. Just as well.'

It was a big consolation to the old hag to see another skinny girl pass back through her doors, begging for soap. Why had Mimi thought she'd be any different?

At the second tub on the left, she agreed with the woman that she'd take part of the load in return for three centimes. Two to keep, one for tomorrow's soap. The woman wasn't interested in chatting, and Mimi was glad. Shrouded in steam, with the din of the engine drowning her thoughts, she scrubbed till her hands were raw, then went home and collapsed into bed.

Weeks, a month slipped by. The piles of centimes built into francs. Pixie came and went, a ghost from another world, haunted and scared, and unreachable through her wall of drink. Not a second had passed in all that time when Mimi wasn't frantic about Colette, but, thank God, she still had time and the precious contract that the notary had written up. No matter how hard she worked, how many mind-numbing hours she spent scrubbing to the rhythm of the steam engine at the laundry, droplets clinging to her clothes, she was always there. As Mimi let the gossip of violent marriages, sickly children, new boyfriends, bastard boyfriends, honeymoons, funerals, hopes and shattered dreams wash over her, the laughter and screeches bubbling up like puffs of steam, she couldn't get her Colette out of her head. Was she lonely, afraid, unhappy with that loveless woman? Did she go to sleep every night crying for her papa, not understanding why he'd left her alone with someone who didn't love her? Did she wonder about her dead *maman*, imagine her as beautiful and kind, that somehow she would come to life and rescue her one day, as she herself had imagined her own papa emerging from the shadows of a Montmartre street, tanned and smiling, with a pile of presents and a bag full of apologies for abandoning them?

Mimi was good at washing clothes and put her all into it, and today was her best quota yet. Nine dresses, seven of them two colours, with fiddly lace and trim, and three sets of bed sheets, stained with God knew what. All clean, folded and delivered, money pocketed. When she arrived at her tenement, she barely had the strength to climb the stairs and she liked it that way, so she could sleep without thinking too much. Giggles rang out from the widow's old apartment. A grubby boy with the cheekiest face stuck his tongue out at her and streaked past, nearly sending her flying. A young woman appeared at the doorway, distracted and stressed. 'Christophe! You come back here and help like I asked you. There'll be no hot chocolate unless you do!'

The boy clumped back up the stairs, hands in pockets and his *maman* kissed him on the head as he passed into the doorway. The scene behind Mimi was like a kick in the stomach. Their room wasn't much bigger than hers, but it was scrubbed to within an inch of its life. A fire blazed in the little grate and something bubbled on the stove, probably the boy's *chocolat chaud.* The small bed doubled as a makeshift sofa by means of a threadbare throw, and next to it on the floor was a little pallet piled with blankets, a nest for the boy. The man who'd given her the matches sat on a rickety wooden chair by the fire smoking a pipe. A cosy, warm, domestic tableau. The mother ushered the boy inside, gave Mimi an indulgent raise of the eyebrows by way of apology for her son, and closed the door.

Why had she listened to Jean-Baptiste, to Marie-Thérèse and Edo? She didn't need anything for Colette but to love her. Because of Maman, and Rafi, and everyone she knew, she didn't know there was another way. It was simple, always had been, or how had the human race got to this point at all? All you had to do was to stay sober and healthy, keep them alive, and the rest was as natural as a mouse in a hole with its babies. She had a job at the laundry, a room that she could fix up. She'd protect Colette like a lioness, like she'd protected herself, and everything else would just work itself out.

CHAPTER 20

Mimi cleaned herself up as much as she could in the tin bath, and shook out her silk day-dress. It was a bit crumpled, but it would do, and thankfully she still had the matching gloves to cover up her raw hands and forearms. The gloves hurt her tender skin, but she gritted her teeth, and set out for the Left Bank in the impractical silk slippers that complemented her dress.

'La-di-da,' shouted the gaggle of ragpicker kids who gathered to escort her to the end of the road, swinging their hips and pouting. 'Nicked it from the laundry, did you?'

Mimi spun round and roared, sending them scattering and giggling at the shock, and turned the corner. At least her little girl had a mother, unlike these cheerful, vulnerable mites.

She must have practically floated all the way to the villa on the Left Bank where Marie-Thérèse was holding her daughter hostage. Colette belonged with her, no matter what society thought was best. No one could know better than a mother, and her father knew it too, in the end.

A ragged servant opened the door and assessed their visitor with pursed lips.

Mimi held her gaze, hoping she would pass as a fine lady in her crumpled dress.

'Is Madame Beauregard at home?'

'Who may I say is calling?'

'Mademoiselle Bisset, on an urgent matter.'

The servant invited her in to wait on the bench in the hallway, then shuffled off. There was a slit in the silk fabric on the bench that hadn't been repaired. Dustballs rolled in the corners of the chequered marble floor, the banister was dull and unpolished, and paint was flaking off the walls in places. The whole place looked like it was dying. Across the hall, the door creaked open and a pair of bright eyes peeped out. Mimi's heart lurched – Colette!

'Hello,' she called. 'Are you hiding? Come out, so I can see you. I think we might have met before. You're the little girl who likes climbing trees, aren't you?'

Colette burst through the doorway and ran across the hall. 'I beat you in a race. You were wearing that dress and I thought you were a princess!'

Colette actually remembered her! Did she understand on some level that they were connected? She was wearing a drab little dress, had lost her chub and rosy cheeks, and a bit of her shine. Mimi was tempted there and then to steal her daughter away, take her back to her room and light a fire in the grate, feed her on hot chocolate and love, rock her to sleep in a comfy nest, and make the whole of Paris her playground. But it was impossible. They'd have to hide away and live on nothing, and her daughter didn't know her from Adam.

'You were very fast. Do they still take you to the park?'

'Not since Papa died. I have to keep quiet, do my work, not upset my aunt and not add to her troubles,' said Colette importantly.

'What work do you do?'

Colette took a moment to count on her fingers, lips moving

with the effort. 'Eight fireplaces and twenty hundred pieces of silver.'

Marie-Thérèse swept into the hallway, scuttling like a spider across the marble floor, twisting her mouth at the sight of Mimi and Colette together.

'Colette! You have work to do. I've told you before, no one wants to *see* a maid.'

Colette ducked away before Marie-Thérèse could swipe at her. Good girl, she had her wits about her.

'I hope you weren't thinking of striking that poor child?' Mimi said in her best toff's accent.

'What the hell are you doing here? We said seven months, and I have my information. Edo Manet has seen sense and thrown you out on the streets where you belong only two months after I last saw you. That didn't last long, did it? Unless you have the ten thousand francs we agreed, which I doubt, I don't want to see your face again.' Furious blisters of spittle formed at the corners of her mouth.

'I've come for my daughter.'

Marie-Thérèse narrowed her eyes and straightened up. 'She's not yours to take, my dear. As you see, she is well looked after here. I couldn't possibly release her into God knows what with a *fille-mère*, girl-mother, from the slums, however finely she's dressed for the occasion. Who knows what kind of behaviour secured you *that* gaudy piece of tat?'

That's how they did it. Put you down, cited rules you didn't get, ground you into the dirt with their eyes, then fixed you with a rictus grin to show you how reasonable they were. Two could play her game.

Mimi smiled back. 'But I'm her mother and *you* clearly dislike her. As you know, her father bequeathed her to me on his deathbed. I understand your concerns, and she has of course been a financial burden to you since his death.'

Mimi held out the bag of coins she'd scrimped. Marie-Thérèse opened the bag greedily and counted.

'Twenty francs? This would barely cover a week's expenses.' She pocketed them nevertheless.

'It's all I have, but I can get more. I can sign any documents you want me to as surety and I'll love her enough for you and Jean-Baptiste and the whole of the Beauregard family.'

'Men might fall for your manipulative begging, but I can see right through your game. Her inheritance would buy you a brothel's worth of jewels and enough absinthe to drown Montmartre. It would be criminal to hand her over to a girl like you.'

She was a witch, but Mimi was desperate. Perhaps if she stopped fighting her, and just told her the truth, there'd be a chink in her armour. And the truth was all she had left.

'Please, you've got me wrong. A day hasn't gone by when I haven't thought about her every minute. You can see how much like me she is. I thought she would be better off here, with Jean-Baptiste, and it's a sacrifice that nearly killed me, but knowing she was happy and healthy and cared for made it bearable. But now you have her hostage in this loveless shell of a house, and I'll never raise the money you've asked for. You've got this house, and other money, and everything you need, and I want her back where she belongs.'

Marie-Thérèse's features set. 'Since you're so interested in my affairs, you might as well know that this house will barely pay your erstwhile lover's gambling debts. Life might be simple where you come from, following your animal lusts and needs, but it's not like that for us. I've already told you: Colette will stay with me and I will relinquish her within the terms of our agreement, in five months' time, for double the amount settled on her head, or I will keep her and do as I will with her. At six years old, she will be sold to a respectable household to undertake domestic duties, and her prospects there will be far superior to any she may have with you. Did you think I didn't know about you and Edo Manet? That he has seen sense, thank the Lord, and tired of you, and you are back in your hovel where you belong? I have set out my terms, and unfortunately for you, your charms won't work on me. I would be prepared to accept the sum of ten thousand francs on the terms we agreed. In the meantime, I have asked my servant to fetch the police. I have reason to believe you intend to kidnap my ward, Colette Beauregard, who is legally mine. If I were you, I'd leave now before you get yourself into deeper water. I say this with your welfare in mind, my dear. And, of course, if you want any hope of seeing Colette again.'

'What you're doing is wrong, and you know it. I wish you had died instead of Jean-Baptiste. At least he had a heart!'

She'd be no use to Colette in jail, and she had no choice but to leave. Love and desperation had made her foolish. How did she imagine an emotional appeal would make the slightest bit of difference? But she had to try. How could she have just stood by with so little hope of meeting Marie-Thérèse's terms? But life didn't work like that, not for the likes of her, anyway. Youth and beauty may bring a little fleeting luck, but it didn't last long. Dear God, she wished she'd just snatched her there and then and wrapped her up in silk and fed her hot chocolate and smothered her in kisses, given her the doll in the yellow dress and consoled her with stories of the zebra on the boulevard Montmartre. She'd weave tales of her handsome, Italian grandpapa who could jump across the air light as a squirrel on the circus trapeze, about her beautiful grandmama who loved dancing, and cared for her little Mimi like she was china, who in turn loved her own Colette more than the sun and the moon and the stars.

Mimi kept walking, not even sure where she was going, tears blurring her way as she crossed the Pont Neuf, over the swollen, surging Seine, and through Les Halles, where the market was in full swing. Blood dripped from great slabs of meat on the butchers' blocks, fishwives gutted silver-striped mackerel, their eyes glazed gold in death, barrow boys pushed piles of cabbages fresh from the farm, the bloom on them still dewy as new-borns. Ragged girls a few years older than Pixie sold straggly bunches of flowers or boxes of matches, skin weathered before their time, their looks squandered in return for food and shelter, staring hunger in the face with a desperate smile at the passing gentlemen. Mothers ushered their offspring out of the way of the barrows, hurried them past the ex-whores with their cheap flowers, and pointed to the seafood stalls, garnering wide-eyed delight from their children, delightfully entranced by the shells and slithers and sparkling ice.

Mimi pressed on past Opéra where she'd danced with Edo and the gang, where they'd been the golden couple, and ripped off the gloves from her tender washer-woman's hands. *Don't think, just keep walking,* until she arrived back in Montmartre.

At the bottom of the Butte, a big top rose up, strung with bunting which whipped in the bracing breeze. Behind the temporary fencing, elephants trumpeted, lions roared and the barrel organ pumped out its fairground tune. The circus was back with its surreal world of make-believe.

The turnstile boy called out. 'Mintaka! Over here!'

It was the stable boy, her zebra's keeper, and he clicked her through the turnstile.

Nothing had changed, and it was a relief to be distracted for a moment. The grass was patchy from overuse, the burnt smell of candyfloss combined with hay and manure hung on the air, and exotic washing – the cast's costumes combined with bloomers and everyday smalls – was strung between the caravans. The caravans themselves were exactly as she'd left them, and the pastiche classical scenes proclaiming the strength,

beauty or idiosyncrasies of their occupants looked old-fashioned, garish and tired.

'How's my zebra doing, can I see him?'

'In fine fettle; come on, it's the least I can do after...' He
stopped short. 'Are you OK?'

'Just a bit of a limp, that's all. Everyone says I have nine
lives.'

'One's enough for me if that's what you have to go through
to get another. Glad to see you made it through, though. We
weren't sure for a while.'

He let her into the stables and told her he'd wait. She
walked down the stalls to look for him, and there he was, in all
his monochrome glory. Tif, his head hanging curiously over the
gate, sniffing the air at her approach.

He flattened his ears and lowered his head to nudge her. He
hadn't forgotten. She put her forehead on his, let his warm fur
comfort her, stroked his soft muzzle, whispered his name, and
wept. Tif's flanks twitched and his tail swished, but he kept his
head right where it was to catch her tears.

She told Tif everything, and he listened, nuzzled her,
nudged her for hay, and stamped as she talked. He tolerated her
hugs, her need for closeness and a quiet ear, with regal
resignation.

She noticed how many colours made up his iris: dark brown
with honey and sand highlights, a reddish tinge in places, white
and silver patches where the light caught. For the first time in
months, she found herself imagining the colours she'd mix to
make an exact match, the brush to create the glassy effect, the
fine tip she'd need for the streaks of colour, how she'd blend
them, and line his eye in black kohl.

It was almost like he was whispering it to her in his zebra
wisdom. *You and me are misfits, displaced, different. If a zebra
can live in Montmartre, why can't a girl from the slums be a
painter?* She couldn't go back to the laundry, and those caravans

with their tired old cartoons could be her canvas. The circus was a world apart, which didn't ask where you came from, or where you were going. She'd pour all her love for Colette into her art. It was the only thing she could think of to ease the pain and longing.

CHAPTER 21

Drawing helped Mimi forget, and remember. The designs for the tumblers' caravan were strong and light at the same time, how she imagined her papa. The menagerie drawing represented their homeland with bright colours and symbols from India and Africa, and the clowns were stylised Pierrots and harlequins to delight her daughter.

She sketched every night until she ran out of candles, then woke as soon as the sun rose and drew before the laundry, until her sketchbook was full. When she was satisfied with what she'd done, she tied the leather binding, hooked it under her arm and set off to the circus.

Monsieur Dejean turned the pages.

'I've never seen anything like these. People expect a certain style.'

'That's because they don't know any different. Cirque d'Hiver is famous for its daring and creativity, but everything you say about yourself in pictures is old-fashioned and tired.'

This man must have seen a hundred waifs and strays plying their meagre wares, looking for a way out. He handed back the sketchbook, a flicker of recognition showing in the twitch of his moustache at the sore, flaking hands that took it from him.

'People fainted in shock and horror at the last exhibition I was at,' said Mimi, 'just from seeing a picture in a style they weren't used to. It was new and daring and fresh and told the truth and people hate that, but they love hating it.'

That made him laugh. He was a showman, always looking for something to shock, scare or delight his audiences with.

'All right. I know Mintaka doesn't give up till she has her way, however hard things are for her, and I won't ask questions about that passion burning in you so hot it hurts. You have your reasons, and everyone here is running away from something; it's what makes us the best circus in France. My performers put all their hopes and dreams into the show every night and the audience feel it and give us back theirs to keep for a while.' He opened his drawer and put a circus armband on the table in front of her, to identify her as a worker, gold dust in Montmartre. 'We owe you. You nearly died working for us, and we look after our own. I can give you money to buy whatever paints you need, but that won't leave much money aside for wages, and we're moving on in the spring. You are welcome to come with us, but I suspect you have something here to keep you in Paris. Either way, we have twenty-one caravans on site, each with its own unique artwork that you can paint over and use as a blank canvas. Work through whatever is eating at you, and I trust you to create something astonishing, and worthy of us.'

Mimi stood outside Boum Boum's caravan. It felt right to start there, with the clown that she'd seen Colette giggle uncontrollably at with her papa. He was also the quick-witted man who'd saved her life. Monsieur Dejean had been generous, and an array of paints in every colour were laid out on the dust sheet, and the circus technicians had rigged her up a movable scaffold on wheels. The November weather was kind; the sun shone bright and crisp, and the leafless trees made filigree sculptures against the pristine sky.

Prising off the lid of the paint, she smiled for what felt like the first time in months. It was the exact saffron-yellow she'd asked for. It would need two coats to cover over the elaborate paintings on Boum Boum's wagon, but the work was cathartic. Each stroke of bright colour shut out the old world, and heralded a new one, full of possibilities. After a few hours, the wagon was a blank of gradated colour, ready for her artwork.

In the afternoon, she painted over the acrobats' wagon in indigo, working until the light failed and cold descended with the setting sun. At dusk, two familiar figures appeared as she climbed down the scaffold. Jules and Juliet in their pre-performance overalls, arms outstretched.

'Come here, my little gamine, I want to feel your mended bones so I know you're not a ghost,' said Jules.

Mimi hugged him and choked back tears, gripped his hands to feel the reassuring strength she'd craved since the day they missed.

'You know there's a job for you back in the sky if you need it. I will never drop you again, my precious little star. Come back; this work is beneath my brave girl, a job for a labourer.'

'You didn't drop me, I fell, and I'm happy doing this. And thank you, but I'm never going back on the trapeze.'

'I can only do a double somersault since you flew away from us; I lost the nerve for the triple. The sight of you so still under the gaslights haunts me every day. But here you are, as beautiful as ever, if a little too thin.'

Juliet stood next to him, arms folded, more jittery than ever, hopping from foot to foot to keep herself warm, skin luminous as the moon in the evening light.

'You're back in the bosom of your family, my darling; I'm glad you came back to us,' she said kindly, but she was spooked.

Mimi knew how it was in the circus. She'd fallen and she was bad luck, and even if she could rationalise it, Juliet's nerves weren't up to overcoming a trapeze artist's superstitions.

'I'm just here for the winter, to paint these wagons. And don't worry, I couldn't bear to come and watch you, even if Jules *is* only doing a double nowadays.'

Juliet's jitters quietened a little and Mimi busied herself with clearing away her paints, securing things for tomorrow's work while they chatted about nothing. Juliet was the only other soul apart from Rafi and her friends who knew about Colette, but she didn't breathe a word or ask about anything. Mimi was grateful for that. All she intended to do was work and sleep till she'd finished painting her wagons. Everything else was just tainted memories.

Mimi worked every day, and winter worked against her. The days grew shorter, and Mimi cursed the sun when it began to sink, its last rays teasing her with vivid light that brought her paintings to life, before snatching it away as it sank over Montparnasse. Rain and wind stopped her for a while, until the resourceful circus technicians rigged her up a tent to cover the wagon she was working on, and extended her days by running gas lights to wherever she was painting. There were days when she hated every single brushstroke she made and she started again from scratch, sometimes several times over, begging more paint from Monsieur Dejean than he'd budgeted for. It had to be perfect.

At night, she studied the performances, sketching furiously to capture the essence of each act. She sketched the trajectory of the horses' hooves on the sand as they galloped fluid as air, their riders turning arabesques with effortless determination. Boum Boum's innate sadness made him funny; Monsieur Dejean could out-toff any gent with his elaborate turn of phrase and command of the audience, twirling his moustache to emphasise a long word. She'd promised not to watch the trapeze, but she did anyway, hidden at the back in the darkest row. Smudged lines captured Juliet's delicate jitters, diffused images the gasp of the crowd as she stepped out onto the wire, a few pencil strokes the net of her tutu. Jules stretched out to catch Juliet from the swing, but Mimi never drew the moment of the catch, rather the split second before, to portray the whole point of the act. Will he snatch her out of the air in time?

Sometimes, in the auditorium, she saw her former friends there, carrying on as they always had. Renoir, Monet and Degas sketching what they saw, stealing the acts and remaking them as their own. She longed to tap them on the shoulder and leaf through their sketchbooks, compare notes, shout with them about the critics, argue about the finer points of bristle or sable, linseed oil or walnut, share tips on the truest pigments. Occasionally, Berthe Morisot joined them and Mimi was consumed with jealousy as she chatted with the others. Was she drawing something to show Edo, asking his advice on her sketch of Harlequin and Columbine, whether she'd portrayed the love between them with her pencil marks while he lost himself in her stormy presence?

She couldn't face them, though, and she didn't want to risk ever bumping into Edo. She was still furious with him, and missed him at the same time. It was like an open wound, all mixed up with her longing for Colette. Was she already sold, against the law written in the contract? There was still a little time, but making the funds was impossible. It was all she could do to keep going day to day, without bringing up painful feelings towards Edo.

Christmas brought families queueing at the turnstiles. There was excited chatter and giggles, wayward boys escaping their parents' clutches and sneaking into the stables to bother the animals, tousle-haired girls begging their *mamans* for a palomino pony like the ones in the ring, and a spangled costume to match their bridles. If Colette were here, she would be escaping with the boys to the stable, or slipping backstage to take in the colours and chaos, just as Mimi would have if her parents ever took her to the circus.

Mimi worked harder than ever. Every little girl holding her *maman's* hand with unquestioning trust was a rebuke, a fat rosy cheek peeping out from a velvet hood a vivid reminder of what could have been. She avoided everyone, even Rafi, spending every hour she could working, or backstage, sketching, pitching in with anything that needed doing. It was her way of chasing away her longing for Colette, forgetting her dreams of life amongst the artists with Edo, or seeing the pity and worry in Rafi's eyes. She didn't need any of it. Only Tif knew that she cried most days, when he silently caught her tears in his warmth, and understood.

By January, eleven of the wagons were complete. Some of the performers hated the transformation and complained bitterly, uncomprehending of the shapes and loose lines. Others saw how just a few blocks of colour and a suggestion of a line caught the moment and fired their imaginations more than any crude facsimile ever could.

She'd taken everything she'd seen from the new Impressionists and made her own style, from the Japanese influence, to the sometimes brutally frank depiction of faces and feelings, drawing them how she perceived them. There were beautiful moments, too: the magic of the ring, the limits of human strength, drama and pathos.

Monsieur Dejean loved it, especially the heated arguments the newly painted wagons engendered, and commissioned posters which the circus hands plastered across Montmartre on damp walls, old windmills, street lamps and shop windows, dodging exasperated *gendarmes*.

One bitter January afternoon, the reluctant sun feeble and

low, Mimi was painting a menagerie wagon with her idea of a bright African scene in reds and yellows, the animals silhouetted, with pops of colour on their circus saddles and bridles, when two figures appeared out of the gloom, torn posters in hand.

'So *this* is where our pet cat has been hiding all this time.'

'Wild cat to you, and mind where you step with those great boots; you'll spill my India yellow,' said Mimi, delighted to see Renoir and Monet standing there amongst her paint pots, despite her resolution never to see them again.

'I see your period of exile hasn't softened your tongue,' laughed Monet.

'I'm feral now, and I bite.'

'These are fascinating,' said Renoir, holding up a poster of Harlequin and Columbine. It was one of her favourites, a washed-out blush background, minimal line, and blocks of colours and shapes depicting their passion for each other.

'It pays better than the laundry,' said Mimi, plunging her paintbrush into turps to stop it drying out.

Monet took the poster and waved it dramatically at her. 'Darling, you've never been good at lying. These aren't just cheap illustrations for food money. These are considered and controlled, despite the appearance of throw-away ease. It's almost as if you'd learnt from the master.'

'I make my own art,' replied Mimi, busying herself with her paint, uncomfortable at Monet's reference to Edo. He was right, though she didn't want to admit it; it was his work that inspired her own style.

'What is wrong with you, always blundering around and sounding off without a thought about the person you're showing off to?' Renoir chastised Monet. 'More importantly, how is our little kitten? You look far too gaunt and, if you don't mind me saying, a little haunted.'

Dear Renoir, always the gentleman, but she'd rather have

Monet to deal with. She was so used to being alone with her thoughts and her paints that too much sympathy might just crack her right down the middle.

'Oh God, you're right, just look at that brave face, what was I thinking? Now, Mimi, we've found you, and there's nothing you can do about it, so the least you can do is take us to the circus bar and talk to us for a bit. I promise to tell you about getting thrown out of a hotel, starkers in the middle of the night, when some crude hotel manager positively insisted I pay the bill earlier than funds allowed.'

'I suppose you'd been living there for at least a month, guzzling his best truffles and Chambertin?' laughed Mimi.

'You know me better than I know myself,' replied Monet, holding out a lace-cuffed arm for her to link, as if he owned Paris.

They helped her pack away her paints and brushes and they made small talk easily enough, but there were more elephants in the room than she'd painted on the side of the wagon, and she prayed they wouldn't pry.

Monet told her about ending up in the street naked after being thrown out of his hotel on his honeymoon in Trouville. Luckily, his new bride thought it was hilarious. Mimi hadn't met his wife, Camille, but she'd need nerves of steel to be married to this dilettante. He was to be a father, and God knew how he'd be able to support a wife and baby, when he could barely support himself. Nevertheless, he loved his wife and had married her when she fell pregnant. More than she could say for the men in her life.

'A born lord,' roared Renoir. 'When his tailor had the temerity to ask him to settle his bill, Monet said he'd take his custom elsewhere, so the poor man changed his tune and said it was an honour to dress a gentleman.'

'He saw sense in the end,' said Monet.

People went gooey over a haughty smile, a lace cuff and floppy haircut, but good for him if he could get away with it.

It was wonderful to be in the warmth of the bar, flanked by her two reprobates, shooting the breeze and telling tall stories to make each other laugh, but as the bar began to empty for the beginning of the show, and they'd downed their third brandy, the two stood up to leave.

'We miss you,' said Renoir. 'There's no one to dance away the night with, or make us laugh at the Folies, or tell Monet to stop showing off. And I know Edo misses his favourite muse. He's hardly worked since you left.'

'I'm sure there are a million girls queuing up to work for the genius rebel aristocrat,' said Mimi breezily. 'As you can see, I'm busy with my own projects.'

'That sounds very grand for standing in a damp field in the middle of winter painting circus wagons,' said Monet.

'But they're fascinating nevertheless,' added Renoir, tutting at Monet's bluntness. 'We had no idea those green eyes were collecting and logging technique and ideas. It's like you've taken everything our artistic collective has wanted to achieve, and remade it into your own, a fresh take on all our principles of line and colour and the ephemeral moment, then wasted it here, on the great unwashed.'

'The great unwashed are my people,' said Mimi hotly.

'Ours too,' said Monet. 'But, unfortunately, an artist's only hope of real success is still the Salon. They've got a stranglehold over collectors' opinions, and consider themselves to have the most delicate artistic sensibilities based around classicism and tradition but choose to ignore the life that's happening right under their nose.'

'Why don't you submit for this year's Salon?' suggested Renoir with a warm smile.

'That'd put the wind up 'em,' said Monet.

'Just to see the shock on their faces when you turn up with a canvas. It'd be a hoot,' added Renoir. 'If anyone's got the nerve, you have.'

'Do you really think I'm good enough?' said Mimi.

They both laughed, rolling their eyes.

'Of course not, a woman never could be, that's just a law of the universe, but for the fun of it, things are so dull without you around,' said Monet.

They meant to be kind, but *this* was why she'd hidden away since she left Edo. They'd never accept her as an artist, only as a curiosity from the slums who could match their repartee and be their muse, even dabble in her own ideas, as long as she stayed on the right side of the canvas.

'Bugger off, the pair of you. I'm not stirring up that hornets' nest for your amusement. I've got honest work to do here.'

'At least come to the Salon des Refusés.'

'The Reject's Salon, what the hell is that?' asked Mimi.

'Darling, that's what you get from hiding away in this field all winter. *Everyone's* talking about it. It's an exhibition for artists who were rejected from last year's Salon. There are so many artists and so few spaces in the Académie, that they're holding this for the rejects. Durand-Ruel's had a big hand in it, and he's chosen the most controversial pictures he can find, alongside traditional artists he can sell to polite society for portraits. The critics are sharpening their knives as we speak. Edo's got at least two paintings in it.'

'I'll think about it,' said Mimi, mainly to get rid of them. The sound of Edo's name still hurt.

'It's actually against religious law to hide your light under a bushel,' said Monet as he kissed her goodbye on both cheeks.

There's no light left to hide, thought Mimi as she waved them off, faking her best muse's smile.

As soon as they left, Juliet's jittery arms enfolded her.

'I heard what they said, and I saw your reaction. Don't pretend. They're right about one thing, though: you've been hiding, I've hardly seen you since you started on your painting. I'm not sure how you manage to be so elusive, but you're never quite where I expect you to be. Forget them; why don't we have a party, just us, and you can forget whatever is eating you for a while? I won't ask, we learn not to at the circus, but let yourself go, just for tonight.'

Mimi watched the night's performance with Pixie, who was delighted to get a free ticket. Anyone who didn't know her would have thought she was sober, but Mimi knew better. Her friend was a bit too loud, found the jokes a little too funny, and stamped on the feet of the gentleman next to her so many times that he moved seats. There was also the tell-tale sweet-sour smell that followed drunks about like the scent of death.

Mimi never tired of watching. Every night was different, and it was the nuanced differences, the changes of mood, the atmosphere created by the audience, which informed her drawings and helped her distil the essence of every act.

Afterwards, Mimi and Pixie stood shivering on the dewy grass at the entrance to the hall of mirrors where she'd arranged to meet Juliet. The audience were filing home, and windows lit up in the wagons as the performers retired on this crisp January night. Juliet arrived, still in her trapeze costume wrapped in a wool shawl, and produced the key. Inside, they lit candles and hundreds blazed back at them.

'Fuck me, it's like heaven,' said Pixie.

The hall of mirrors was a series of corridors lined with gilt mirrors and elaborate plaster columns, stretching off in every direction. They stepped forward and banged their heads, turned around and banged them again, giggling. The mirrors were so highly polished that the only way you could avoid bashing into your own reflection was to hold your hand out in front of you.

Mimi lost Pixie and Juliet, though she could hear them chatting and laughing somewhere in the maze. It was disorienting and strange and, without your usual senses to depend on, almost like floating. Mimi walked further in, seeing herself from angles she didn't recognise. It was exactly how she felt, lost in a hall of mirrors, out of control, not knowing which way to turn, bumping into her own reflection in a world where the rules were different. There had to be a logic to it, but someone else had the key. How could it be right that Marie-Thérèse could hold onto a child that was rightfully hers? How could the rules be so unequivocally stacked against her? Why was it that Renoir and Monet and Berthe Morisot could submit to the Salon and not her? It was just built that way. You could spend hours stumbling around in here, or you could smash right through the elegant edifice and march straight out, head high.

'Mimi, there you are!' Pixie and Juliet were holding hands, leaning into each other, flushed with the fun. It was the happiest she'd seen Pixie since she could remember. Mimi wasn't sure how long they'd been in there, but when they left, the moon was up, full and bright, the evening star its anchor. What would it be like to have a constant companion that rose and fell with you without fail? Such comforts were not for the likes of her. Perhaps that's why she was born so strong.

Back at Juliet's caravan, the three girls snuggled up and chatted. Pixie made them laugh with her wild stories of gentlemen in back alleys, or kicking the cancan and watching men practically faint at a flash of bloomer, 'a piece of bleedin' frilly fabric, talk about easy money!' The toff who used an upturned jewelled slipper to stub out his fags and kept a poor fangless snake in a basket in the corner. She'd scarpered quick when he told her what he wanted to do with that. Pixie told a brilliant story, but it was her way of making it all right, an exotic tale that wasn't really happening to her.

Mimi was permanently exhausted, her nights broken with

dreams and terrors, so when she felt herself drifting off, she crept away, leaving the two to chat, and snuggled under a blanket on the bench in the living area. It was nice to fall asleep with the sound of friendly voices nearby for the first time since Edo. She'd cut herself off too much, and the directionless feeling from the house of mirrors descended over her.

The moon anchored by the evening star reminded her of Rafi somehow and when she woke in the morning, she was conscious she hadn't dreamt of Colette. It was a relief, but also a worry. In a superstitious kind of way, it was her only connection with her, and she didn't want to ever forget how she looked, her husky little voice, or how defiant she was when she was afraid.

She wrapped herself in the blanket and crept into the room where Pixie and Juliet were sleeping. The two were tangled up together, sleeping so peacefully, everything entwined, Juliet's straight blonde locks fusing with Pixie's Titian curls. The bottle of absinthe Pixie had insisted on was still unopened on Juliet's bedside table. It was a kind of miracle, unacceptable to society, but perfect for them.

She closed the door as quietly as she could, and left.

CHAPTER 22

By early spring, the wagons were all finished, and anyone wanting to look modern in Montmartre was beginning to adopt a similar style for their posters, especially the new cabarets that were springing up all over the Butte on the sites of the old mines, vineyards and derelict windmills.

The Cirque d'Hiver were packing up to move on and, within a week, all the magic and drama would be delighting towns in the South, then crossing the border into Italy.

Pixie was leaving with them, and Mimi wouldn't miss the drunken sham her friend had been, but she'd miss the woman she'd become. Since the night of the hall of mirrors, Juliet and Pixie were inseparable, and the insightful Monsieur Dejean had given her a job. Every night, a swaggering matador in braided silk trousers, scarlet waistcoat and a broad-brimmed hat extracted haunting laments and spirited Flamenco from a battered gypsy guitar while the Spanish riders encircled him, galloping to the music of their homeland.

The matador was Pixie, hair tucked under her hat, which she threw into the crowd at the end of the act, red curls tumbling to her shoulders in triumph, whilst Juliet blew kisses from behind the scenes, her jitters almost conquered.

It wasn't a happy ending, exactly. Never a day passed when Pixie didn't want a drink, and sometimes she was difficult to live with. But they loved and understood each other, taking turns to be the anchoring star, and the circus embraced a love that the rest of society would despise them for.

A part of Mimi wished she was going with them, but how could she leave Paris when Colette lived there? The seven months was up, and even if she couldn't meet the terms, she had to do something.

Mimi stood at the top of the road waving, as the wagons trundled down the rue des Martyrs. Pixie and Juliet waved a silk slip at her out of their window till they turned the corner, the technicians blew kisses and Monsieur Dejean clicked his heels and saluted her with a wink. Last in the line was the menagerie, and Tif's wagon. He didn't even give her a backwards look. And why should he, he was a bloody zebra, she told herself. But she'd miss him most of all. Who would she talk to about Colette now?

Monsieur Dejean had left her with double pay and a bonus until they came back as the Cirque d'Été, the Summer Circus, begging her to join them again when they returned. He was sure he would have something for a gamine who could turn her hand equally well to avant-garde illustration as to defying death without a safety net. She knew what she would do with it. It was five months since her visit to Marie-Thérèse's villa. Five months since she'd seen Colette. Her time was up, but there was no way she was going to give up. If Marie-Thérèse really was as poverty-stricken as she said she was, she may take a different view of a bag full of money as surety to buy a little more time, even if it was nowhere near the sum she'd laid out for the purchase of her daughter.

She ran her finger over the latest notch she'd made to

imagine Colette's height. Surely she'd be taller? Mimi smoothed down her green striped silk dress. She hadn't worn it since the last time she'd visited, and she was horrified to see a papery moth escape, and a hole in the hem. Never mind, it was unlikely anyone would notice. Putting every last centime of the money Monsieur Dejean had given her in a leather bag, she made sure it was deep in her pocket. Every other chancer in Montmartre was a pickpocket or a thief, and she wasn't about to give anything away.

There were two demons she wanted to conquer today – Marie-Thérèse, and the Salon des Refusés, the Reject's Salon. They were right, it was almost as big as the Académie's Salon, and all Paris was buzzing about it. Renoir had begged her to go to the opening and pressed a ticket on her. Edo and Berthe were exhibiting alongside Renoir, Monet, Degas and the rest, and the idea of seeing the controversial works that were rejected by the Salon was irresistible. The place would be packed, so the chances of bumping into Edo were very slim. The circus was a world apart, and she'd hidden there for too long. And why should Edo stop her from going anywhere?

Stepping out with her parasol and gloves, her hat secured with a mother-of-pearl pin, no one would ever know she'd spent the last few months in overalls up a ladder with a paintbrush in her hand, thinking of nothing but her daughter and the world of art she'd left behind. At the boulevard Haussmann, she turned onto the rue de Richelieu, then crossed the river at the Pont des Arts. For the first time since Edo, she felt that maybe things could turn around. New shoots pushed through cracks in the paving, tight little buds blossomed from winter wood and ducks hatched ducklings without a care in the world, not knowing yet what predators might snatch them away.

On the rue Bonaparte, Mimi passed Edo's studio and tried not to remember. Opposite, the queue was snaking through the gates of the gallery, and she slipped in behind two gentlemen who were talking loudly about the races. There was such a crush that no one took a blind bit of notice of an unchaperoned woman in their midst, not that she'd have cared if they had. She had no false virtue to protect in return for money and a roof over her head.

Handing in the ticket Renoir had given her at the desk, she joined the crowds in the exhibition rooms. The din was deafening as voices melded and bounced around the high ceilings, women fanned, men escorted and studied. The whole place was electric. Mimi had to fight her way through to get to see the paintings, which covered every inch of the lofty halls.

She scanned the catalogue, and found what she was looking for: Édouard Manet, *Le Déjeuner sur l'Herbe* and *Olympia*.

In a side room, armed guards protected the artworks, and mothers ushered their precious charges past, shushing them when they asked why there were soldiers. After checking her pockets, they admitted Mimi into the room, and there they were. *Olympia* and *Le Déjeuner sur l'Herbe*, the pictures Edo had painted of her. Except they weren't her any more, they were someone else. A red-haired girl, who shared her defiant look, stared out at her. He'd painted her over as she'd asked, but she was still there in the pose, in the inspiration. In *Olympia* he'd kept the black cat, but he'd changed the colour of her red choker to black, and swapped the peony for an orchid. Laure, an African model she'd met at the Lapin Agile, was handing this new girl flowers, probably from an admirer. Was that a message that the painter was no longer the admirer? Mimi let herself think so.

Le Déjeuner sur l'Herbe transported her right back to the day on the banks of the Seine, when everything seemed possible. The pose, and the languid atmosphere was still there, but it was no longer her, or Renoir and Monet. How appropriate it all was. That life was never hers, and now it was as if it had never existed in the first place.

A scuffle erupted outside the room, interrupting her reverie.

'It's not art, it's a grotesque cartoon!'

'An affront to common decency.'

Mimi ran out to see what all the fuss was about. The guards were doing their best to contain a gaggle of men and women, including a nun, who were trying to get into the exhibition, knives at the ready to destroy the pictures.

Durand-Ruel, the dealer, was there, taunting them in front of a gathering crowd.

'The man's a visionary. He's just painting what he sees. Every one of you is a hypocrite if you deface his work in these hallowed halls of make-believe.'

'Disgusting. The man who painted this is a base animal!'

It was then she saw Edo, looking mortified, Berthe at his side attempting to pull him away from the scene.

She'd tried to forget his almost golden glow, his tall straight figure, the way he clenched his jaw when he was upset. Berthe looked rebellious and protective of Edo at the same time. It should have been Mimi at his side. It was her who inspired the pictures, her who looked directly at him unashamed, her who helped him create his greatest works yet.

The scuffle died down, and the big exhibition hall drained of people, all crowding into the little side room containing Edo's pictures. He'd left before he'd seen how famous he'd be. People hated anything new, or against the rules, but they loved it too. And these pictures weren't just sensationalist. They were unlike anything any of these people had seen before, yet referred back to, and built on, all the classical tropes they'd just been admiring in the main halls. They were real, and now, and spoke to the viewer, perhaps about things they'd rather not acknowledge, but no matter, it was his best work, and he couldn't have done it without her.

In all the fuss, she hadn't noticed his other portrait. This one was of Berthe, a close-up of her head and shoulders, in mourning clothes. A frothy silk and net hat framed her pale face, wisps of hair gave her an alluring, reckless air, and the expression was exactly her. Enquiring, neurotic, clever. A bunch of soft violets pinned at her breast gave the picture its name, *Berthe Morisot au bouquet de violettes*. It was acceptable to name this society belle, the woman he was mad about, but not Mimi Bisset. He must have painted this after she'd left, probably without another thought about his green-eyed muse from Montmartre.

Why should she care after all this time? Of course she cared. She loved him, she loved this world of artists and salons and breaking the boundaries, and she desperately wanted them all back. But there was a very good reason why she'd left them, just as much as they'd rejected her. Colette.

Pushing through the crowds to the exit, she navigated the grand streets to the Beauregard villa. Would Colette recognise her, run to her like she had the last time she visited? Her papa had died last summer, and it was now spring, and she hoped and prayed that Colette had kept her spirit and defiance since her aunt had put her to work as a maid for her. She could run rings round that old witch Marie-Thérèse, and... Mimi had no idea if Marie-Thérèse would be willing to negotiate when she got there, but she had to try. Had to keep trying. She'd stayed away long enough for Marie-Thérèse to think that she'd scared her off with her threat of calling the police, and arriving unannounced was the only way she could hope to get a glimpse of her daughter and somehow make sure she was all right.

Turning the corner to the row of beautiful villas, she was filled with a sense of optimism. She was her mother, there just had to be a way, a key to help her navigate her way through the hall of mirrors, she just had to keep trying. Even if it took her years.

When she arrived at the Beauregard house, it was as if she'd run down one of the mirrored corridors, only to bash into cold, hard glass. She was as stunned as a bird who'd flown into a window.

The tall gate was hanging off its hinges, the courtyard was springing weeds, and the windows were shuttered. Mimi banged on the front door so long she bruised her fist. There were no servants left behind to manage the house and straining to see through a chink in the shutter to the parlour revealed empty rooms. There wasn't a stick of furniture, no sign of life whatsoever.

Mimi wasn't sure how her legs got her to the next-door neighbour's house to rap on their door and enquire, but thank God the maid was polite.

'I'm sorry, I don't know, ma'am. We woke up one morning and they were gone, lock stock and barrel. I feel sorry for all those traders who pitched up with their bills to find they'd scarpered without a trace. All the servants left her, and she was a cruel mistress by all accounts. All she had left was that little maid who was barely big enough to lift a pitcher, poor mite... Listen to me, I've said too much. Did she owe you, too?' said the maid when Mimi couldn't hide her devastation any longer.

'Yes, she did, a huge debt,' said Mimi. *She has my child.*

The maid tutted, eyes lighting at a potential piece of juicy gossip. 'Well, you aren't the first person to come knocking, or the last, I'm afraid. But I can tell you now, no one knows where they went, they left no forwarding address, for obvious reasons, I suppose...'

Mimi didn't wait to hear the rest because she couldn't trust herself not to scream. She wanted to howl at the moon in rage and pain, but her throat was so tight she could hardly breathe. At the Pont des Arts, she ran down the steps to hide in the damp shadows under the bridge.

She would never see Colette again. Her daughter would be sold, and subjugated by a family who wouldn't even treat her as human. She'd seen young girls from the slums sold to big houses without a care for who their masters were, and some of them were beaten, or worse. Please, God, not her baby.

Spring rains had swollen the Seine so much that it threatened to breach the flood walls. Mimi stepped forward, to the water's edge. The river was murky and deep, and there was a menace about it in the darkening day. The stinking effluvia of Paris was caught up in these waves rushing out to sea, hypocrisy swirling along with the shit and blood and semen and disease that affected every human, rich or poor, in this blue-grey city of dark and light. If she took another step forward, she'd be part of it, just another lost cause amongst the seething mass of humanity who loved, hoped, stole, murdered, deceived, and ultimately cared about no one but themselves.

A crowd had gathered on the bridge above, and there was excited chatter, then screams and cheers as a single wave surged around the bend in the distance, sweeping up everything in its path.

'La Barre,' someone shouted, the crowd clapping and whooping. It was the Seine bore, the spring tide that brought a single wave barraging down the river and out to sea. It had such purpose and force, and Mimi stood transfixed. Let fate make her choice for her; she wasn't afraid.

She faced it full on as the bloated wave rolled over the cobbles and swept her into the freezing water.

The wave sucked her under, and she choked in the black swell, lungs burning, water roaring in her ears. Fate had made its choice. Time slowed. The pain would be short-lived, and then nothing, her worries over. But her body wouldn't give in; something forced away the voices and replaced them with inhuman strength fuelled by the agony of her burning lungs. She fought with everything she had, thrust upwards, surfaced, saw a commotion on the bridge; they'd seen her! Before the tide turned her full circle, she was disoriented, flapping her arms wildly to stay above the water and breathe. *Colette, Colette,*

Colette, she couldn't die. The eddy at the back of the wave bashed her against the flood wall. She felt a pair of arms dragging her, spluttering and screaming Colette's name. She had to live.

Vomiting water and bile on all fours, hands patted her, sat her on the cobbles, wrapped her in a spare shawl, squeezed the water from her hair, asked her name. Poor love, they murmured. The day she'd warmed herself on the bank with Edo and the boys on a sunlit afternoon after the river had snatched her into a different current flashed vividly by. Loneliness crushed her amongst the kindly crowd. A laundress had a dry dress in her load, a gentleman went to fetch hot, sweet tea from a nearby café, another insisted on paying for a hackney cab.

'What address shall I tell him, where's home?'

She didn't have one, not really.

'Boulevard des Capucines,' she said mechanically. She hadn't seen Rafi in almost a year, but he was the closest she had to family.

CHAPTER 23

Mimi hadn't been to Rafi's new apartment on the boulevard des Capucines, but here she was, head pounding, emptied out. She knocked on the freshly painted door, and when he opened it, she just sobbed on the threshold.

'Mimi!' He stepped out of the doorway, looked both ways, then pulled her in. Only then did he give her a stiff hug and Mimi pressed her face into his rough woollen lapel. 'What on earth has happened to you, your hair is dripping wet! Hush, come in, come in, sit by the fire and tell me everything.'

He ushered her into a chair by the grate, where a fire was licking high up into the chimney.

'It's Colette,' she managed.

'Of course it is. Nothing else ever made you cry. *Breathe*, and try to tell me. Here,' he said, folding a blanket round her shoulders, 'you're shaking like a leaf. What the hell has happened?'

She gathered herself. There was a whole wall of shelves filled with his books, an expensive quill sitting on a writing table, a jumble of Japanese prints, oil paintings and scribbled notes on the wall above it, and a separate kitchen just visible beyond a panelled door. The whole place had a calm, homely feel. At least one of them was all right.

It took her a long time to tell him because just saying the words made it too real all over again. She told him the Barre, the wave, had taken her by surprise, and she wasn't even sure herself what was going through her mind at that moment. He had to stop her several times too, because it all came out in a jumble of Jean-Baptiste's last words, Marie-Thérèse's terms, the locked-up house, and Edo.

Rafi kicked the fireplace. 'I knew that bastard didn't deserve you! He can't see past his own arse for his aristo friends and daddy's money, even though he pretends to love his rebel artist image. What a fucking—'

'Raphael! Is somebody here?'

A woman appeared at the door, key in one hand, untying her bonnet with the other, beaming, but her face fell at the sight of Mimi, and Rafi rushed over to kiss her. She must have been about Mimi's age, pretty, but a little pinched, and her shabby clothes were clean and pressed as a new pin, like a reproach.

'This is Mimi, my friend from Montmartre, the one I told you about,' he said carefully.

'Indeed you did,' said the woman, looking Mimi up and down. 'Is something the matter?'

Mimi pulled the blanket closer to her and stared into the fire. How could she even begin to explain?

The woman looked askance at Rafi. 'Aren't you going to introduce us?'

Rafi looked beseechingly at Mimi. 'Meet Mademoiselle Béatrice Dulle, my...' Rafi was stricken, trying to get a word out.

'Fiancée,' said Béatrice emphatically.

'How lovely, Rafi didn't tell me,' said Mimi dully.

'Oh,' said Béatrice, disappointed.

'We haven't seen each other in quite some time,' added Mimi formally, instinctively jumping to Rafi's aid.

Mimi excused herself as best she could, refusing Rafi's desperate offer of a hackney cab. She just had to get out of there.

'Please, you have to let me help for once,' he said.

'Really, let her do as she pleases, she's perfectly capable of using her own two feet,' said Béatrice with a tight-lipped smile.

Mimi couldn't blame her. They'd both seen the look in Rafi's eyes when she said she was leaving, Rafi's hug goodbye a little too long.

She walked all night to try to think, make sense of it all, a mean sliver of a moon watching her with a slit eye, until the sun chased it away, its brightness careless of her plight. When she reached the rue Becquerel, she crawled up the stairs to her room, past the little family who were just boiling a kettle for breakfast, cosy as dormice, and closed her eyes tight, drowning in regret.

But it wasn't enough to close her eyes and wait for sweet sleep; Colette was out there somewhere, needing her, and Edo had stolen all her dreams. She didn't want to hide away any more; Colette was the best thing that had ever happened to her, and she had just as much right as any of them to make art, to confront people with their own hypocrisy. She still had her circus money, enough to buy all the paints and canvases she wanted, but she didn't want them hidden away. She wanted them at the Salon.

Mimi slept fitfully, every detail of her near-drowning coming back in vivid pictures, the wave engulfing her in muddy cold, her burning lungs, the muffled roar of water. Strange details too: a bottle with a colourful Bières de la Meuse label she'd grabbed in desperation, the slimy bolts on the underside of the Pont des Arts, a pale face in the crowd like a moon, the shuttered Beauregard villa, the maid's gossipy words about her daughter, Colette counting on her fingers. She slept the rest of the day, and most of the night and woke with the sun, furious and hungry. Damn the whole bloody lot of them.

They'd all be at the Lapin Agile tonight and she couldn't get it out of her head. She knew that Edo went every evening from 5 p.m. to 7 p.m. to gather his disciples, and there was no way any of them would miss the chance to join the post-mortem of yesterday's opening. The Impressionist gathering would be almost as important as the *vernissage*, where they'd rail against the Salon and the crowds flocking to shock themselves with *Olympia* and *Le Déjeuner sur l'Herbe*, then rail about how disgusting, how ugly and immoral life was. Didn't they understand about real life?

Anger spurred her on to build a fire, boil up enough water for a bath, wash the pain off her face and go out to battle. Never mind the moth-eaten dresses in her little cupboard; one of the girls from the laundry had got a job at Worth, and Mimi needed to look the part. A bribe was enough to persuade her laundry friend that no one would notice just for one night, and Mimi left the most fashionable couturier in Paris in a scarlet silk dress with a figure-hugging bodice, and a hooped skirt that took up nearly the whole pavement on the narrow Montmartre backstreets.

The Lapin Agile was so packed she could barely open the door and it was standing room only, but the Impressionists were at their usual long table, piled with vol-au-vents and savouries, Monet stuffing them as quickly as he could so he wouldn't need to buy dinner, Renoir offering them around. It was a full house – Edo was there, and at his side, Berthe Morisot, leaning in to hear him above the din, a half-smile on her Cupid's bow lips.

Mimi took a deep breath, threw back her shoulders and pushed through, elbows angled against anyone who thought she was fair game.

Monet leapt to his feet, spilling his wine. 'The Lady in Red, our little cat is back. Come and sit right here,' he said, shoving a glowering Cézanne along the bench to make space, but Rafi was at her side before she could get any further.

'Mimi! I was so worried about you. I came to find you at your apartment, but it was all closed up.'

'Rafi, you and I both saw Béatrice's face when she saw me. You're getting married now, and any friendship between us isn't fair on her. We're not children any more.'

'Don't shut me out,' he said, but Monet and Renoir were already there, pulling her to the table.

'We knew you couldn't hide in that big top forever.'

'How could I when I knew that this hotbed of iniquity and outrage is missing its leading muse?' she said, sitting at the table and looking directly at Edo.

Edo raised a glass. 'We've missed you,' he said, looking directly back. 'It's been miserable without you.'

Monet fell off the bench, fluttering his hands over his heart. 'Stop! The muse and the genius reunited. It's too romantic!'

Renoir gave him a hand up. 'The divine inspiration and the tortured artist!'

'Have another vol-au-vent and spare me your purple prose,' laughed Mimi, but Edo couldn't take his eyes off her. 'I went to see your pictures at the Salon des Refusés,' she said.

'The critics have panned them, it's been a nightmare,' said Edo, darkening. 'But where have you been?'

'Painting.'

'For the circus. We found her there toiling away, and they're not half bad, for a woman,' said Renoir.

'Unfair!' said Berthe.

'Yes, it is unfair,' agreed Mimi. 'But not quite so for you, though; it's just the laundry girls that don't get to show, isn't it, Edo?' It was maybe a low blow to Berthe, but Edo deserved to hear it.

'I told you she bites,' laughed Monet.

'She's right, though. I've seen her work and she's good. Why shouldn't she be selected?' said Berthe.

'I agree, but you know those bastards, they'll barely accept anything from us,' said Edo generously.

The *us* hurt.

'I mean it, I want to exhibit at the Salon. I have the kind of paintings they'd accept, a whole series of a mother and daughter that I love and I've put everything I feel into them...'

Edo blanched at that.

'But Berthe's doing that already, and come on, let's be serious about it, there isn't really room for another woman, however talented,' said Renoir, trying to be kind. 'She's an anomaly as it is.'

'My dear, if you really have designs in this direction, I suggest you read this first,' said Degas, slapping a copy of *Le Figaro* on the table and pointing to one of the passages. It was a review by the infamous Albert Wolff.

'...There is also, as in all famous gangs, a woman. Her name is Berthe Morisot, and she is a curiosity. She manages to convey a certain degree of feminine grace in spite of her outburst of delirium. Not a thought has been spared for the public. Why, only yesterday a man had been arrested in the rue le Peletier after leaving the exhibition because he was biting everyone in sight...'

Mimi looked up at Berthe in sympathy. 'What supercilious crap! That man loves the sound of his own voice too much.'

Berthe tossed her head rebelliously. 'I don't give a damn about that rag. Mimi darling, you look so beautiful in that dress, and it's wasted here with all these ragbags. Would you join me for a glass at the Café de la Paix? We can plot how we're going to conquer the Salon together, and I have an idea I want to put to you.'

Mimi accepted. She hadn't left Edo because she'd wanted to, but because she had to, and seeing him again tonight was torture, so she was grateful for an excuse to leave. She was intrigued, too, by what Berthe had to say.

As soon as they were seated on their velvet banquettes in the elegant dining room, Berthe leaned over and fixed her with those dark doll's eyes.

'You know he hasn't been the same since you left.'

'He's found the time to paint over me, and make another portrait of you, though.' Even though she'd asked him to, it still hurt.

'Darling, you mean the one with the violets, of me in mourning dress? Edo's already married. A woman in my position could never be with a man who's already taken.'

'But you would otherwise?'

'Please, hear me out. I'm marrying Eugène, his brother. That's why Edo painted me in mourning dress, to say goodbye, but he never laid a finger on me.'

'But he wanted to so badly, he painted you as if he had, that was obvious to me. Do you love his brother?'

'He's the closest I can get,' she said candidly, twirling her cocktail stick. She looked her in the eye. 'You know it's possible to love two people?'

'You love the two brothers?'

'No, for a man to love two people. I believe Edo does. You and me.'

She'd known it all along, of course, but to hear the words was kind of a relief. Mimi took a sip from her champagne coupe to gather her thoughts.

'Yes, but not completely. He'd make a respectable woman of you, if he had the chance, but you're unattainable, and maybe he likes that. With me, he loves the daring muse, but that's not everything I am. We only got to live in his other world, of art, and studios and living on the edges of society.'

Berthe's eyes filled with fervour and she waved Mimi's comments away with a flutter of her hand. 'That's exactly what my idea is about. I'm not free, not even in my art, but you are. You showed me your mother and daughter pictures, and they're beautiful, and if you tried hard enough, you might even get them shown at the Salon, but you could do something much bolder, something that would be more honest, and bring more scorn down on your head than even Edo's pictures have brought upon him. His ego is bruised, but you and I both know they'll make him famous.'

'He couldn't have created them without me, but I'm disposable as far as him and all his artists friends are concerned.'

Berthe shook her head and pressed on. 'What's so compelling about Edo's pictures of you is that they're so honest. When I saw you gazing out of that picture, so confident of his respect and lust, I couldn't sleep all night.'

'The first time I saw that picture of you, sharing a secret with the viewer, I knew he was in love with you and I didn't sleep either.'

Berthe put her hand on Mimi's. 'That's all in the past, now. You can do something that will shock the whole of Paris, if you can get it into the Salon. Why don't you paint a male nude? Not a classical one, but in the same vein as Edo's *Olympia*? Real, with human desires.'

It was genius, like the idea had always been there, but Berthe had drawn it down and given it a name. But what about respectability and Colette? All that was in the past now, and she had nothing to lose. She'd never give up on her, and she could see how this could be her best chance of realising her Salon dream, and making a lot of money. She'd seen how Edo's uncompromising realism had brought him derision, but also fame. He was a groundbreaker, a visionary, and why shouldn't she do the same? Berthe didn't want to say it, but Mimi had nothing to lose like Berthe did. That was her burden and, perhaps, her gift.

CHAPTER 24

Sunday morning was the model market in Pigalle, and it was a thrill to be doing the choosing, rather than being chosen.

The Italian girls draped themselves around the fountain to appeal to the classicists. Seamstresses, laundresses and courtesans gossiped and paraded the square, wearing their Sunday best, lifting their skirts to avoid the open sewers and detritus in the gutter. The girls with babies hushed them, showcasing their best Madonna and child attitude. A baby screamed, another giggled with that heart-stopping gurgle of delight only tiny children uttered. How casually their mothers bounced them, or sang to them, or even ignored them for the nuisance they were. Mimi wanted to shake them and tell them to treasure every single second, keep their soft skin close to theirs and never let them go.

Amongst them all, standing out like a candle in the dark, with a luminous, serious quality, was Victorine Meurent, the model Edo had used to paint over her in *Olympia* and *Le Déjeuner sur l'Herbe*. She could see why, with her red hair, grounded confidence and contemptuous stare. The artists were reverent around her, and she had a disdainful way of making them think they needed her much more than she needed them. Victorine would be a kindred spirit, if Mimi wasn't on another mission.

There were a few men amongst them in hired soldier's uniforms, or a Parisian's idea of a shepherd's outfit, in rustic kerchiefs, straw hats and stained smocks. These were the men who were the goatherds, disciples and infantrymen in the great allegorical paintings. Now Mimi was here, the idea of approaching them was daunting as they loitered, chatting and smoking and eyeing up the girls. Never mind. With her travelling paintbox and a palette under her arm to mark her out from the other girls, she buttoned her jacket right to the top, tucked a stray hair under her hat, and approached a soldier, a short man with even features and an unthreatening presence.

'Not sure about a girl who wants to paint a dick rather than suck it, darling. If you'll do both, I'm yours, as long as you pay me,' he said loudly for the entertainment of the other men.

Before she could reply, they were buzzing round her like flies on shit.

'I'll do it for free,' said a soldier with a crooked nose.

'Tell you what, I'll raise you. I'll pay her, so get to the back of the queue, mate,' said a shepherd, cupping his package like it was God's gift.

'Enough!' she yelled, loud enough to stun the bastards into silence. 'None of you sad specimens could afford me,' she said evenly. 'And if any of you ever want to work again, I'd wash out your sewer mouths. My father runs the Académie, and he wouldn't want your filth anywhere near his students.'

They smirked, but backed off long enough for her to stride away with a little of her dignity intact. What was she thinking? That she could change the world by carrying a paintbox? That was just a fraction of the derision she could expect, but they wouldn't stop her. A male nude by a woman should be just as acceptable as the other way round. There'd been wars, and revolutions, and great inventions, but people still couldn't accept that simple concept. What a bunch of ignorant, blinkered, dyed-in-the-wool philistines. And that was just the male models, never mind the rest of bloody Paris.

Mimi did everything but paint. She made a canvas so big that she had to move the table to fit it against the wall. If she needed to stand back, she bumped into something, but she was determined. First, she grounded and primed the canvas in neutral colours so her portrait would stand out. Then, she spent hours at the Louvre sketching the male statues, perfecting the male form on hundreds of pages, planning the picture she'd present to the Salon. It would have to be technically perfect if she stood a chance of being accepted, and she knew every nick and chisel mark on the *Borghese Gladiator*, the myriad nuances that made *Marcellus as Hermes Logios* appear deep in thought, the depiction of the Tiber River as a middle-aged man, and the devices the sculptor had used to make him wise and believable and autocratic.

But it was no use without a live model. For it to be truly great, she needed to look into their eyes and draw their body and their soul. An idea started to form in her head as she sketched her way through a sequence of Hermes statues. He was the Greek god of eloquence, like her own Rafi, who expressed himself best through words. Rafi loved what the Impressionists were doing, and he was the only man she knew who would even contemplate the idea of being a model for her. He didn't give a damn what society thought. Béatrice wouldn't approve, and who could blame her? But as Rafi always said to her, his Mimi didn't think of reasons why not. For the first time since last summer, when she'd climbed a tree with Colette in the Tuileries, she was his Mimi again, the one that always found a way out.

. . .

Just for the hell, to see if she still could, she jumped the bollards on the boulevard Haussmann. She only made nine, but that was because her skirts were longer and fuller nowadays and she caught it on the last one. At the Café de la Paix, Béatrice and Rafi were waiting for her at a table near the window. Rafi stood and kissed her on both cheeks under fierce scrutiny from Béatrice. Nevertheless, Mimi lent down to kiss her warmly, but Béatrice wasn't having any of it, staying seated and cutting the second kiss short.

They made small talk for a while, Rafi squirming, his kind heart wanting to keep both of them happy, but Béatrice didn't make it easy. She sulked if Rafi addressed more than one sentence to Mimi and talked over her at every opportunity. Mimi let it pass. She owed it to Rafi to try to like her, and she did her best to see what it was that attracted him to her. She was quick and sharp, a girl from the slums, like her, who worked hard at her job in a hat shop, and she was proud of Rafi's success as a writer. But there was something almost too efficient about her, and she had a schedule for Rafi which Mimi was sure he would tire of. Monday, meet her at the hat shop and take her for a Kir, Tuesday tidy his apartment and review wedding venues, Wednesday dinner with the parents... she lost track after that. When their coffee arrived, Béatrice put her hand on Rafi's proprietorially.

'Anyway, what have you invited us here for, we're intrigued, aren't we?'

Rafi nodded uncomfortably. Damn him, why couldn't he just be himself around her?

'It's an unusual request, but entirely above board. One I didn't think could be asked without you being here,' said Mimi carefully.

'Go on, I'm intrigued,' said Béatrice, though she clearly wasn't judging by the bored look on her face.

'Rafi knows this already, but it's my burning ambition to be an artist, to be exhibited at the Salon. You'll think I'm completely mad, I know, but there's always a first time for everything, and the best art is about pushing boundaries, and changing perceptions, holding a mirror up to society.'

'Good luck with that, but I don't suppose it's going to put much food on the table.'

So, she was one of those, always closing interesting things down.

'If I'm the first to do something, if I'm recognised, I think it will. Especially with the idea I have for my next work.'

'Mimi, what are you planning? I haven't seen that spark in your eye for a long time,' laughed Rafi.

She took a deep breath. 'I want to paint a male nude, from life, and life-sized.'

Béatrice nearly spat out her tea. 'What's that got to do with us?'

'I can't do it without a live model, and I wanted to ask Rafi, with your permission of course.' She kept her face neutral, as if it was the most reasonable request in the world.

Rafi and Béatrice answered yes, and no, in that order.

'Raphael, you know that's impossible...'

'I'd ask you to be there too, of course. It's totally acceptable at the École des Beaux-Arts. The girls there are treated with absolute respect. It's essential for anatomical study, and the male sculptures in the Louvre are incredibly beautiful and everyone eulogises about them, so it's nothing new, apart from they were all sculpted by men. I've known Rafi forever, like a brother. I know how it must sound, but will you think about it?'

'Bea, if anyone can make it work, she can.' His intelligent eyes shone and Mimi knew he'd be thinking it through to the end. Dear Rafi, he'd be able to see the audacity, the sheer cheek of it, the layered meanings of the piece, the new barriers broken, the reception at the Salon, the scathing reviews, the shouting and discussions, the gradual acceptance...

'Darling, I'm not averse to it, not at all, it's an interesting idea, and who would I be to stop you?' said Béatrice. 'But we only have three months before we move south, and there's so much to do, I just can't see how we'd both fit it in. I'm so sorry.' The incline of her head and the tight-lipped smile was meant to put an end to it.

'I'm sure we could find the time; there's Friday afternoons...' said Rafi.

'No. I've told you before, every minute is allocated to making the necessary arrangements.'

'It will take over two months' worth of Fridays just to move across Paris with a few sticks of furniture?' said Mimi. She shouldn't speak hotly to her, she knew that, but the fire in her belly was coming out through her mouth.

'It's not southern Paris, it's the South. As in Aix-en-Provence, where my parents are. We'll need help with the children and it'll be lovely to have my family just around the corner.' She smiled indulgently at Rafi.

'You're pregnant?' said Mimi.

At this, Béatrice baulked. 'Certainly not, we're not married yet!'

All Rafi could do was smile apologetically at her. 'It's a train ride away, we'll be back and forth...'

'I doubt it,' said Béatrice, picking up her gloves and putting them on a little too aggressively. 'Once we're there, it's going to be far too far to travel back very often. But you're welcome to visit once we've settled in,' she added, looking to Rafi for approval at her magnanimity to his childhood friend.

'That would be delightful,' replied Mimi, draining her tea to hide her shock. Why hadn't he told her? How could he leave her? But he had every right to do whatever he wanted, it was just that she'd always thought he'd be there.

She left as soon as humanly possible, rushed through the diners at the Café de la Paix, who were gossiping and laughing in their silk dresses and top hats, chinking glasses, flirting and swapping scandal without a care in the world.

Outside the revolving door, she gulped in the fresh air to steady her breathing, then set off along the boulevard des Capucines.

'Mimi, wait!'

She spun round. Rafi was waving his flat cap at her like he used to when they played in the streets together. He ran to catch up with her.

'I'll do it.' He smiled, hands on his knees to catch his breath.

'Don't you need a pass?' said Mimi.

'There's a break in the schedule on Wednesday afternoons,' he replied with a wry smile. 'It's when I do my writing. I rent a studio nearby for when I need complete peace and quiet. Béatrice never comes there, so she doesn't need to know. You can use it as your artist's studio if you like. I'll write and pose for you, you paint, and it will be our childhood dreams come true, sort of.'

She jumped up and hugged him tight. 'You're an angel,' she said.

'You know I'd do anything for you, don't you?'

'Apart from marry me,' she said jokingly.

'I'd better get back before I'm missed,' he said, retreating.

Sometimes she wished she'd kept her big mouth shut.

CHAPTER 25

Rafi's studio was modest, nothing like on the scale of Edo's, but there was enough room for both of them, and Rafi was happy to shift things around for Mimi to get the best light. His desk was squeezed in by the door, surrounded by piles of *l'Opinion Nationale,* encyclopaedias and his favourite books, whilst her things took up most of the room.

It was the first time she'd ever had a space dedicated to painting, and she fixed everything up just how she wanted it. There was a picture rail, where she hung all her paintings of Colette, from her baptism, to sleeping in her crib, to their imagined picnics and trips to the seaside. She was her inspiration, her guiding spirit.

All the paraphernalia lined up on the scrubbed pine table was a work of art in itself. There were pretty glass bottles containing her Venetian turpentine, white gesso for priming, and her three favourite mediums of slow-drying poppy, pale linseed and glossy walnut oil. She fanned out her smudged paint tubes in rainbow order, and arranged her paintbrushes in two categories of boar's hair and sable, then again into rounds, filberts, flats and fans. The canvas was taller than her, and she'd bought a huge easel to support it. She'd starve for a week to afford it, but it was worth it – and apart from Edo and his rich friends, she didn't know many artists who actually ate regularly.

In front of the easel was a daybed, the kind Rafi had slept on all his life until recently, a poor man's space-saving sofa by day, and a bed at night. She dressed it with a bolster, simple white sheets and a red eiderdown. All the male nudes she'd studied were of men in athletic poses, as gods, or warriors. Hers would be a naked man, just woken from his night's sleep, looking directly at the viewer. It was a nod to Edo's *Olympia*, but it would also turn the convention of the female reclining nude on its head. To her knowledge, no one had ever painted a simple picture of a naked man in a domestic setting, in a prone pose, and she would make it beautiful, profound, and worthy of Rafi.

Mimi plumped the bolster and rumpled the sheets, contemplating the colours and techniques she'd use to convey the folds and shadows, arranging every last detail, until Rafi arrived with a book tucked under his arm.

'You're going for the jugular, I see,' he said, bouncing on the bed.

'Men sleep in a bed and wake up in the mornings, don't they? I thought you were in love with the idea of realism.'

'Yes, but only when conveying realistic prostitutes, my dear, and they don't know any better. I don't mind slumming it for fun, but no one wants to see the actual truth.'

They giggled.

'Did you bring the book?' said Mimi.

He gave her book he had tucked under his arm. Charles Baudelaire, *Les Fleurs du Mal*. It was perfect. This book had so enraged polite Parisian society with its themes of corruption and lost innocence, oppression and love that it was banned within a month of its publication, only to be reinstated on its literary merit.

'It's genius, Rafi!'

She'd asked him to bring the book he thought should be featured in her painting, and he couldn't have chosen better. It summed up everything she was trying to do, the hypocrisy of society, the cruelty, the beauty to be found in the dirt and on the edges of society, and Rafi understood. He wasn't afraid, and neither was she. She didn't want to just paint pretty pictures, she wanted to *say* something.

'If you insist on exploiting my body in order to shock the whole of Paris into some kind of egalitarian utopia, I might as well make the most of it. Now, where do you want me?'

He undressed behind the broken screen she'd found dumped in a Montmartre backstreet, and sidled out cupping his manhood, with a dopey look on this face.

'Well, this is unusual, I'm not really quite sure where to put myself.'

'Just imagine you're in the garden of Eden before the unfortunate apple incident, and you're ignorant of how evil your flesh is.'

Rafi looked ruefully around the room. 'I never really expected Eden to look like this, or to be quite so chilly.'

Mimi pulled the casement windows shut, trying not to laugh at the goose pimples that had formed in protest.

'I didn't have this trouble with the statues in the Louvre. Just lie on the bed; you can pull the blanket over you till I'm ready to start. I was hoping for a malleable model, not a demanding diva.'

'I don't have to do this, you know that, don't you?'

'That's where you're wrong, my friend. Of course you do; you should know by now I always get what I want.'

'That's certainly true when it comes to me. I barely even remember saying yes,' he said, pulling the blanket over him.

'Just lie there till I tell you to move.'

She'd been dreading the moment he emerged from behind

the screen, naked, but he'd made it easy and warm and friendly, like he always did.

Pulling on her paint-smattered artist's smock was like finally being her, and she got straight to work arranging him on his side, one hand propped up on the bolster, the other holding his book. His legs were relaxed, one knee up, his sex comfortably resting on his thigh, his gaze directly at her, as if he'd just read a page and looked up, caught unawares. On his bedside table was his revolutionary's cap, an inkwell, quill and paper, and pooled on the floor in front of him, a red slip, to indicate a woman's presence somewhere in the room.

The tableau she created was perfectly commonplace and innocent on the face of it: a man just waking, light streaming in from the east, looking up over his book to say good morning to his lover. But the details were incendiary. A revolutionary writer, a naked man, reading a banned text which pushed at the boundaries of public morals and called out hypocrisy, lying on a single bed, a clear indication of the couple's unmarried state.

Rafi was more sinewy than she'd imagined for a man who spent a lot of time at his desk. His skin was very pale, but his muscles were defined, and there was a vulnerability about him naked which she hadn't anticipated.

Blowing on a piece of willow charcoal, she sketched the first outlines, and they fell into companionable silence, Rafi taking the opportunity to proofread his work while Mimi drew. It was so peaceful being completely absorbed in the task, with Colette looking down at her in happy poses from the picture rail. There was so much to say, about Rafi's marriage to Béatrice, about the day she'd run to him after the spring bore had swept her down the river, but neither of them mentioned it, like a spell they didn't want to break.

By the end of the day, she'd drawn the major outlines, and Rafi had to go. It was frustrating, she could have continued for hours, but she only had a fraction of him, and that was enough for now. When he'd gone, she inspected the drawing on the life-sized canvas and felt as alive as she had the split second before the catch on the trapeze. She'd make it technically brilliant, beyond reproach from a classicist's point of view in terms of execution and composition, but it would be her own vision, unlike anything the Académie had ever seen.

Mimi worked on the canvas for the rest of the week, filling in the details where she could without Rafi being there, drawing the folds of the sheets, the shape of the bolster, the window behind the bed, studying the way the sun poured in through the window every morning, and the shadows it cast on each part of the composition. On most afternoons, she obsessively visited the Beauregard house to see if there was some glimmer of life, spotting a little sprite with dark hair and a defiant scowl flit past the cracks in the shutters, before realising it was a bird, or just a shadow, a new punch in the stomach every time it wasn't her Colette.

She poured everything into the picture, rubbing out and starting again until she was satisfied, and the drawing was complete and accurate. On the next Wednesday, when Rafi arrived, she was ready to begin applying the layers of paint, her favourite moment in the whole process.

'Give me a second to get through the door. Really, give a man some dignity!' said Rafi when she was so impatient to start that she barely said hello, pristine brushes at the ready, palette knives lined up, fat tubes of colour waiting to be mixed, a world of possibility and promise and combinations that couldn't wait a moment longer.

Rafi took up his pose, adhering to the marks she'd made to make sure he was in the exact same place as last week. Nothing could be left to chance and every detail of the composition was fixed securely in Mimi's mind, a military operation to create the appearance of a transitory moment.

'I wonder if this is how a slab of meat feels on a butcher's block,' said Rafi.

'Slabs of meat don't answer back. Please move your left elbow back a couple of centimetres, that's it, then don't move!'

First, she made a tonal palette for the eiderdown, in cadmium red, zinc white, brilliant yellow and burnt sienna. Choosing walnut oil as her medium, she slicked the paint on thickly with a palette knife, a bright gloss of colour, the point of no return, the beginning of something unknown, but wonderful. Next, she used a sable filbert to blend and build, picking up every nuance of the undulating fabric.

'You know you flare your nostrils when you dip your brush in the paint,' teased Rafi.

'I've told you the rules. I'm the genius artist, you're the passive model who will be made great only by my superior vision. It's best if you try not to have a personality.'

'That's not what you told me when I took the assignment.'

'Stop talking! It makes you move, and ruins everything.'

'A bad workman blames his muse.'

Weeks turned into a month, and it became the most natural thing in the world for Rafi to arrive at the studio, kiss her on both cheeks, put a cheese and ham baguette on the table next to her paints to make sure she was eating, then take off his clothes, and resume his pose, holding up his book. She found herself saving up stories from the week to tell him, which gave everything a lighter edge. Sometimes they met at the Lapin Agile with the others to shout about the new rip-off taxes from the annexation of Montmartre, or rail at the latest Wolff review in *Le Figaro* before dancing on the tables, but mainly on the nights when Mimi knew Edo wouldn't be there. When he was, there was an uneasy truce between them, a superficial politeness that was so strange after their deep intimacy, and she was still attracted to him. She could tell he felt the same, too, and often she'd look up from a heated conversation with Cézanne about how simple shapes could convey a mood, or an argument with Degas about a model's contribution to the success of a painting, and she'd find that he was already looking at her.

She told the gang that she'd be submitting for the next Salon, which they thought was a hoot, but they didn't really believe her. As selection day drew nearer, they all got the jitters, and arguments broke out about which paintings would make the grade, and whether their dealer Durand-Ruel held enough sway with the selection committee.

On days when everything went wrong and she stamped her feet at wasted paint and threw her paintbrushes at the wall for not complying to her wishes, Rafi spurred her on. When Rafi hated the words he'd spent all week labouring over, Mimi reminded him he was Hermes, god of eloquence, and he should have faith.

Some days, she almost felt happy, but Colette was her counterpoint, the minor chord to the melody, but also the spirit that kept her going, and fuelled her fight against hypocrisy. If she ever saw her again, she'd show Colette she could be anything she wanted, tell the world the truth, no matter where she came from or what society dictated.

CHAPTER 26

If Mimi wasn't so delighted with her portrait, she'd be sad she'd finished it. Finishing it meant only a few weeks to go before Rafi married Béatrice, and went to live in Aix-en-Provence, 700 kilo-metres away, and weeks by train and horse to get there. But it also meant that it was ready in time to submit to the Salon selection committee, and she could take her chances against all the other hopefuls. The Impressionists at the Lapin Agile complained bitterly about the committee, and it was true that they were dyed-in-the-wool traditionalists, but they knew talent when they saw it. Hadn't they selected Edo's pictures, despite the outrage they must have known they'd cause?

Mimi made Rafi close his eyes ready for the great unveiling.

'It had better be good after freezing my arse off week after week.' He smiled.

Mimi led him to the exact spot she'd planned for maximum impact and stood back.

'Open your eyes now!'

'*Que c'est magnifique*, it's magnificent,' he said quietly.

His body was blue stylised shapes, but his phallus was hyperreal and rendered in life-giving gold. Intense yellow sunlight streamed in through the window, at odds with the flat blue-grey Paris light, to denote his flight south. The quill, inkwell and revolutionary's cap were silver, to represent his sword and shield, and the discarded slip on the floor was recognisably that, but also a pool of blood to symbolize a woman's cycle, and childbirth. Rafi's face was perfect, capturing his warm, quizzical look and his sharp intelligence in beautifully layered brushwork, the flesh tones muted and subtle, and she'd given him green eyes, her own colour, not his brown, to denote her reflection in his gaze. The Baudelaire book was gold, diffusing into the air around it, like a divine being, the book of difficult truths.

'It's everything I knew it would be,' said Rafi. 'It's daring, unique, disturbing and beautiful all at once, like you, and it's full of heart and wit. It's wonderful, Mimi, but you know they'll never accept it?'

'Did you think I could catch a zebra, or learn the trapeze and be the great Mintaka, or master oils and create a portrait that is like nothing else you've ever seen?'

Rafi shook his head. 'I'm glad to see I've got my old Mimi back with a vengeance, but be realistic – how do you think you're going to succeed where nearly every other aspiring artist in France has failed?'

Mimi thought back to the day, a lifetime ago, they went for their walk through Paris, from the Gare Saint-Lazare to the École des Beaux-Arts, and she'd told him she'd exhibit at the Salon. She was annoyed then when he shot her down, and she felt the same flicker of irritation now. Typical Rafi, always the pessimist. She rubbed her hands together to chase away the thought.

'I'm not sure yet, but I have to get it there by this afternoon, and you promised to help me wrap it and take it.'

The paint would take months to dry, so Mimi had devised a huge pochade box to transport it without smearing it. When they'd fitted it and secured it ready to take, along with her favourite picnic scene with Colette, Mimi turned to Rafi.

'I'm going to miss this painting. It's all I'll have left of you when you leave Paris.'

'I wouldn't worry too much; you won't be able to move for it in your apartment when the Salon rejects it and sends it back,' he teased.

'I'm serious. What am I going to do without you?'

'What you've always done. Forge your own path, get yourself into trouble, come out smelling of roses,' he said ruefully.

'Will you look for her when you go to Aix?' Mimi asked abruptly, looking at the pictures of Colette on the picture rail.

'What makes you think she'll be there?'

'Nothing, it's just she could be anywhere, and I can't search the whole of France alone.'

'You can't search the whole of France, full stop. Mimi, you've got to accept it. I've seen the way you look at those pictures of her and sometimes it puts you into a black mood for the rest of the day. You're torturing yourself. You gave her up for good reason, for a better life. If she's anything like you, she'll get through and rise above everything. And there are a lot of mothers who would kill to have their daughters put to a respectable trade, rather than end up in the laundry, or worse, a *maison close*, a brothel. Jean-Baptiste was suffering, possibly even delirious when he asked you to take her back. Leave it be, and start again with a man who deserves you, and whoever you choose, make sure they understand you, everything about you, and that they're kind. You're young, you can have more children, but you're not giving yourself a chance.'

Even Rafi, the man who knew her the best of anyone she'd ever known, still didn't get it. She would never give up hope.

'You'll understand when you have children. You never forget, there's a thread that attaches you forever, a rule of the universe that means you belong together. She has my eyes, my mother's fingernails, she sees the world the way that I do, I just know it. And the longer the separation, the harder it gets, knowing that I'm missing all the precious moments that I'll never get back. I know it's impossible, but just promise me you'll look for her anyway.'

'OK, I promise,' said Rafi.

Dear Rafi, he only ever wanted the best for her. She felt the same about him, too, and she had to ask him the question that had been burning before he left this little studio forever.

'Do you love her, your future wife?' asked Mimi.

'We're good together, and I want a family. Isn't that what all orphans crave?'

'But you have a family, me,' said Mimi.

'No one will ever have you completely,' said Rafi, busying himself with some papers on his desk. 'Come on, let's get this to the Salon before it's too late.'

The picture was ridiculously unwieldy as the two carried it gingerly down the boulevard des Capucines, and crossed the Pont des Arts to the Académie. There were several near misses, one when a horse got spooked and bolted, and another with a boy who was concentrating more on his hoop and stick than where he was going.

At the submissions desk, a clerk addressed Rafi.

'Name?'

'Mimi Bisset.'

'I only need the artist's name,' he said irritably.

'That's me. Mademoiselle Camille Madeleine Bisset, artist.'

It was the first time she'd said it, officially, and it felt amazing.

The clerk looked at her over his pince-nez. 'I've seen it all, now,' he muttered.

'I have two works to submit: this one, entitled *Study of a Mother and Daughter*, and the life-sized one in the pochade, a classically inspired work entitled *Hermes Reading*,' said Mimi as the clerk stared in horror.

They escaped while his mouth was still flapping at the sheer nerve of her, and they staggered giggling out of the gates, and onto the street, arms linked.

'He looked like someone had stuck a red-hot poker up his arse, then twisted,' said Mimi.

'I'm not sure it was the Hermes he was expecting,' laughed Rafi, walking backwards to face her.

Rafi defied Béatrice's timetable to go for a celebratory drink with Mimi, but after half an hour he rushed off, not wanting to upset his fiancée. Bless Rafi, sometimes he was too noble for his own good.

Mimi sped home, walking on air, and when she got back to Montmartre, the second good thing of the day happened. The circus was back at its spot at the base of the Butte ready for the summer season, and she couldn't wait to tell Juliet and Pixie everything.

A few days later, Mimi was at the Lapin Agile with the gang as Eugene arranged the vol-au-vents in front of everyone on the table. Every year, in honour of the Salon selection results, he made them in the shape of sweet ticks and savoury crosses. Every person around that table wanted to devour the sweet ticks, the reward for being selected, and Mimi had never wanted anything so badly in her life. Everyone was there, and Rafi and Pixie had joined her for solidarity. Each artist had a sealed cream linen envelope in front of them, embossed with the hallowed Académie des Beaux-Arts stamp. However much they loved to hate the institution, these were the people who would make or break the fortunes of all of them.

'You first, Edo. Where you lead, we follow,' said Monet gravely, serious for once.

'Absolutely not, ladies first,' Edo replied, smiling like a fool at Berthe.

'All right, I'll go first, pray for me!' said Berthe. She crossed herself dramatically and opened it very slowly, careful not to tear the envelope, then pulled out the letter, kissed it and held it to her heart. 'They're taking my favourite, *Chasing Butterflies*!'

'And so they should, the ungrateful bastards,' laughed Edo, hugging her.

Berthe hugged him back, then took a delicate bite of a sweet pastry tick. 'You next.'

'Open it for me,' said Edo.

For God's sake, she's marrying your brother, thought Mimi.

Berthe opened it and held it up for everyone to see. '*Le Balcon*! Oh Edo, it's your best so far.'

Mimi was floored. The last picture he painted of her, the night she left him. It wasn't lost on Edo, either. He raised his glass in Mimi's direction and sipped with the half-smile she loved.

Renoir was showing *Luncheon of the Boating Party*, the work he'd sketched on the day they all caught the train to the river, and Monet's works were rejected, along with Cézanne's and Degas'. Everyone joined in vociferous damning of the short-sighted, bigoted cabal that was the selection committee, eating a cross or a tick from the table according to their selection status.

'What about Mimi?' said Berthe when everyone else had opened theirs.

'We'd completely forgotten!' said Monet. 'I wish I'd been a fly on the wall when *you* turned up with a canvas.'

'I bet most of them were too old to take the shock,' joined Renoir.

But Mimi wasn't listening. As the assembly roared and bashed a drum roll out on the table, she picked up the envelope. While it was neat and sealed in expensive cream linen paper, there was still hope, everything to play for.

'Come on, you're killing us,' said Monet.

'Take your time,' said Rafi, putting a comforting hand on her shoulder.

'Open it,' said Edo encouragingly. 'Let's see if those waxworks have a modicum of taste between them.'

'Fuck 'em if you're not in, you don't need them anyway,' murmured Pixie as Mimi peeled back the fold.

It was there in black and white, but she couldn't quite believe it. She passed it to Rafi to check.

He whooped. 'Maybe there *is* justice in the world. They're taking one, *Study of a Mother and Daughter*!'

'A toast to Mimi's *Mother and Daughter*.' Renoir stood, glass aloft.

'Our very own pet, at the Salon!' said Monet, slightly bitchily.

'Talent *and* determination. A feat against all the odds,' said Edo, holding his glass her way. 'I salute you.'

'To me!' Mimi joined the clinking with her Kir, feeling like she could fly. But it wasn't enough. 'They didn't take *Hermes Reading*,' she said to Rafi when the commotion had died down and the gang settled back in to damning the Académie with great gusto.

'They were never going to, Mimi. I love that you ever thought they might. And Monet's right, I bet there were some near heart attacks when they unveiled it, but you have to be realistic. However much everyone here rails against them, they have a public audience, and the world just isn't ready for it. They needed armed guards for *Olympia*, for goodness' sake. Imagine, yours would need its own locked cell. It's just too controversial.'

'How controversial?' said Durand-Ruel, the Impressionists' art dealer and supporter.

Mimi spun round.

'Very.'

'Tell me more,' he said.

'I thought the art dealer, Durand-Ruel, would take *Hermes Reading*,' said Mimi to Tif as he munched some hay from the flat of her palm, 'but he said it wouldn't be worth his while, I'm too unknown. Am I the only one in Paris who's prepared to take real risks? Not just easy ones, like *Olympia*, which has a well-known society man behind it, but one which *means* something, which would take Paris by storm. By that, I mean exhibiting a picture of a male nude by a girl from the slums.'

Tif snorted and stamped his foot.

'See, even you're shocked. But I just know it has to be seen, like everything in my life has led to this point. It's difficult to explain...'

'Juliet told me you came in here to talk to the zebra,' said a warm southern French accent that unmistakably belonged to Jules.

Jules Léotard, her erstwhile trapeze partner. Mimi smiled ruefully at him.

'He's the only one who understands,' she said.

'Intelligent beasts, zebras,' replied Jules.

'More than most humans.'

'Pixie told me about your picture, and the Salon.'

Mimi gathered herself. Of course it *was* good. 'It's wonderful that they're taking my mother and daughter picture.'

'But it's the swing, not the triple somersault.'

'Exactly. I want to make people *feel* something.'

'I still have nightmares about the moment you fell.'

'It wasn't your fault. And I would never have started painting, which is my life.' *Along with Colette*, she thought.

'I'm superstitious; you know all us trapeze artists are. I dropped you, and I must make amends. You need your picture to be famous in order for this dealer to exhibit it for you?'

'He's a businessman. He thrives on scandal and controversy.'

'I know a reviewer, Albert Wolff. He comes to the Egyptian camp for love when we're in Paris. He's a beautiful man.'

'With a mean pen. He's the Impressionists' worst enemy.'

'He's the most widely read art critic in Paris, by a country mile. If I ask him to, he will review your picture. And I'm sure such a sensitive soul as Albert will be horrified and outraged by what you've created.'

Tif brayed and stamped in his stall.

'Tif thinks that's the best thing he's heard since I rescued him on the boulevard Montmartre.'

Jules clicked his heels and saluted. 'Then I shall make it so, my bright star.'

Mimi studied the Salon exhibition poster on the lamp post as she waited by the news stand for the first edition to arrive. The cart arrived piled high with journals, and when the first bale of *Le Figaro* newspapers landed on the ground by the stand, the boy flicked out his penknife, sliced through the string and gave her the copy off the top.

'As promised. What is it you're so desperate to see?'

Mimi opened at Wolff's review, and the boy's eyes widened.

'Bloody hell, I wouldn't want to be you, that hurts,' he said, sucking in air and whipping his wrist to make his fingers snap.

'What do you mean? It's the best article the man has ever written and it's wonderful being me!' said Mimi, pressing a coin in his palm. 'Give me two.'

She ran all the way to Durand-Ruel's gallery on the rue des Petits-Champs and slapped the paper on his desk triumphantly.

'Here.' She pointed. 'I told you he was going to write it.'

Durand-Ruel picked up the paper, a smile spreading over his face.

Imagine if Pandora's box was a painting, and you wished to unleash every one of society's ills to fly at will into the Paris air just by looking at it, then you would be delighted with Mademoiselle Camille Bisset's Hermes Reading. *If eloquence is defined as the ability to communicate a story, then this painting is true to its title. It tells the depraved tale of a woman of uncertain virtue and is rendered in a life-sized mockery of everything you hold dear in civilised society. True, the composition and technique are impressive, the image arresting, and there are some uncomfortable truths about French society, but to call this art? This garish perversion is worse than anything you might have seen from this young woman's partners in crime, the Impressionists, and the sheer audacity of it is breathtaking. See it at your peril.*

'This is gold dust,' he said, putting the newspaper down like it was on fire.

After the review, Mimi spent many happy evenings in the Lapin Agile. It was May, and the gang gathered under the trees and spent long nights talking and dancing and anticipating the Salon. Renoir and Monet were ecstatic.

'Our very own depraved laundress of questionable virtue, with a paintbrush like a dagger,' said Monet as he waltzed her around the courtyard. 'My ideal woman.'

'The avenging angel of the slums,' said Renoir, escorting her to their table.

It was a triumph. Jules went back to performing his triple somersault, and women continued to faint at the sight, and the clamour to find out where Parisians could go to see and be horrified by Mimi's painting built to a crescendo.

On the Wednesday before the Salon, Durand-Ruel summoned Mimi to his gallery.

'I have two pieces of news for you, both good.'

'Give me the best one first,' said Mimi.

'I've found a place to exhibit your picture, opposite the École des Beaux-Arts. My intention is that every single person who goes to the Salon will then come to view *Hermes Reading* to indulge themselves in a bit of affront, then go home to their noble residences to carry on as they always have, ideally denigrating your name in order to make themselves feel more virtuous than ever. The point being that your name is on the lips of every man with a chequebook within a thirty-kilometre radius.'

'I admire your commitment to art and social justice.'

'It's my way of being committed.'

'But only if there's commission in it.'

'Well, you've got me there. Now, do you want to know where this great exhibition hall is?'

'The Palais de Justice?'

'No. Edo Manet's studio. As you know, it's right opposite the École, and it will be easy to herd them in like sheep after they've been edified at the Salon. Let's face it, after that load of whitewash, they'll be ripe for a bit of excitement.'

Mimi's heart was racing. 'And Edo has agreed to this?'

'He suggested it after he saw the review. Something about making amends, I think he said. I suppose that means something to you?' he said casually, smirking at Mimi's discomfort. 'You don't object, do you?' he asked disingenuously.

'What's the second piece of news?' she said, changing the subject.

'I have an American buyer who's just about single-handedly keeping all you starving artists going with his love of the avant-garde. Luckily for you, he can see your potential.'

'He's buying?' Mimi couldn't believe she'd get actual real money for the thing she cared so passionately for. It didn't seem right to get paid for something she loved doing so much, but this made her an artist not only in her eyes, but in other people's too.

'Something of such notoriety couldn't command less than fifteen thousand francs. He's a friend, so I've given him my best price. He's happy to show it at Edo's studio before it's shipped to America. With, in my opinion, great foresight, the Americans are lapping up everything that the Impressionists are producing, and you're the newest and most daring of them all.'

Mimi's world was spinning. 'Fifteen thousand francs is more money than a laundress could hope to earn in a lifetime. Would you say it again, just so I can be sure I heard right?'

Durand-Ruel, a portly man, came out from behind his desk and spun her in a little waltz around the gallery. 'Fifteen thousand francs, my dear, fifteen thousand francs.'

'It's all my dreams come true at once; I could kiss you!'

Durand-Ruel fell back into his chair. 'Please don't, I'm not sure the old ticker could take it. And please be sensible. What you get in your pocket after my commission is twelve thousand francs, so don't get above yourself.' He gave her an indulgent smile. 'Now, who shall I write the cheque out to?'

'How should I know? I don't even have a bank account.'

Twelve thousand beautiful, glorious, golden francs. A life-changing amount of money for anyone, but for Mimi it was manna from heaven. Enough to buy her daughter back, if only she could find her.

CHAPTER 27

The last time Mimi found herself outside the door of Edo's apartment, she was anticipating a week together in a world of art and bewitching nights, a perfect world of their own creation. Today was different. She was on business, with Durand-Ruel at her side, but that didn't mean she hadn't worn the green dress that matched her eyes, and the supple leather lace-up boots she knew he loved.

When he opened the door, he greeted them both formally, and she breathed in his familiar smell of starched laundry, turpentine and the lemon of his favourite cologne. His hand in the small of her back when he kissed her hello still set her senses racing, despite everything. She missed him; he gilded her life and added another dimension to the one she knew. But that was then.

'I vaguely recognise this place, I'm sure I've been here before.'

'As far as I'm concerned, you never left. You're here every time I start a new painting, with those eyes challenging every-thing.' He turned to Durand-Ruel and shook his hand. 'She's the best muse I ever had, and she was always going to be a great artist.'

'Careful, you'll have her head swollen and I need her at her easel, striving,' said Durand-Ruel. 'A man has to make a living,'.

'And so does a girl, and this one is a bit in love with you for everything you've done,' said Mimi to the dealer.

'All just enlightened self-interest, my dear. Now, Edo, will you show us the way?'

If Mimi's papa was somewhere out there, she hoped that he'd be as kind as this man was to her. He didn't want anything from her but her work, and that was unimaginable in her world, until now.

The studio was almost exactly as she remembered it: the morning sun streaming in through the ceiling-height windows, a neat tea table laid out for them with Edo's favourite china, the chaise longue, the wood burner crackling in the corner. But Edo's pictures that were usually hung higgledy-piggledy from the picture rails, leaning against the walls, half-finished on easels, were gone. The only picture was hers, hung in pride of place on the biggest wall space. Mimi looked at Edo wide-eyed. After telling her that she'd never exhibit at the Salon, he'd given over his studio to her painting completely.

'It deserves to be seen,' he said.

'I think your last critique of one of my works was "competent".'

'I was an idiot then,' said Edo.

'Well done, my friend. You're right, it deserves to be seen, and I'm glad to see you cleared the space. There'll be a great deal of swooning, perhaps even the odd fight, so good that there's plenty of floorspace for people to react. I've invited the newspapers, too. Honestly, I could have sold them tickets, so many of them want to come, and I've had to give the devious bastards time slots to make sure they all get to see it. Expect nothing but vitriol, my dear.'

'I thrive on it, clearly,' laughed Mimi.

They made all the arrangements they needed to about the invigilators who would guard the picture, a one-way system around the space, and ushers to control the crowds. When Durand-Ruel stood up to leave, Mimi took her gloves off the table to join him.

'Mimi, can you spare me half an hour of your time?' said Edo.

She hesitated.

'I have another meeting, so I must rush,' said Durand-Ruel. 'Don't keep my new protégée talking for too long, she needs her beauty sleep.' And before she could protest, he was gone.

Mimi put on her gloves ready to go. She'd already been through the pain of leaving him once.

'You're right, you should go after the way I treated you,' said Edo. 'But I've lived with your painting these last few nights and I've hardly slept. You've achieved everything I've ever wanted to in technique and composition, but the style is unique to you. For that, I'm proud to have had some hand in your development, even if I was too stupid to realise it at the time. But that's not what kept me awake at night. I'm one of the hypocrites you want to confront with this picture, and I've been as blind as every other idiot who can't see what's right in front of them. I was wrong about you, and about your daughter. I want to help.'

This was exactly the magic she'd hoped to weave on the general public with her picture, and here was Edo, changing his mind about everything! But it was pointless now.

'It's too late for that. I was desperate, and you were too scared and proud to do anything about it, and now she's gone, and I have no idea where to find her.'

'That's just it. I didn't want to come to you with empty promises, so I made some enquiries. I think I might be able to arrange a meeting for you with Marie-Thérèse. We have the same lawyers as the Beauregards, and as you're all too aware, even the law is not above a little bribery and corruption.'

Mimi allowed her heart to beat a little faster, to hope. 'Oh Edo, you know where she is? Take me to her right now! I have money and I'll give anything to get her back. I don't want my daughter with that old witch a minute longer than she has to be. It's been torture not knowing where she is.'

Edo held up his hand and sucked in his breath. 'It's not quite that simple. She owes her lawyers, too, so even they don't know where she ended up, but they have some leads, and they expect to track her down within days to bring her back to Paris.'

But her mind was racing full speed now. 'Please, God, or anyone else who's listening, they've got to find her. Do they know anything about my little Colette, is she well, is she happy?'

'They're pretty sure that Marie-Thérèse will be in touch again on her sixth birthday. That's when Jean-Baptiste's money is settled on Colette, so there's no way that she'd harm a hair on her head. My mother knows Marie-Thérèse Beauregard of old. If there's money to be made, Marie-Thérèse will be meticulous. I've arranged that we arrive at the lawyer's office at the same time as they do... if you're happy for me to come with you.'

She could have hugged his beautiful bones.

'Edo, there is nothing I would love more! You're bringing me Colette, and I thought I'd lost her forever, I hardly dare believe it. You know she's got black hair and my eyes, and she's the cheekiest little scut you'd ever care to meet, such a handful, but clever and sharp as a pin. She'll run rings around us all and I'll never let her out of my sight again.'

Edo laughed. 'By the sounds of it, she might have different ideas.'

Mimi thought back to the day she stormed out of his apartment, how he'd turned his back on her and left her to suffer.

Now she realised he'd suffered too, in his own way. He was taking huge risks for her, and giving her everything she'd ever wanted... a reputation as an artist, and Colette.

'Thank you, Edo, for doing this. There's a part of me missing until I bring her home.'

'I was a coward. Mimi, can you forgive me? When it really came to it, I was as bad as everyone else who's let you down in your life, but please, let me make it up to you.'

A lot of water had gone under the bridge, and she'd nearly been swept away with it. And things were complicated. Now wasn't the moment to make any decisions, after everything she'd been through.

'You want me back now Berthe's marrying your brother?'

'I want you back, that's all. Berthe was a fantasy, you're real. You asked me if I could love all of you, and I can. You and your daughter can both live in the apartment on the rue des Batignolles and you can take her on trips to the seaside, pack picnics and swing her in the sunlight like you always wanted to. You know I have my own family, and I can't change that, but we can live the life we always promised ourselves. We can both paint, and I'll support us all and to hell with what anyone thinks.'

A year ago, this would have been everything she'd ever wanted, but she wasn't ready to trust him yet.

'I can't think of anything till I get Colette back.'

'Move into my apartment, and get it ready for her. I ask nothing in return, apart from your forgiveness. Even wild cats need a home for their kittens.'

The way he smiled, with a dimple on one side, the rings on his fingers like a pirate's, his long limbs and golden hair, the way he loved science, but with an artist's heart, the way he painted her in symbols and made her feel dark and sweet at night, all flooded back.

She kissed him then, and she let herself linger too long while Paris busied itself on the street below.

'I need to think,' said Mimi, breaking away.

'Take your time,' said Edo. 'I'll be here.'

She left, reeling and on fire, and ecstatic about Colette. She'd always reached for the light, and now the light had finally reached for her.

CHAPTER 28

The Salon was heaving, the crush so big that Mimi was worried she might drown in a spring tide of crinolines in every colour of the rainbow. Who knew that there were so many toffs in Paris, but here they were, strutting their stuff, loudly showing off their superior knowledge.

'Gustave Courbet's peasants are sooo charming, one could almost see them as human...' 'Fantin-Latour's still lifes are exquisite, but Cabanel's allegories are the best. You haven't heard of him? Not many people have, but I make a point of studying him.'

Nobody was talking about the Impressionists, their pictures were either skyed, or in the least visited rooms, but Mimi didn't care. Her picture, the one she loved most, of her and Colette was hung at the Salon, with her name on a little plaque underneath. She'd bring Colette here to see it one day soon.

Edo squeezed her arm. 'Nothing more than you deserve,' he said. They'd agreed to go and find hers first and it was in the room at the back, hung higher than any human could hope to see properly, but Mimi savoured the moment. It might be a back room, but there were still pillars, and marble floors, and the excited din of thousands of people curious to see who the Salon deemed the best in the land, and she was one of them.

In the main room, Renoir's *Luncheon of the Boating Party* was garnering murmurs of approval and she could see why; it was delightful. It was the beautiful gang on a summer's afternoon in an expansive tableau, the men in boaters and white singlets, the women in beribboned straw bonnets, silk jackets and muslin blouses lounging, chatting and sipping wine, glasses and bottles reflecting the light on the table, all under a golden haze of youth and promise, an abundance of it, elegantly squandered in carefree disregard for the precious hours slipping away.

'Remember that day?' said Edo.

'How could I forget, I nearly drowned!'

'You looked so happy and wild, like a river spirit.'

'It's the only time I've ever left Paris.'

'I'll take you to the sea, and watch the breeze take your hair and spin it with the sun. It's a different light there, bouncing off the waves.'

'I've always wondered what it would be like to feel the sand between my toes, eat oysters and drink champagne beside the ocean.'

'I thought you two weren't talking,' said Monet.

'We're not, we just couldn't get away from each other in the crush,' said Mimi.

'That's not how it looked from where I was standing. Can I prise you two away from each other? I've found Edo's piece, in room number twenty-two.'

'Is that still in the building?' said Edo.

'Hardly. It's up three flights of stairs, and most people have given up by the second floor. Nevertheless, it's there, and I have to say, my friend, it's a work of genius. I'm just bitter that they didn't feature my work this year, which is better than the lot,' said Monet, half-jokingly.

'You're young, my friend, with a long career ahead of you.

You won't need the Salon when you really get going,' replied Edo.

But everyone needed the Salon, didn't they?

In room twenty-two, a few people were disinterestedly regarding Edo's *Le Balcon*, and Mimi's heart dropped into her boots. She was no longer in it! Berthe was sitting in the place she had been, and someone she didn't recognise was standing in Berthe's place. A man stood behind the two women, strangely disconnected, while a young boy was just visible in the room behind them. He'd even changed the peony into a hydrangea.

'I wasn't the only one who was angry,' said Edo.

'I prefer it how it is,' said Mimi. 'I'd rather not remember that night.' Despite their current entente cordiale, and his attempts to make things up, she couldn't quite forget that he'd dumped her in her moment of need. That was the real Edo, just as much as the one currently at her side.

'Me neither,' said Edo. 'But I remember all the others.'

The clock struck twelve in Saint-Sulpice.

'It's time. Are you ready for this?' said Edo, looking concerned for her.

Mimi held up her fists. 'I'm a street fighter.'

The Salon de Réalisme, alias the solo exhibition of Mimi's *Hermes Reading*, had been open half an hour, and the gang had all agreed to be there at 12 p.m. sharp.

Outside the exhibition, a protest had already begun, with a gaggle of worthy upholders of decency gathering on the pavement outside.

'Profanity is not art!' shouted a tight-lipped woman.

'Ladies, do not enter!' shouted a red-faced man Mimi would swear on her life she'd seen backstage at the Folies, fresh from watching the dancing girls fling up their skirts.

That was the cue for a bevy of society ladies to push past to see for themselves, accompanied by their gentlemen, who were in a hot-headed rush to be the first to enter.

Durand-Ruel stood at the door, handing out catalogues for his gallery, greeting visitors with an important smile. He had a way of making them feel like connoisseurs with insightful, daring taste in art, and he was working today's crowd with his usual aplomb.

Inside Edo's makeshift gallery, Mimi could have burst out laughing. The gang – Renoir, Monet, Berthe, Degas and the rest – were in a corner, leaning against the wall, arms folded, or hands on hip chatting, looking on in utter contempt.

Two ladies were already laid out flat, being fanned by friends or concerned escorts, who were spitting blood at the atrocity their delicate companions had been subjected to. Others were huffing and puffing, speechless, or muttering about common decency. A few among them were more contemplative, and a couple of brave gents moved closer for a better view, admiring the brushstrokes, and analysing the symbolism.

'Disgusting,' said someone behind her and Mimi spun round, defiant. It was Albert Wolff, the reviewer, beaming. He gave her a wink. 'I've never seen such an abomination in all my years in the craft of art criticism.'

'And your review has ruined my reputation.'

'Delighted to be of assistance,' he said.

'You could have kept your opinion to yourself, but you chose to share it with the whole of Paris, and now look what you've done. These poor ladies are horrified.'

'Aren't they? Poor darlings will be telling everyone about it.' He kissed her hand with exaggerated ceremony. 'Seriously, though, you have talent, and your work is unlike anything I've ever seen, and I've seen a lot, good and bad, I can tell you. And you're also so much fun to review... Promise me you'll keep going.'

'It's my life,' said Mimi.

'Then my work here is done,' said Albert. 'The Salon is going to be so dull in comparison, but the editor wants a full review, so you'll have to excuse me. It would also be detrimental for me to be seen in your company, I'm sure you understand.' He smiled.

'Thank you,' said Mimi.

'Anything to see Jules back to the triple again. Seriously, the thrill!' And he left, nodding curtly to Durand-Ruel on the way out.

'How could you even *speak* to that man,' said Edo. 'He's my worst enemy.'

'Keep your enemies close is my advice,' replied Mimi.

No one suspected Mimi was the artist, despite knowing it was by a woman, so she was free to mingle with the crowds and hear what they had to say. Growing up in the slums she'd never cared what society thought of her, and she was impervious to the supercilious toffs who all had an opinion, enlightened or not. But when Rafi came marching in, hands thrust deep in his pockets and wearing his most disgruntled injustice scowl, she ran to him.

'Isn't it wonderful!' she said, gesturing to the crowds, and the picture in pride of place.

'Have you *heard* what they're saying about you? I could fight every one of those snooty wastes of fucking space. Haven't they got anything better to do?'

'Thankfully not, and you'd lose,' said Mimi.

Rafi regarded her. 'You're not upset?' he said, lightening a bit.

'That the whole of Paris is talking about my picture? *Our* picture! That what I've done evokes such extreme emotions, and everyone's studying it to work out what the hell I'm trying to say? I'm not upset, I'm ecstatic.'

'And so she should be, it's a work of sublime genius, and I'm grateful to you, my friend, for being the only man in Paris brave enough to model for it,' said Edo, joining them with a proprietorial hand around her waist.

He held out his hand for Rafi to shake, and he took it stiffly.

'I could never refuse her anything, and she never needed to prove her talent to me,' replied Rafi. 'Would you excuse us for a moment?'

Rafi pulled Mimi to one side.

'You're not back with that swaggering, self-satisfied toff, are you?'

'Rafi, I thought you liked him!'

'Never have. While you're with him, you've got no chance of meeting someone who'll treat you properly. He'll dump you again, just you wait; he's using you as his trophy muse while your star is in the ascendent, that's all.'

'That's where you're wrong. Oh Rafi, I've been dying to tell you. He's found a way for me to see Colette again, and he's offered me his apartment to live with her.' Mimi told him about the lawyers and the possible return to Paris and Rafi listened carefully. 'I haven't decided yet, but he really means it, and he wants to make amends. He's so talented, and I can't help admiring everything about him, and he's prepared to do anything to get me back. His apartment's so *right* for Colette, and we can paint together and be kind of a family, an unconventional one, but who cares about that?'

'That's quite a list, but if I were you, I'd slow down a little. You have your own money now, and you've fought so hard for your independence.'

'What's it to you anyway,' she said, disappointed he didn't share her optimism. 'You're going to be hundreds of kilometres away with your new family.'

'Sooner than I thought, Mimi. Béatrice is furious about the painting; she read the review in *Le Figaro* and has barely spoken to me since. She'd never come and see it for herself of course, but I had no idea she knew Monet's wife from the hat shop, and she let slip that I was the model.'

Mimi was secretly pleased. It was about time the little prig saw Rafi for who he was.

'I'm sorry, I had no idea it was going to be quite so infamous,' she said, only lying a little. 'But she'll get over it, won't she? Let's meet at the Café de Paris tomorrow, just you and me, for old times' sake. I owe you dinner at least for braving the modelling couch all those weeks.'

'When I say sooner than I thought, I mean this afternoon. Béatrice wanted to bring the day forward with all the fuss around the review. I came to say goodbye.'

Mimi had known this day was coming, but not now, not today. How could he leave her when everything she'd ever dreamed of was happening?

'Really, you can't hog her for the whole of her exhibition. Mimi, can I steal you? There's someone I'd like you to meet,' said Edo, holding out his arm for her to link.

At least he was here, wanting her, and helping her with Colette, not abandoning her like Rafi was about to, like everyone had all her life.

'I suppose this is goodbye then,' said Mimi breezily, not wanting Rafi to see her devastation. 'Don't worry about me, everything is perfect.'

'I'm glad to see it,' he said, but he didn't look it.

'I'll come and see you in the South.'

'Not if I see you first,' he replied, referencing their favourite childhood put-down.

Edo pulled her away, and just like that, Rafi was gone.

The gang all had something to say about her painting. Monet loved it for the diffused light around Baudelaire's book, Renoir for the way she'd captured the expression on Rafi's face, and Degas was a bit disgusted by the blood on the floor, but he understood the significance. It was unanimously lauded for its freshness, the colours, the atmosphere and the symbolism, bringing together all the Impressionist principles they held dear, of capturing the fleeting moment, realism and portraying the truth, free from social convention. But with Rafi gone, it felt empty and meaningless. What was the point if he wasn't there to witness it all?

All the while, Berthe was quiet, standing apart from the group and contemplating the work. There were a few quizzical looks from the crowd, shocked that a woman could so obviously stare at a man who had just woken from a tryst with his mistress, naked as the day he was born, but she wasn't one to bother about that.

'It's wonderful. So honest, yet so evocative of everything that's gone before from all the greats. And the model, he's the writer who comes to the Lapin Agile, isn't he?'

'Yes, Raphael St Pierre, we've known each other all our lives,' Mimi said, almost choking on the words.

'It's the expression you've caught so beautifully. The vulnerability, the longing, the desire. Darling, that man's madly in love with you.'

And it hit her like lightning. Madame Vadoma's prediction. *A man who cultivates the weeds will bring success, but without him there'll be no happiness.* In her superstitious moments in the middle of the night, she remembered her prediction, and vaguely thought of Baudelaire with his *Les Fleurs du Mal*, the flowers of evil – weeds, in other words – the book that Rafi was holding. But now it made complete sense. And the old witch was right. It was Rafi, always Rafi!

Mimi ran, and outside the rain was heaving down in sheets. At the bottom of the steps, a crowd assailed her.

'That's her! She should be locked up! Trollop, blasphemer, *grisette*!'

They blocked her way.

'What have you got to say for yourself?!' shouted one of them.

'I'm all of those things, and proud of it,' she shouted desperately. There was no way past the crowd. She would have to go through. And before she did that, they would need a show. 'I was born in the wrong place, at the wrong time. I was an orphan and I grew up on the streets, and I had a child out of wedlock and I love her more than I ever thought was possible. And now I'm an artist, whether any of you like it or not, with things to tell you. If you can't face up to the fact that everyone is naked under their clothes, however fine or expensive, that's your problem, not mine. Now, if you'll stand aside, I think I might be in love with my model, and I have to find him!'

A man emerged from the crowd and manhandled people aside. 'She's in love. Let her through!'

'He's a lucky man,' shouted another.

'Only in Paris,' giggled a lady holding a snuffling bulldog.

Mimi left them to it. Saint-Sulpice struck three as she raced along the Left Bank. The rain lashed and the wind was fierce, billowing her hat and slowing her down. She ripped it off and let it fly, the wind catching it up and flinging it into the Seine. At Notre-Dame, the bell struck the half-hour and her dress was soaked.

'Need a lift?' said a passing cabby, slowing to her pace.

'How long to Gare de Lyon?' she said.

'Ten minutes at most, hop in.'

But they got stuck behind an overturned cart and the horse was spooked, with fruit and vegetables everywhere. Precious minutes ticked by, the driver helping to turn the cart back up and gather up the produce. The quarter-hour sounded, and Mimi couldn't stand it any longer. She could run as fast as any Parisian nag, so she jumped out and doubled her pace, crossing the Pont d'Austerlitz to the sound of her heartbeat.

At the Gare de Lyon, she scanned the departures, in such haste that the destinations blurred: Grenoble, Dijon, Geneva, Chambéry, Lausanne... Marseille! Platform two, in three minutes.

A whistle blew, and steam billowed under the glass roof.

'Ticket, please.' An officious man in a uniform stood by the barrier.

'I don't have one, but I have to see someone before that train goes.'

'I've heard that one before. Ticket.'

The train spewed steam, doors slammed, people on the platform waved handkerchiefs and Mimi sprang over the barrier from a standing start.

'Oi!'

The steam subsided a little, and there he was standing in an open carriage door, black curls escaping his favourite cap, a porter handing in a suitcase to him.

'Rafi!'

He squinted through the smoke.

What the hell was she going to say to him? And what about poor Béatrice? But before she knew it, the words came out anyway.

'Don't go!' But the engine roared and stole her words.

The porter closed the door and Rafi waved through the window. She ran up the platform to reach him.

'I need you. I love you, stay!'

He strained to hear her, shaking his head, and he disappeared in a billow of steam and grit, which blinded her as the engine fired. Tears mixed with the rivulets of water pouring down her face. The train began to pull away, and she bent double in exhaustion and the pain of him leaving.

When the steam cleared, she straightened up to trudge home, but there he was, standing in front of her on the platform, his warm, intelligent dark eyes like an embrace, loving her, just as Berthe had said.

'What did you say?'

'I said I love you.'

He kissed her, wiped away her tears and wrapped her in his

jacket to dry her, and held her tight. The train hooted and disappeared, taking Rafi's other life with it.

'I always knew your green eyes would get me into trouble.'

'You're in deep, now. You know I'm the most infamous artist in Paris and I'm unstoppable?'

'To me you're just Mimi Bisset, and that's enough, but never stop being unstoppable, will you?'

'I wouldn't know how if I tried.'

'That's why I love you, why I've always loved you.'

He spun her round, and set her down, brushed a stray hair from her cheek and kissed her again and she could have sung her good luck to the sky, above the clouds and the rain, for the whole of Paris to hear.

'But what about Béatrice?'

'I was saying goodbye to her. I couldn't stop thinking about it since the day you asked me if I loved her. I didn't, but I couldn't admit it till I saw the picture, and I realised *I* was being a hypocrite. And then when I met her at the station, she'd heard about the riot because of your exhibition, and she said she could never marry me, and she wanted to go south to her parents alone. It's better for her that way, because I could never have hoped to love anyone else, however hard I tried.'

They walked hand in hand along the banks of the Seine, the spring rain streaming down in rods, quivering on the roses and swirling pollen in gossamer whirlwinds around them.

At the Tuileries, they threw bread for the ducklings and talked about the home they would make for Colette in a villa near the river, a train ride away from Paris, and she'd have her own swing and a little dog, and the most loving mama and papa a girl could ever wish for.

'I think I knew for sure when you rode up my street on that ridiculous zebra, starry-eyed with your find. Then I lost you to the circus.'

'You'll lose me again if you're not fast enough....' Mimi ran into the maze and Rafi followed, chasing her round double-blind switchbacks laughing wildly till she came to a dead end, and he caught her and kissed her, pressed her into the fragrant hedge until they broke apart, dizzy with each other.

'You promised me dinner at the Café de Paris earlier today. I believe a lady always keeps her promise.'

'You believe correctly. I'll pay of course. It's the least I can do after making a fortune from your body.'

'Those are words I never thought I'd hear.'

At the Café de Paris, they arrived soaked and euphoric and waiters fussed around them with silver salvers and warming brandy. The room was a blur of candles, chatter and clinking glasses, and they talked until they realised the waiters were whistling loudly and stacking the chairs around them.

A bright full moon hung sharp against the lacquered sky, anchored by the evening star, and Rafi pulled her close against the cold until they arrived at his apartment. On his single bed, he undressed her slowly and made love to her until the sun rose and warmed them from the east, the golden light she'd painted in *Hermes Reading* enveloping them both in its honeyed glow.

CHAPTER 29

'Your little girl needs a father, and Rafi will be a much better one than I'd ever be,' said Edo magnanimously.

Mimi couldn't help feeling a little disappointed at how easily Edo accepted her and Rafi. She sensed he might even be relieved. There was no doubt that he would have taken her and Colette in, but he was who he was, and it would have gone against everything that was acceptable in his world, and she didn't blame him for being afraid.

Berthe was right again about something, too. Maybe it was possible to love two people. There would always be a little corner of her heart for Edo, but he was a fantasy, she realised. He was the world she dreamed of being a part of, of art and hazy boundaries between the slums and society, where rules didn't apply. But that world didn't really exist, apart from in the cabarets and backstreets, and the life they'd planned together could never last. Now she had more than she ever dreamed of. Her own world, with her own rules, and her clever, warm, talented Rafi.

'Are you ready?' asked Edo.

'As I'll ever be. What if she's afraid of me?'

'You're her mother, you'll know what to do.'

Today was the twentieth of June, Colette's sixth birthday, and Edo's lawyers had confirmed that Marie-Thérèse would visit the Paris office with Colette in order to secure the amount settled on her. Mimi had her striped green silk dress repaired, and was careful to wear the exact same outfit that she'd worn the two times she'd met Colette, so her baby might have at least a little familiarity.

Edo handed her into the carriage and they sped across town, past the Cirque d'Été onto Opéra, and stopping at the rue de Rivoli in front of a glossy black door. *Soulier & Montant Avocats*, read the brass plaque. It looked so official, and she'd never dealt with lawyers in her life. She could face down hostile crowds, fly a trapeze, and jump ten bollards in a row, but officialdom felt terrifying with so much at stake. In the slums, the law was always stacked against you, and Mimi's heart was in her mouth. What if it all went wrong?

'Trust to what is right,' said Edo. She wished she came from a world where such trust was rewarded.

As they walked up the stairs, the mahogany banister polished to within an inch of its life, Mimi heard Marie-Thérèse's cut-glass tones.

'Really, I don't understand the delay. It's a family matter, and should be straightforward. We have a train to catch, don't we, Colette?'

Colette didn't reply, and it was all Mimi could do not to fly up the stairs two at a time and answer for her. Her hands were shaking too much to hold a pen, so Edo signed the visitors' book for them both and finally they were admitted to the office. Sitting opposite a harassed-looking solicitor were Marie-Thérèse and Colette, dressed in shabby travelling clothes. Colette looked pale and drawn, and much taller than the latest notch she'd drawn for her on the door frame. Mimi smiled at her, but Colette hung her head, while Marie-Thérèse exploded.

'What on earth are you doing here? You ran out of time, my dear, as I thought you would. And, Édouard Manet, I thought you had better taste than to consort with that little minx.' She snatched Colette's hand.

'Ai,' yelled Colette, twisting away, quick and slippery as an eel, but Marie-Thérèse caught her again.

'Monsieur Montant, please ask your secretary to call the police this minute. This woman is here to embezzle my niece's fortune. Colette' – she gritted her teeth into a smile – 'I told you. It's very important to behave, and I'll give you a sugar mouse if you do.'

Her act was pathetic. Mimi unfurled their agreement and laid it out on the table. 'We have a contract. I'm a little late, but it should still stand.'

'You're hurting me, and you never give me sweets or anything nice. Let go!' Colette yelled.

'If you don't let her go, I'll call the police myself!' said Mimi. 'And if anyone is embezzling money, it's you, you witch.'

Colette began to giggle and Marie-Thérèse patted her head stiffly. 'She is a funny lady, isn't she?'

Mimi winked at Colette, and she smiled back shyly, slipping away from her captor. She was an angel.

'Stop showing off,' said Colette.

'I beg your pardon?' said Marie-Thérèse.

'It's what you say to me when I say things I don't mean, and you tell me off. Now you're doing it and no one's saying anything, and you shut me in a cupboard for a whole day with no supper when *I* do it.'

'A very good reason why we should get on with proceedings, Colette,' said Edo. 'We're here to give you a new home, with your *maman*.'

Colette folded her arms and shook her head. 'Maman is dead.'

Mimi crouched to her height and held her gaze, saw the familiar spark of her *maman's* eye, the quizzical arch of an eyebrow she recognised in her own reflection when she didn't comprehend. 'This might be hard for you to understand,' she said gently, 'but I'm your *maman*. I loved your papa very much and he loved you, and before he went to heaven, he asked me to look after you.'

Marie-Thérèse gave a snort worthy of Tif the zebra. 'Very touching, when there's ten thousand francs at stake, I'm sure. Monsieur Montant, this young woman abandoned her child and left her to us. We've done everything for her, and brought her up in a respectable home, and now there's money to be had, she's back to squeeze as much as she can out of my darling niece.'

The solicitor busied himself with scrutinising the documents, clearly uncomfortable with all this to-do. Edo joined him to point to the salient phrases in the papers.

'Is Papa watching me from heaven?' Colette said, tears glistening.

'Yes. He's happy that you and I will be together again.'

'Nonsense! Can we dispense with this charade? Colette and I have a train to catch.'

'I don't want to go back there! It's dark and boring, and you're mean, and I want my papa!' said Colette, her face screwing up ready to cry, just the same as she did when she was a baby. But she didn't cry, and Mimi wished she'd open her mouth and bawl and shout and wail and let it all out, and soak her dress with her hot tears.

Mimi rounded on Marie-Thérèse. 'Anyone can see she belongs to me. She has my eyes, my hair, my olive Italian skin and, thank God, my spirit! Colette is coming with me and I'll never let her out of my sight again. You said to me last summer that you would sell her to me for ten thousand francs. Shame on you that you would sell a human being, or keep her from her mother, but luckily for you, I'm from Montmartre. I understand how money talks.'

'And I suppose you're here to tell me that money doesn't matter, that just because you squeezed out another little brat to litter the gutters, that gives you the right to her? Well, the law doesn't work like that. She is legally mine, and whatever game you're playing here, it won't wash with me.'

'What if I had a banker's draft for ten thousand francs? Yours without the burden of the brat, as you call her.'

'She calls me that all the time, especially when she's angry,' said Colette.

'No one should call you that,' said Edo kindly, as Mimi showed the banker's draft to the solicitor.

He pressed his glasses up his nose and squinted.

'It's legitimate, and made in your name,' he said, handing it to Marie-Thérèse.

'You can take Jean-Baptiste's money too, I don't want it. I just want Colette.'

Marie-Thérèse rearranged her features into something resembling human. 'If you're happy to relinquish twenty thousand francs, that should go some way towards her keep for bringing her up thus far, and help me with the shock of poor Jean-Baptiste's death. And if Edo can vouch for the character of this young woman, I could consider releasing her, as long as I know she'd be well looked after.'

'Your concern is touching,' said Edo. 'And yes, I can vouch for Mademoiselle Camille Bisset. She's an artist, a free spirit, and one of the most extraordinary people I have ever met. And I know she'll protect Colette like a lioness.'

'Then I will take you at your good word. At least I know that you are from a decent family,' she said, looking down her nose at Mimi.

'And at least I know that I am rescuing Colette from a bad

one,' said Mimi, smiling sweetly. She was getting the hang of this toff thing.

'Am I going to your house?' said Colette shyly.

'Yes, you are. You'll have your own room, and lots of dresses and toys, and do you like hot chocolate?'

'Yes!'

'You can have as much as you like.'

The solicitor beamed and dipped his quill in the inkwell on his desk. 'Splendid. It's all settled then. If you can bear to wait, I'll draw up the adoption papers now to ensure the legal transfer of Madame Beauregard's ward to her mother. I find these things are best done straight away, to avoid any confusion. And, I must say, it's moments like this that make my job worthwhile. You are peas in a pod. No one could mistake the fact that the two of you are mother and daughter.'

'Let's just hope that she teaches her good morals,' said Marie-Thérèse.

'She was never going to learn them from you, was she?' Mimi could only take the toff thing so far.

'Will you be my new daddy?' said Colette to Edo.

'No, no, your new daddy is waiting for you at home. He will never replace your papa, but he will be as kind to you as he was, and he loves your *maman* very much. But I can be your uncle, if you like?'

'Do you like hot chocolate?' Colette asked Edo.

'Delicious!'

'Then you can come to tea.'

Mimi hugged her angel and felt her silky hair on her cheek, her little warm body in a trusting embrace, and tried not to weep for all the lost years. If Colette could do it, so could she.

CHAPTER 30

Mimi surveyed the scene and fixed it in her mind to keep. A balcony looking out onto a milky green sea, muslin curtains fluttering on the veranda, a stone balustrade mellowed by the sun, the steps leading directly down to an endless strand of pale, fine sand. And there, perfectly framed in the centre of it all, a young girl in a yellow dress twirling with the wind like a dandelion clock, spinning for the sheer joy of being alive. She was seven now, a whole year older, a blissful year where Mimi had delighted in every moment, the childish giggles and tantrums, nightmares, lost milk teeth, and enchanted wonder at new discoveries.

'Maman!' Her voice carried on the breeze.

'I'm coming!'

Mimi kicked off her shoes and ran, the sand deliciously cool and soft between her toes, arms flung open. Colette jumped up and hugged her, all rosy cheeks and hot hands, the sea scattering the sun behind her, gulls' cries carrying on the salty air.

'Race you to the sea!'

Her cotton dress billowed, revealing skinny brown knees, and her vivid green eyes fixed on the water's edge, determined to win, perfect little feet making watery prints on the shining sand that glossed over the moment she passed.

'I beat you!'

'Not again,' laughed Mimi, holding her hand as the waves caressed their feet with freezing foam.

Colette found a heart-shaped shell and gave it to her. 'I love you to infinity.'

Mimi sluiced it in the sea and held it up to the sun, the pearlescent underside a gleam of pastel colours.

'It's like a mermaid's tail,' said Mimi.

'I'd rather be a pirate,' said Colette, fighting her with an imaginary sword.

'You're brave enough to be one, but even pirates need lunch. Papa is waiting for us on the balcony and once we've had a hearty feast, we can hoist the mainsail and set out for Xanadu. I hear it's lovely there at this time of year.'

'Is that far away?'

'Very.'

'But I like it here,' said Colette.

'Then this is where we'll drop our anchor for at least a week.'

'Good. And after that, we can go home, and I can play with Gisèle.'

Gisèle was what Colette called the doll that Mimi had saved for her all those lonely years without her. Mimi had suggested the name, her mother's. Colette had solemnly agreed that it was just right for her doll, and Mimi had hugged her to hide her tears.

Rafi was waiting at the top of the steps for the two of them, dark curls lightened by the sun, arms folded with his head to one side with a smile as warm as the balmy air.

'What's this wild flotsam and jetsam washing up at my villa?'

'We're dropping anchor here for the week, but we still need to look out for enemy pirates.'

'Aye aye, captain! And what about your second in command, you look like you've worked her too hard on deck,' said Rafi, putting a protective hand on her stomach.

'I'm fine. I'm so happy, Rafi! And all this sea air will help him, or her, grow strong.'

'We'll leave you to your easel after lunch; the light is perfect, I think? Colette and I have a very important puppet show to watch on the boardwalk in town, don't we?'

'Hooray!' said Colette, hugging Rafi. 'Can we get a hot chocolate at Café de Morny?'

'They are saving your favourite table, Mademoiselle,' said Rafi, bowing.

After her little family had left, Mimi mixed ultramarine with zinc white, terre verte and phthalo green for the sea, then yellow ochre, titanium white, alizarin crimson and cerulean blue for the sand.

A girl in a blue and white striped dress sat on the sand, hand on her straw bonnet, while her companion stood, grappling with her lacy parasol which had turned inside out in the wind whipping off the sea. They were both laughing, and the waves crashed, the sea rougher than it was this morning, tossing the sailboats that hugged the shore, their white sails swelling.

Mimi chose her brush, a bristle filbert, to begin the scene. She knew the buyer that Durand-Ruel would sell this to. She had several collectors in America, and one, an oil baron with a taste for her seaside landscapes, would be sure to take it. The Americans were taking a real interest in the Impressionists and were pretty much keeping them all in food and clothing thanks to their open minds and taste for the new.

The gang had all begun to marry and have children, and they lived near to each other by the river outside of Paris, painting, mingling, picnicking in each other's gardens. Feckless

Monet was the most successful of them all, and moved his family to a ramshackle place with an enormous garden nearby. With the money he made from his painting, he was obsessed with creating his next masterpiece, a garden full of Japanese bridges and lily ponds, which he painted a million times over with a masterful eye for colour and light. He'd dreamt of them, he said, since the day he rescued Mimi from the drink that summer's afternoon in Chatou a long time ago.

Renoir was becoming known for his affectionate portrayals of opulent balls, sunlit picnics and idyllic family scenes, and Berthe was nursing her baby, Julia, cossetted by her attentive Eugène, who worshipped the ground she walked on. His life was devoted to her and Julia, and unlike most husbands, he was happy for her to work, making up for her slightly casual attitude to her baby, who she adored, but who came second to her painting.

Mimi slicked a highlight on the girl's bonnet and tried not to think about Edo. His career had taken off too, but he wasn't well. No one knew what was wrong, but he found it difficult to stand at his easel for long periods of time, and his eyesight was failing. He was still the handsome, talented, society darling she'd always known, but a nagging feeling inside knew that his light was ebbing, and she couldn't bear to think of it.

The thought of Edo made the scene in front of her all the more precious. He was the first of them who had valued the ephemeral moment, the fleeting beauty of life captured on canvas. And she intended to rejoice in every last minute of whatever she had left of it. Colette had her own swing, hung under the apple tree, and she spent happy hours watching her in the dappled sunlight. Rafi wrote a regular column for the *l'Opinion Nationale,* and the two of them still sometimes danced around the rooms in their villa after they put Colette to bed, just to remember how many rooms there were, and to glide on the polished floors in awe of their good fortune. You could fit two of her Montmartre rooms just into the drawing room, and their garden had its own orchard, and flowerbeds and a terrace where they could watch Colette climb as many trees as she liked.

In Paris, the circus would be packing up into her painted wagons and heading south. Pixie would play her matador to new crowds, Juliet and Jules would dare death to snatch them out of the air night after night, and Tif would fly round the ring in his glittering bridle, a supple Romanian beauty turning arabesques on his back.

And Madame Vadoma would be laying out her tarot cards in her starry tent. A girl in a yellow dress, a cat, a river, an artist's palette, and a man who cultivates the weeds. She would sit back, and close her eyes. 'All is well,' she'd whisper, at least until the next shuffle of the cards.

A LETTER FROM HELEN

Dear reader

I hope you enjoyed being whisked away to nineteenth century Paris and immersed in the world of the Impressionists as much as I did. I'd love to stay in touch, so if you'd like keep up to date with all my latest releases, just sign up at the following link. Your email address will never be shared, and you can unsubscribe at any time.

www.bookouture.com/helen-fripp

We often think of Impressionist paintings as cosy, nostalgic works that adorn chocolate boxes and grace our grandmothers' walls with sentimental depictions of dreamy landscapes, but this perception couldn't be further from the truth.

The Impressionists were revolutionaries, pushing at every boundary of societal and artistic convention. Paris was in a state of flux, half of which was a medieval city with stinking, narrow alleyways, open sewers and tenements crammed with disease, prostitution and poverty. The other half was a building site, with Baron Haussmann's wide, clean boulevards in construction, resulting in much of the Paris we know now. The *Belle Epoque* was just beginning, and opulent nightclubs hosted aristos and slum-girls alike in a riot of glamour and clash of cultures. Trains, which offered unprecedented movement and travel to the growing middle classes, were the Titans of the day with their mighty steam engines powering the length and breadth of the country. Everyone and everything, it seems, was on the move.

It was these circumstances, and these people, that fascinated me when I sat down to write The Painter's Girl. 1860's Paris was the perfect place for a girl like Mimi, full of ambition and talent, with a lust for life, to slip through a chink in the status quo and make a better life for herself.

History hasn't always been kind to the models and muses who posed for the Impressionists. Ellen Andrée is dismissed as a degenerate by the shocked critics in Degas' painting, *Absinthe*. 'Heavens! What a slut. A life of idleness and low vice is there upon her face, we read there her whole life,' said one eminent critic. In fact, Ellen Andrée was an accomplished actress with fierce intelligence who had fought her way out of the slums. Victorine Meurent, who glares audaciously out of Edo Manet's *Olympia* looking directly, and nakedly, into the viewer's eyes was branded a drunk and a prostitute. In truth, she was a brilliant artist and talented singer, violin and guitar player who would go on to live a long and prosperous life. My Mimi is an amalgam of all the girls who appear in the paintings that are so familiar to us, yet of whom we know so little. In particular, I was inspired by Suzanne Valadon, who was a trapeze artist in the circus until she fell at the age of fifteen. She went on to become a muse, then an artist in her own right, smashing the conventions of the day. She grew up in Montmartre in poverty, her mother was a laundress, and she never knew her father, but she was obsessed with drawing all her life, stealing pencil stubs and drawing all over the walls of her mother's apartment, and climbing the tenements to sketch the ant-like people scurrying in the boulevards below.

'I was wild and proud... drawing was a way of brazenly rejecting established artistic and gender conventions,' she later said. She was known for her physical daring and stamina, her abandonment to the wild parties of the day, and for appearing in the sunlit balls and picnics painted by the Impressionists, in particular, Renoir.

Whilst Valadon is an inspiration, she was active a little later than the time my novel is set, and Mimi is entirely fictional, a representation of all those girls who appeared in the paintings of the day.

I have conducted extensive research and have created a Paris, an artistic community, and a society that was true to history, but I have taken liberties with the timelines of some of the famous paintings, and the dates they were created. All of them exist, many of them are familiar and fêted works of art, but some of them may have been created much later in the artist's career than presented in my book.

Having studied them all so closely, I'll never look at a river in the summertime again without seeing Monet's luminous highlights on the ripples, or Renoir's friends idling away a summer's afternoon. The Boulevards, elegant balconies, glittering nightclubs and Paris streets belong to Edo Manet now, and Mimi's triumphant zebra ride through the streets of Montmartre will be in my mind's eye every time I climb to the Sacré Coeur to watch the sun set over the magical city of light.

Thanks,

Helen Fripp

www.helenfrippauthor.co.uk

facebook.com/hfrippauthor

twitter.com/@helenfripp

instagram.com/helenfrippauthor

ACKNOWLEDGEMENTS

Huge thanks to my editor Ellen Gleeson whose encouragement, insights and occasional, much needed handholding have helped me bring Mimi to life. Also to Katja, my friend, critic and fairy-dust sprinkler extraordinaire, and my agent Kiran Kataria who's always there with the right advice. Every 't' has been crossed, 'i' dotted, and facts meticulously checked by the brilliant proof-readers Jade Craddock and Becca Allen and I am hugely grateful for their diligence.

Love and thanks to Nick, Tara, Charlie, Mike, Nick F, Fran, Polly, Laurie and Jemima who I'm lucky to know and love.

Printed in Great Britain
by Amazon

80557515R00166